JACOB'S LADDER

JACOB'S LADDER

John Andes

iUniverse, Inc.
Bloomington

JACOB'S LADDER

iUniverse books may be ordered through booksellers or by contacting:

iUniverse
1663 Liberty Drive
Bloomington, IN 47403
www.iuniverse.com
1-800-Authors (1-800-288-4677)

ISBN: 978-1-4759-7783-7 (sc)
ISBN: 978-1-4759-7784-4 (ebk)

Printed in the United States of America

iUniverse rev. date: 02/18/2013

Six deadly sins: Deceit, dishonesty,
duplicity, anger, hatred, and revenge.
One immutable redemption: Unconditional love.

I

"Defense. Defense. Big D. Come to me."

Three minutes later the gaggle that is the defensive squad of the thirteen and fourteen year old boys Varsity Giants team of the Tampa City League is milling around Jacob Baker, their coach, mentor, father confessor, and fill-in father to some.

"Line up on the ball and face me."

Another minute.

"What is with you girls today, you're slow. Are you asleep? Line up. Now turn around and look away from me."

Another minute as the linebackers figure out how to perform this complex task.

"When Robby and Amos tell you Louie, what does that mean? Tell me and show me one at a time. Nose tackle?"

"Coach. When the call is Louie, I know I have to swim; reach with my right hand and arm to the right side of the center's helmet and twist my body as I knife past his right side. All the while, I keep my eyes on the QB and find the ball. All of this is done from a crouched position. I do not stand up until I am in the backfield."

"Good. Stand easy, Gene."

"Left tackle."

"The same action as the Nose."

"Right tackle."

"The same action, coach."

"Left end."

"Bang the end so hard he gets a grass stain on his pants. Then I go four yards deep and turn to my right. Bang, bounce, and box, coach. I never take my eyes off the ball."

"Right end. Same as the left end; bang, bounce and box, coach."

"Inside line backers."

In unison they yell, "Follow the ball, not the man in the backfield and wait for the man with the ball to commit to a running side or slot. Then attack."

"Right outside linebacker."

"Knife between the end and the tackle and take an angle to the ball."

"Left outside linebacker."

"Spy the end and the steps of the QB, and be prepared to drift with the end to avoid the blocker or slide with the sweep, coach."

"If the end does not block our end, what will you do?

"Come down on him like rain. Keep him from getting away from the line of scrimmage."

"Wing linebackers . . . right side first."

"If there is no flanker, I drift toward the line of scrimmage and up field to close off the reverse lane to my side. If there is a flanker, I hit him before he gets started. I knock him on his rump, coach."

"Left side?"

"I must spy the backfield, look for the ball, and drift outside to close off the sweep."

"Wings, remember, the Eagles pass to the flankers about twice a quarter. So the harder you hit the flanker the very first time he's standing there like a little girl waiting for the bus, the less likely he will want to be a flanker. And, the less likely he will go out for a pass."

"Good. Now what about Roger . . . to the right."

The process and actions are mirrors of Louie. Stanley is straight ahead. The interior linemen know to bring their hands up under the offensive linemen's shoulder pads and drive them back into the backfield. This push is essential. Push back is not acceptable, because it means that the offense has control of the line of scrimmage. Once in the backfield hands are raised to stop the pass. Stanley 2X is a set play in which the two outside linebackers blitz between the ends and tackles. This gives us seven on six or seven and a sure way to disrupt sweeps and off tackle slants.

Pre-game repetition of responsibilities is key to success. They understand. A far cry from nine weeks ago, when they all wanted to be the quarterback or they wanted to blitz in a confused manner. They believe in the concept of team defense. Each player has a role. Each role is part of a large plan. The fact that Champions Varsity is 5-0 and has allowed only two touchdowns so far this year corroborates the team concept.

After Louie, Roger and Stanley, they take a lap, and huddle around me once again.

Four questions.

"When do you move?"

"We move at light speed at the snap of the ball."

"At the snap of the ball, what do the linemen not do?"

"We do not stand up until we are in the backfield or we will sit down on the bench."

"How do you tackle?"

"We tackle around the knees, because if the knees don't move, the player doesn't move."

"And, how do you play?"

"We're gonna trip old ladies and bite the heads off babies."

"Take another lap and huddle around me."

Upon their return, they surround me tightly and we jump up and down grunting like apes for thirty seconds.

"Who are we?"

In unison, "Giants."

The cherubic man-child marauders are ready.

In the fourth quarter as I watch my defense smother the helpless Eagles, a glint of sun catches my eye. Snapping my head around I spot a chocolate black BMW 750M with tinted windows slowly pulling away from the side of the playing field. Parents and families don't leave before the post game celebration of sodas and chips. Why now? Who? That's the trouble with being paranoid. Always wondering about the unusual.

Six wins and no losses going into the break. The second team played very well in the second and fourth quarters. They need more playing time before the playoffs so rotation won't weaken the overall effort. Only two practices next week, no game, then two practices the week after. We all need a break from the rigors of the season so far. The second half of the season is the tough half.

II

The intricacies of formal attire have intrigued me for years. The pleated shirt, studs, cufflinks, braces and cummerbund are contrivances, which add up to a beautiful appearance. From coaches garb to shower and shave, and the magnificent attire of modern man in less than 90 minutes. It's like construction. Just much less time. A beautiful house from bricks, paint, wood trim, and glass takes much longer.

Four times a year I resurrect my tux. Bought by my parents in celebration of my 18th birthday, the satin and cotton costume still fits . . . with substantial modifications over the decades since. Bigger in the waist and chest. Thank God, the expansion of the latter was greater than that of the former. Not by much. A regimen of running and working out in the gym three times a week for years has kept me fit and healthy. Best of all, it has more than compensated for the all-too-frequent over indulgences of drink and food.

The many small light bulbs above the expanse of mirror in the vanity create enough heat to initiate sweat on my brow and upper lip. This is the two-sink vanity she loved so much. She used to spend what seemed like hours sitting at the counter applying the delicate hues and tints from her pallet. Her attention to minutia was intense. The result. Near perfect beauty. The problem. Time, alcohol and drugs consumed during the process pissed me off something fierce. We were always late. In the beginning of her decline, she would arrive at gala receptions with a buzz. Later she was stoned. Finally she was hammered. Then no more. It's been years since we went to one of the Grand Previews at the Museum of Art.

Events reserved for patrons, who would ante an additional $500 per person for the complimentary cuisine and cocktails. After five years of the special assessments and donations, your name would be etched on the huge brass scroll by the front door. Plus, you would receive an 8 x 10 glossy of you, the mayor and the curator. Our names, along with 30 others, were inscribed beneath the year of our recognition. I keep the photo of Heather, me, the mayor and his wife, and the museum director on the sideboard in the living room. A reminder of what had been, and could have been, but will never be.

I'm not sure if I was aware of the significant change in her health and demeanor. It just became obvious to me one Friday night. Maybe I had seen the disintegrating evolution, but chose not to see it coming. Maybe I was just blind. Love and marriage do that to people. Maybe I was preoccupied with my struggling business and young son. Self-centered people tend to look inside for strength and comfort, and thereby ignore changes in the world around them. They put "other than self" on hiatus.

My Bally slip-ons have the patina of success. There is no polish stuck to the tassels. Gold ring and bracelet. Cuff links and studs inherited from my grandfather. Because I am right handed, I have some difficulty inserting and affixing my right cufflink. Cash, Visa card and driver's license inside right pocket. Car key and house key only. A foulard of royal blue, maroon, and yellow paisley peaks from the breast pocket. I do not look like a coach; I look like a someone from the society page.

The baby sitter has already taken the motherless child to the living room for a conversational updating. The kind expected between a 14-year old and a 20-year old. Eugene Baker, Gene, is my life. For him, I would do anything. Love him, protect him, and support his growth to manhood. Teresa Maldinone has been Gene's babysitter since before he became my sole responsibility. She is a junior at the university.

Majoring in health care administration. I've known Teresa and her family for years. She is good, honest, and loves Gene. Somewhat attractive in a youthful-exuberance way.

Gene's daddy is ready for another trendy evening with the city's power brokers. Old money that had the dream of the museum. New money that put the fund raising campaign over the top. And, the no money faction seeking an audience or just association. No recognition will be granted until years of deferential proximity have been endured.

"Can dad have a hug before he goes?"

Slightly embarrassed, he nods. Gene's smile is a sign that he is returning to mental health. His eyes give off a mixed signal. He is not terribly pleased I am going out, but he is pleased to be with Teresa. He is embarrassed to be considered a boy to his dad in front of this young woman. Ah, the agony of puberty.

"Have a fun night at the museum."

"It's a grown-up schmoozing evening. Not high on the fun list. I'll be home before midnight and you'll be sound asleep. Teresa, you know where the telephone numbers are. See you guys later. Love ya."

The modified BMW 320i has been washed and waxed and glistens under the fluorescent lighting of the condo garage. I bought the car before Gene was born, and have invested a substantial sum into its maintenance and improvement. It's my toy. The trip to the museum takes twenty minutes. Slowly driving the nine miles from one end of the shoreline to downtown, the lights illuminate the palms . . . sentries to my trip. Black-shadow guardians precisely 100 feet apart. They are not threatening, although they are huge and often sway with the evening breeze as if they were alive. The strobe . . . light . . . dark . . . light . . . dark . . . can be hypnotic. The clicking of the tires on the concrete roadway is rhythmic and further induces tranquility. Legitimate drugs. I begin to see Gene's eyes. Once sad and round, now beginning to glisten with the joy of life and squinting from a regular smile. I never want to see the sad eyes again. After nine miles of mind expansion and physical decompression, I am at peace. Valet parking at the cultural complex is a true luxury since the garage is part of the museum and performing arts center. What the hell, it's party night.

The party started at eight. It is now nine fifteen. Fashionably late enough to be noticed. My invitation lists the sponsors and the artists in the *Decade of Russian Constructivism*. The registration desk is run by the docents dressed in gowns of the time. They are flanked by guards costumed in near-perfect state military uniforms. These guards are husbands, sons or fathers. The entrance sets the mood. Exchanging my numbered, thermograved card for a nametag, I inject my body into the school of neo-intellectual fish that are in a frenzy for culinary delicacies and the food of art. The sea ebbs and flows before me. Faces, hairstyles, heads bobbing with conversation and laughter. The occasional hand wave across the crowded room reveals the limited number of gene pools among the frozen chosen.

"It's good to see you again, Jacob. How long has it been?"

Solomon Tuggs. Former member of the Circuit Court. Now retired to private practice and for $500 per hour counseling young lawyers as to the whys and wherefores of the local judicial system. Giving them knowledge to help them cut through the red tape and bullshit, which are the local law process. Solomon and I are kindred spirits. Our fuses are short and we are, to say the least, outspoken. As a result of these personality traits, both of us have gotten into social squeezes, from which only abject apologies have saved us. Humble pie has been a staple in our diets.

"Solomon, or should I say, your Honor. We only meet at these large social events, because this is where the city feels comfortable with both of us being in one very large room. I suspect there are hidden forces, which strive to keep us apart. Like they keep gasoline and a flame separate. These forces know you and I are liable to explode if not diffused by a multitude. That said, it's always good to see you. Where is your charming, and much better half, wife? Or did she let you out of the house without a chaperone tonight?"

"Gawd no, Jacob. She'd never let me out on the town alone. Particularly since she must have known you'd be here. I suspect she is in some corner with a young man. It does her good to be flattered and flirted with. She is a lot more interested in me after an innocent evening with one of her faux toys. Keeping one eye on me and one eye on him, the warden has the best of both worlds. Can I buy you a drink?"

"That's a great idea. I was afraid no one was going to offer to slake my thirst."

Three lines to the bar are twelve deep. There is a good chance that this is the second or third trip for many of the attendees. The majority of the revelers will not drive home tonight. They arrive early, fill their stomachs with too much drink and either stay at the hotel across the street or call a limo to take them home depending how deep in the hinter lands they dwell. I start to grin at the thought that these are the same people I always see in line at the bar at every big event. And, they must be thinking the same thing about me. If they can still think clearly. They seem to be friendlier, more open while standing in line. When they go back to the main floor, they will form huddling cliques to whisper about the latest company take over, divorce, or other malady that has befallen one of their own. There is a truce now so that their brains can soak up and tongues be loosened by alcohol. Solomon and I are now belly to the bar. Umberto, a fixture at all the Grand Previews is smiling. He has already poured our drinks. Solomon tips accordingly for the premeditated service.

"Now, if you'll excuse me, Jacob. I want to find my warden. Matrimonial duty and all that. Have a good evening. By the way, I saw Beatrice Consolo in the main hall a few minutes before you arrived. She looks terrific. Just thought you'd like to know."

With the parting shot he dove back into the mass of swimming humanity. Beatrice Consolo is the daughter of the three-term mayor and a former almost love interest of mine. During the worst of the recent past, I thought I wanted to be with Beatrice. Maybe I just wanted to be with a woman who would reaffirm my masculinity. Any woman. Other than a couple of dinners and socializing at public galas, nothing happened. I was just not emotionally ready for a woman other than my wife. Before Heather's death I was depressed, frustrated and angry. After her death I was angry and confused, yet strangely relieved. I had not seen Beatrice for a year. She is working in Tallahassee. Some senator, seeking reelection on the back of the migrant farm workers needed a Committee Leader with a name. Beatrice needed a cause. An ideal public union. Her face is not to be seen in the tide of well-dressed humanity.

Music, barely audible above the chatty din, radiates from the Northwest corner of the Main Hall. Strings, including balalaika, horns, and piano replicate the harmonies of the art's era. A nice touch by Valentine March, the Museum Director. He is always creates a Grand Preview worth the money and worthy of its name. Six food stations serve only Russian fare . . . from common chow to elitist delicacies. Cortez catering is the best. Tito is a culinary genius to complement Belinda's business acumen. It doesn't hurt that she is the sister of the president of the university, who just happens to be a huge force behind the museum. Each table is ten feet in diameter with three tiers of diverse fare. The small plates never hold enough. And how does one eat with a plate in one hand and a drink in the other? Something has to give. But, it's all paid for. So, all must be devoured. Around each of the tables hover the feeders. Filling their plates and emptying them so the plates can be refilled. This process is repeated twice before the gluttons move to the next table.

Perhaps stopping at the bar or requesting that one of the liveried servers fetch a specific drink and find the orderer at the next feeding station.

The food scraps on the floor form a circle eighteen inches from the table's circumference. Like slop around a trough. These scraps are ground into the carpet or carried on the gourmands' shoes throughout the museum. Tracks from one smorgasbord to another. I wonder if these people purposefully fast for twenty-four hours before a Grand Preview so that they can satisfy their hunger at the tables. The same people arrive precisely at the opening bell. Hit the bar. Then do the rounds . . . table to table . . . until they have gorged themselves. Touched every platter. They are the first to leave. They are bloated on rich delicacies, alcohol swims in their blood, and it is not yet 10. Time for bed at the end of a work week on Friday. I wonder if they take home doggie bags of their Last Supper. Maybe it's a game. The one who eats the most from the most stations wins. I'm not sure of the prize, but among a group of the eighty or so older attendees, gluttony could be its own reward. Cortez Caterers insures there is always enough food for every attendee despite the conspicuous consumption of the Eatin' Eighty. What happens to the leftovers? Donations to the Salvation Army Mission? Yeah, sure.

I wend my way through the pulchritude and note the deep cleavage, or dress backs cut to the buttocks, or mid-thigh skirts. To be noticed is the game. Forbidden fruit and flaunting it. They each belong to someone and are there for admiration and titillation. The numerous Daddy Big Bucks stand proudly nearby. Sexuality is a clearer display of wealth and power than clothes. This hinting and teasing are parts of the process of these events. It's as close to publically fucking some stranger as these kept females will ever get. They are frightened to stray from the homestead and all its creature comforts. They know that one sexual transgression leads to banishment. Banishment means nothingness. No

Mercedes. No friends. No money. No country club. No ski trips. No sailing in the Caribbean. These wick lickers will work hard to sustain the sexual double standard into the year 3000. Their indiscretions are with gardeners and auto mechanics. Very hidden from the public eye.

A sly grin and wink lure me to a giggling gaggle of femme non-fatal. I take a long draught of my Balvenie 18 and water, smile, and greet: Isabella Zorro, wife of a transportation *heffe*; Margaret Trane, wife of the area's premier office park developer; Rosa Gutierez, wife of a seafood purveyor and marketer; and Leah Thurston, the wife of the founder of the area's most successful computer software company, *e-bio*. Kissy kissy all around.

"Jacob Baker, where have you been hiding? I haven't seen you for months. Why, I haven't even heard anything about you . . . good or bad. It's as if you have gone underground. Are you really working so hard that you hide from your best friends?"

Bella has a take-charge personality, but she means well.

"Sorry I seem scarce. I've been incredibly busy. The business is booming. Can hardly keep up with the new accounts. Always looking to hire a few good people, so that I can get more business. But, I can't hire new people until everybody is stretched thin and over worked. This cycle seems to be getting shorter. A cycle is damned near addictive. Remember that I'm also raising Gene. I spend every available minute with him doing the stuff guys do. He'll be out of the house all too soon. And I don't want to miss any chances to love him. I promise to be more visible soon. God, Bella talking with you is like reporting to my mom, except your much younger . . . and much better looking."

A sly smirk response.

"How is Gene doing?"

"Thanks for asking, Rosa. He's doing great. The therapist feels he is over the hump. The big hits of degradation, loss, and confusion seem to be fading. I see his smile almost daily and his schoolwork reflects his mental stability. He made the Headmaster's List and he's having a blast on the Giants Varsity."

"Margaret, before you ask, I'm doing great. Any better and I'd have to be twins. And I don't think the world is ready for two of me. Certainly not the business community. Seriously, I'm over the worst of it. Back to working like a slave and being a dad."

"Leah, is Todd here tonight?"

"No, he had to go to Malaysia for a plant inspection. The typhoon destroyed over half of the facility. To keep up with the chip business at hand, rebuilding takes priority. Rebuilding also takes money. Getting money is what he is good at. He did say to tell you hello and he looks forward to catching up with you about next year's business plans when he returns. Oh Lord, I must sound like his secretary."

She was the first secretary. The second one is thirty years her senior. She saw to that.

I've just been grilled at a family reunion by my aunts. Good-natured questioning. But, good natured inquiring minds want to know.

"Have you seen Beatrice? She's here tonight. I'm sure she would want to see you. Stay here let me find her."

"Bella, please no match making. I'm sure I'll see her during my travels through the museum. Ladies, as always it's been a pleasure reporting to you on my life."

One of life's duties. The four of them always cluster. Their husbands form a mirror cluster in the corner. Jocular to those who pass by. My glass is empty. I must find a server or become dangerously dehydrated.

The eyes. I can spot those eyes across a blackened room. One is hazel and the other cobalt blue. No one on this planet or any other in the galaxy could have eyes like that. Eyes that comfort and cajole. Calm and ignite. Sulk and beseech. Eyes that show their owner's depth of emotion. Beatrice Consolo has known since our first encounter in her father's office that she had visual voodoo over me. Tonight the eyes sparkle with anticipation. Is she alone? Not likely. The evening's event cries out for an escort. Me? I wish. As I approach Beatrice and her father, she leaves his side and slides to meet me. Her walk is as graceful and majestic as a dolphin at sea. She takes my arm, turns me toward the Classical Gallery, and delicately kisses my cheek in a warm impersonal greeting. I try my damnedest to remain calm, cool, and collected.

"I was hoping you'd be here tonight. That's not true. I was praying you'd be here tonight. There are a few things I need to tell you. But, now is neither the time nor the place. Can we meet at Bellissimo at 11? Ciao."

She turns and leaves me staring at urns and vases depicting naked guys making war or doing athletic things. Talk about hit and run. I was just run over, but I got the license number of the truck. And I know where and when to find the driver. Get to a quiet place and call Teresa. Tell her to curl up on the couch. I'll be home after midnight. Back to the artsy folks.

III

At 11:10, I am first to enter the shadowed establishment. I secure a table near the open pizza hearth. The café for late night meetings is so damned dimly lit that the table candles are truly beacons. Beatrice was never been on time during our brief almost relationship. My drink arrives, as does she. I order her an Oban on the rocks.

"It's nice to see you, Beatrice. Why all the mystery?"

"You don't waste time on niceties, do you Jacob."

"Sorry. I did not mean to be curt, but Gene is home and I just get a little anxious. Regardless of the babysitter, I want to be with him."

"For the child, you are forgiven."

"What do you want to tell me that you couldn't tell me at the Museum?"

"Thanks for the drink. Cheers. The scuttlebutt around the courthouse is that the unsolved deaths of the mid-level drug dealers a few years ago are being reviewed, and that maybe the case will be re-opened. There is suspicion of cover-up. Something someone overlooked in the original investigation has spurred the interest. I suspect that District Attorney Jack Flaherty and his assistant Stu Pennington have med it their call to dig into the matter. You were involved in the original investigation, right? So, this is a heads up. Not that you have anything to worry about. Just a heads up. That's all."

"Thanks for the information. Without sounding presumptuous, I would say you know more than you're telling me now. Like why the digging and why now?"

"Well, the why, I can only guess. Maybe Flaherty wants to make his reputation by discrediting the former DA and the police department. Like a crusader. His normal caseload would prohibit digging up cold cases just for the fun of it. So, there has to be a real burning issue. I suspect it has to do with the drug trade in town. I don't think he is coming after you. Why would he? Tampa is a major entry point for Andes candy. The dealers who were shot were somewhere near the bottom of the drug chain, but the original investigation stopped with their deaths. There was the assumption that they were murdered by some street low-life. Maybe Flaherty feels that was a cover-up. Maybe Flaherty wants to climb up the chain. Flaherty must think there has to be an end to this beginning. Somebody mutilated the Silvera brothers. Flaherty may think the murders look more like a lesson than the result of an argument over a few grams of coke. If he follows the path from the Silveras to their suppliers and then to their suppliers, he can be a hero in the eyes of the city, state and federal forces. This was not done, at least not to the public's knowledge, by his predecessor. And, I suspect that is Flaherty's window of opportunity. Plus, I heard he will go public with his efforts in a few weeks. This will be his high profile case. His way of letting everybody know who is the new sheriff in town. His way of getting a federal job. Maybe even a presidential appointment. As I said, I don't think he is coming after you, but you may become collateral damage, because of Heather."

"Since you know all the facts, what should I do?"

"I'm sure Flaherty will be questioning all those involved for some snippet of information missed or over looked in the first go. Some connection. I just thought you would like to know in advance that he would be sticking his nose into your life . . . and Gene's life."

"I really appreciate this tip. I'll contact my friend and attorney, Tory Covington, and see if he can short-circuit any extracurricular publicity. Now, tell me the other reason you wanted to see me alone."

"No other reason."

"Let me give you one."

I lean across the café table and kiss Beatrice warmly and deeply. She kisses back.

"That pleasure being enjoyed, I must away to be with my boy."

"Just one kiss in public and you leave me. That's not fair. I wouldn't do that to you."

"Let's expand upon the concept of this relationship. Can you come for dinner on Sunday? I'll cook and clean. Just the three of us. Then after Gene disappears into his teen cave, just the two of us. Now I've got to scoot. See you Sunday at six."

"What choice do I have?"

"If you're not there by 6:30, I'll know your choice."

The drive home was calming. The spinning of my mind became a slow rotation. The drinks. Beatrice coming back into my life. Her warning. The old case about to be reintroduced to society, the newspapers, and Gene. Not fucking fair. Teresa is fast asleep on the living room couch. She is cocooned in a quilt from the linen closet. I call her folks and tell them she is OK, but asleep. Her dad thanks me. Teresa will go home tomorrow. I put extra money under her purse. Gene is curled up on my side of the bed. My pillow. My smells. He is in a safe nest. I slip under the sheet and blanket and drift off.

* * * * * *

There is no game Saturday. Gene and I go to Busch Gardens and Adventure Island. It is a date we made on Monday. A great day of animal watching and water rides. He periodically touches my hand as if he wants to hold it. For a boy this is a big concession to his dad. Stop at Mel's Hot

Dogs for a couple of foot-longs with the works. Home to shower and a well-earned rest. The message light is blinking. Alex wants Gene to come over for dinner and video games.

This is the toughest part of a raising a child. Gene is mine to watch, have, and hold, and then he grows up and expands his universe. This new universe means days, evenings and nights away from me. And gradually, the new universe does not include not me at all. Until he moves away after college, this is not a real loss. It is a loss of companionship nonetheless. Due to the fact that his mother deprived me of his companionship for the first years of our divorce, I don't deal well with being deprived of his companionship now. I try to not let him see this feeling.

He showers first, and packs his bag with sleep shorts . . . he is too old for pajamas . . . clothes for Sunday, two video games and a swim suit. I'll pick him up at three on Sunday. When we arrive at Alex's, I notice Jon and Matt are already there. There may be a bright spot in Gene being away from me. I won't have to deal with the noise and pandemonium of the Fab Four on Saturday night. He gives me a most serious, grown-up nod and disappears up the stairs. I will not see him until the next day. A long day without my son.

On the way back to the condo, I decide I would like a cookout by the pool. Stop at Simon's market and purchase a 10-ounce sirloin, a loaf of Cuban Bread, and some salad from the salad bar. Home. A swim, then the evening's food, drink and a smoke poolside. When I am alone I can indulge my sin of the '60s. Never in front of Gene. And always outdoors so the heavy aroma can drift away. The meal is devoured, because swimming makes me famished and the smoke simply amplifies that feeling. With the tray filled with dirty dishes and uneaten food, I sit back in a chaise lounge to visually grip the last vestiges of day. No one comes down to the pool at this time of evening. They're here in the afternoon and some few trickle down to the water's edge before bed. It is time to smoke the remains and pour a post repast adult beverage.

The double hit is instantaneous and heavy. Time and space blur before me. I am deep within myself. Looking out, I see the building, the pool, and all the lights. I hear the traffic on Palm Ridge Boulevard and music emanating from a condo unit on the seventh floor. The kids must be jamming. The parents are out for the evening. Someone will complain about the racket and the security guards will request that the music and loud voices be tempered. This will occur twice before the jamming stops altogether. It always does.

I see Heather's face and her form as she swims in the pool. Somehow I can't call out her name. My mouth is open, but there is no noise. Climbing up the ladder at the deep end, she grabs a towel and heads toward the lounge beside me. As she walks, she dries her beautiful blonde hair. She turbanizes her head and snaps it back. Blood is oozing from her nose and mouth. Down the front of her white suit. Her eyes are sunken with dark circles. The trickle has become a flow. She sits on the lounge. No smile. No words. Blood now gushing from nostrils and mouth. I can do nothing. Heather collapses in a heap beneath a blood mottle beach towel. She dies. Gene is standing on the other side of the chaise. He is stoically silent. He reaches down and covers his mother's face. Then he dives into the pool and swims away from me. He swims to the other side of the pool, which appears to be a half-mile away. I struggle to get out of the comfortable chaise and unwrap my beach towel. As I get to the pool's side, the towel, heavy with water, becomes entangled in my feet and I trip. I fall hard into the water. The towel is knotted at my ankles, and prohibits me from swimming. The weight begins to hold my face under the water. Panic sets in. I cannot breathe. I cannot reach the towel. The bottom approaches. I push off to breach. Gasping for breath, I call out for Gene. He stares at me, but does not move. I am going down for the second time. Bounce again. This time only my mouth clears the surface. I cry in desperation for someone to save me. I start what I know will be my third and last dive. I feverishly tug at the towel trying to release my feet from the Gordian Knot. It is hopeless. Open mouth. Exhale everything. Inhale completely. Hold mouth shut. As I drift in the aqua environment, I notice the towel knot has become unraveled and the towel floats to the bottom.

The cacophony of the teens as they exit the building shakes me awake. Must leave. Haltingly gather up the towels and platter with plate and food, drink and smoke remnants. In my unit, I place the wicker-handled tray on the kitchen counter. I have been sweating profusely. Shower and to bed. No more dreams.

Sunday. Church and the papers. Local and NY Times. Reading by the open window. On the breeze I hear her voice. No understandable words. Just a sound I know to be Heather's voice. Look outside to the pool and the boulevard. No one. I've got to save this audio chimera for Dr. Batt, my therapist. Time to retrieve the munchkin. Had to wait twenty minutes. He was in no hurry to leave. Nag him about homework. He sequesters himself in his cave. At five thirty I go to his room to tell him dinner will be at seven thirty. He is fast asleep. No doubt no sleep last night. I'll wake him at the appropriate time. I must be anxious about Beatrice. I've checked the time at 5:40, 5:50, and 5:55. The intercom startles me. Answering it, I realize I am breathless with anticipation. Beatrice is on her way. I awaken Gene. He heads for a shower. Something he has not had for a while. The door bell rings, and nervousness nearly overcomes me.

"Hello, Beatrice. So nice of you to come for dinner."

"Hello, handsome, it was so nice to be invited."

She steps inside and kisses me very tenderly.

"Is that OK? Where's Gene?"

"He'll be out of the bathroom in a few minutes. Washing off last night with the guys."

We head for the kitchen.

"I brought the wine for chicken. It should chill for about an hour."

"Perfect timing. Hey, Gene, come in here and meet a dear friend. Ms. Beatrice Consolo, this is my son Gene. Gene, this is Ms. Beatrice Consolo."

"How do you do, Ms. Consolo?"

"Please call me Beatrice, and I'm fine."

"How are you . . . may I call you Gene?"

"Please. I'm fine, too. I should be, I just had a nap and a shower. Now I'm really hungry. Dad, how soon is dinner?"

"Dinner will be at 7:30. If you want a small snack, help yourself."

The first meeting went smoothly. Beatrice followed me into the kitchen. She had to if she wanted to talk rather than yell. Dinner at the counter. Gene inhales his meal, grabs seconds of chicken, and heads for his room. Beatrice helps with clean up. She volunteers for pots and pans. Somewhere between the roaster pan and the two-quart saucepan, I come up behind her and nuzzle her. The baby hairs on her neck stand at full attention.

"That's a cheap trick. I have no way of properly responding without making a mess at the sink."

I slide my hands around her waist and slowly bring them to her shoulders. Cupping her breasts, I apply pressure on her nipples.

"That is precisely why I am doing what I am doing when and where I am doing it. The thrill of hinted intimacy is countered by the knowledge that the young chaperone is just down the hall. We could be discovered doing a naughty thing. The fear of being caught indulging in a very personal pleasure creates ecstatic agony."

Now I am kissing Beatrice's neck and earlobes. I trace my tongue in and out of one ear, down her nape, and into her other ear. She is powerless to react overtly. I suspect she likes the restraint. It heightens her arousal. I had not noticed she had completed her KP chore. As she turns her hands grip my neck and pull my head to her face. We are locked from lips to hips. The passion begins to roil.

"Dad, I'm going to go to bed now. Goodnight, Beatrice."

My son had the good sense to yell from his bedroom doorway.

"What do we do now?"

"We do something or nothing. The something requires that my son remains asleep and we go to my bedroom. The nothing requires that we finish the wine and you go home."

"Neither of those are acceptable alternative actions. But, for the sake of sanity . . . all of ours . . . the latter is the only true course of action. Let us adjourn to the living room."

She sits on the couch with her legs folded under her. I plop into the wingback chair. Our glasses are full.

"You've not dated since your divorce, have you? Or at least no one has seen you regularly in public with a woman. Why?"

"Keeping tabs on me? I'm flattered. I didn't know you cared that much. I owe it to Gene that I'm there for him when ever and where ever. Besides that, I'm still trying to figure out my part in the whole dead spouse-single parent-child-rearing regimen. I was making good progress. Heather died and I was thrown back into the tank of self-doubt and self-recrimination. When I saw what she had done to Gene, I knew I had to focus on the boy. My job was secondary. My own life came in a distant third. Now, I've shown you mine. You show me yours. Why don't you have a live-in, fiancée, or husband?"

"Who says I don't?"

"You're here and we did more than just kiss."

"I've been very busy for the past few years. *Papi's* re-election and now my work in Tallahassee. I can see myself being hoisted up the political ladder. The cause is just and real. We are a nation of immigrants. The process of twelve-hour days six days a week and a picnic with the workers on Sunday doesn't leave much time for me. But, that's not why I am here now. I want something for me. Some pure undiluted indulgence. But, we'll have to save that for another day. Soon. I also came here to continue our conversation of Friday night. For some inexplicable reason, I am concerned about the reopening of the case in which you were tangentially involved. I don't see any reason for Flaherty to reopen the case unless he knows something new or that was overlooked. Some connection between the dead people, the Silveras, and those who were questioned."

"The case, as I understand it, appeared to be very simple. The dealers get a load of really bad cocaine and push it. The stuff is so bad it kills eight people. And not street junkies. There was Heather, Pamela Ortiz, and Bob Merrit, two schoolteachers, a cop, a banker, and that hockey player. They all died the same way. Bled to death. Some exactly where they were doing the lines. Two in their cars. Some in their bathrooms. The cops never revealed why or how the eight bled to death. Strange that they kept this aspect sealed. Then two lowlifes, most likely the dealers, who sold the stuff, are found killed in the most grotesque manner. It could be revenge for one of the victims. Or, it could be a gang mutilation to teach all dealers to stay in line. I mean, they had a bullet hole in each eye. And the noses, tongues, ears, and all the fingers were chopped off. This butchery could only be a signal not to mess with the merchandise. The cops put all the obvious pieces together, reached a socially acceptable conclusion, and closed the case. Decent people were killed by bad guys, who were killed by bad guys unknown. *Finito*. Now the case will be opened for inspection. Like a corpse being exhumed. It's all very curious and I am afraid it may bother or hurt someone about whom I care. So there."

"Now I must leave. I have a full day tomorrow. Telecommuting to the Senator's office. Then to Miami,

Orlando, Ocala and finally Lakeland. I'll be back in town next Friday. My folks will be out of town and I'll be in the house all alone. Soooo very lonely."

Her flirtation is appealing.

"Let's see, did I hear my cue? OK, unless I hear from you to the contrary, I'll be at your place at 2."

The kiss at the door is more passionate and fulfilling than before.

Monday is a school day and a work day. The former starts at 7:30. The latter when I arrive. It's good to be the owner. My office is a brief drive from the condo. There are several people already on the phones when I arrive. The excitement and travails of the weekend will consume at least an hour. My line is blinking.

> *Good morning, Mr. Baker, this is District Attorney Flaherty. At your convenience we would like to talk to you concerning the death of your wife, Heather. We have reopened the case and there are a few details, which we would like to confirm. So, if you would call us, we can set up an appointment at your convenience to review this matter. In advance, thank you for your cooperation.*

Pleasant enough. Almost smarmy. That may be the problem. Call Tory Covington. Fill him in. Have him call Flaherty. Get this matter off my back as cleanly as possible. Now. Before it boils over. What is on today's schedule? Prep for a new business pitch. A car dealer, who wants to be seen as different, yet offers he same fare at the same prices as his competitors. Last month's balance statement for my review. Begin to work on next year's budget. Raises. New hires. New space. Growing pains. And ten calls to clients, present and potential.

My regular first-Monday-of-the-month afternoon appointment with Dr. Batt, tuner of this confused psyche. Why is it that his waiting room, maybe all shrinks' waiting rooms, strongly resembles an antechamber of a mortuary? Dark furniture and doors, and dark green walls are soothing, if not sleep inducing. The brass lamps with the green glass shades calm every nerve ending. The chair seats are overstuffed. No couch. There are no overhead bulbs to highlight any manifestations of mental distress. No flickering neon. The environmental tranquilizer must set up the patients. Knock down the barriers of resistance. After fifteen minutes in this chamber, no one would want to lie or be able to. The decor probably comes in the psychiatrist office handbook. The magazines are properly updated. I am six minutes early for my 2 o'clock. I am always early. I don't care to start early; I just can't deal with the failure of being late.

"Three major events occurred this past week. Beatrice Consolo came back into my life. Big time. Second, she told me that the new District Attorney was about to reopen the case of the deaths, which include Heather's. And third, I had a very vivid dream concerning Heather's demise, Gene being distant to me and my inability to reach him before I, too, die. I know the three events are related. I'm just not entirely sure how. I saw Beatrice at the Grand Preview. We had a drink alone afterward and she came over to the condo for Sunday dinner with Gene and me. In Gene's absence, Beatrice and I necked while we cleaning up after dinner. I felt a big rush of testosterone. She responded to my advances. We are going to meet again at her parent's home next weekend."

"She somehow acquired the information that the case is being reopened and gave me a heads up. To protect me and to protect Gene, she said. After she told me of the legal maneuvering, I had this dream. Not really a dream. More like a drink and drug induced bad fantasy. You know, too much of good things. Heather is swimming, comes back to me and bleeds to death. Gene dives in the pool and swims away. I dive in to swim to him, but my towel becomes entangled in my feet and I drowned."

The rush of events is a big start.

"What do you think all these mean?"

"Because I am a rocket scientist, I know that the dream was triggered by what Beatrice told me. Heather's bleeding to death. Gene being away. My inability to save her or reach him. My failure as the husband and father to protect them both. I thought all of that had been resolved. Now I can reach him and help him grow. So, what's his role in the dream? And, why Beatrice? And, why the damned case again? I thought all of that was well behind me."

"Perhaps there has not been resolution. Perhaps your closure has been a form of denial."

"I haven't denied a thing. Heather was a junkie. She bought some really bad coke. She died. Gene is an innocent passenger in her auto death. I was out of the picture. Living in that one room in Town 'n Country, while she and the boy lived in the Condo on Palm Ridge. The condo that I bought."

"Do you feel guilty about anything?"

"Why should I feel guilty? I didn't kill her? I feel I failed both her and Gene, but I do not feel guilty. She did that all by herself. I stopped using coke twenty-five years ago. She used coke. And Ritalin when the nose candy was not available. She forged scripts every month. Rotated doctors. Bought Ritalin from drug stores in both counties. Ground up the pills and snorted the powder. But, you know all that. I've told you that numerous times before. I feel some blame for enabling her . . . before I concluded that I was doing her damage. I mean, I used to go out to the 24-hour drug stores and pass the scripts. I knew then and know now what I was doing was illegal, immoral, and not truly helpful. But, I was desperate to keep her . . . to help her . . . and her addiction was a strong element of our relationship. It made us each dependent on each other. I wanted so much for her to get healthy. To be the woman I married, or thought I married. I became a real facilitator. Did my actions accelerate her demise? I doubt it. She went into rehab. I put her there. After twenty-eight days, she was clean, subdued and contrite. Went back to painting. As therapy, that was understandable. She was going to twice-weekly therapy, and took prescribed tranquilizers and ant-depressants regularly. She painted at night and slept during the day, so work at the office was out of the question. I lost my partner, my life partner and my business partner."

"I hate to interrupt, but we must continue this at our next session. Would you like to come back earlier than next month?"

"Do you think it would be beneficial?"

"If you would like to come back earlier, it might be beneficial."

"How about next Monday, after I have seen Beatrice? I think that will be another big event that could shake some apples from the tree."

"Is 2PM satisfactory with you?"

"See you at 2 next Monday."

✱ ✱ ✱ ✱ ✱ ✱

The only surprises that work held were the returns of my calls in the morning. If the potential clients are not interested in my company's services, their Presidents do not return my calls. I had three returnees. Surprise! Mrs. Torres was home when Gene arrived and made sure he started his homework. Then she started dinner for her two guys. She leaves at 6:30 when I arrive. That is the arrangement. I always take reading and my laptop home. I have homework, too.

IV

The mayor's mansion was his before his first election. Actually it belonged to his grandfather and was passed to the present occupants via a middle generation. The scion of the family made his fortune in shipping. The ensuing generations expanded the company to include warehouses and bought the truck lines from local ranchers. *SoloCo* recently became a player in e-commerce. High red brick walls surrounding the property are covered with ivy. The concrete planters spill over with all forms and colors of flora. The driveway gate is monitored electronically. This concession to the innovations of the late twentieth century eliminated the need for guards. My call to the house is greeted by playfully.

"Are you alone?"

"Yes."

"Are you naked?"

"No."

"Would you like me to be naked when you get to the house?"

"Yes indeed."

"OK, since I will be naked, will you join me au natural in the pool."

"Yes indeed."

"Hurray! Now hurry."

It's going to be an interesting afternoon. The winding drive to the house increases my anticipation. I park beside the house next to the pool, which is shielded by a 20-foot privacy wooden-stockade fence. As I knock, the door to the pool opens slightly. Unlocked and inviting. I hear the splashing of someone just having fun and not swimming in earnest. Beatrice is in the shallow end leaping, diving, and swimming underwater. This three-step process is repeated and repeated and repeated. Suddenly she leaps onto a raft, spots me, and splays out in an obviously inviting manner. As I rush precipitously toward the pool, I remove my clothes. It's normally difficult to remove pants, underpants, and shoes while running. But, I remember how I did all of this when I was much younger. The goal of the journey facilitates clothing removal. I dive in the deep end and aggressively pull myself to the raft underwater. Swimming beneath the raft, I pull Beatrice off her Cleopatra barge. She swims away. The game of catch is joined in the flesh. No mind games. She springs from the pool, strides majestically to a double chaise lounge, and wraps her glistening body in a huge bath sheet. She dries her hair with a towel then brushes her tresses. I am alone in the water. Climb out of the pool and grab a towel for modesty. Not sure why.

"That was fun. We should do that more often. Would you like a drink? We have all manner of adult beverages in the cabana. Would you bring me a Corona?"

Dazed I walk to the cabana. What just happened? She taunts me with nudity. I touch. Then she dismisses me as if I were an impudent stable hand. I do need a stiff drink, but I'll stick with beer for the moment.

"A Corona for the queen and a Rolling Rock for the knave. Let me ask you, why all the fanfare and then the flight?"

"I'm not sure. I think it's called ambivalence. Desire and fear rolled into one."

"OK, we'll do whatever we have to do to dispel the fear, so that our mutual desires can be fulfilled. Conversation. Vast quantities of alcohol. Song and dance. A few magic tricks. I'll do whatever it takes."

"Let's talk."

"Before you start. Allow me to tell you that I am very confused as to why you are so forthcoming about the reopened investigation. Are you telling me to ingratiate yourself? Are you passing along this information, because someone told you to? Are you providing this heads up so that I can protect Gene and his father?"

"First, no one is telling me to tell you anything. At least I don't think so. Besides, why would someone use me that way? Second, ingratiation is not my goal. Ingratiation assumes a superior and an inferior. You and I do not fall into those categories. Certainly, you are not the former. So, that leaves only alternative three, a simple heads up."

"OK, I accept your explanation for all but number one. It could be in Flaherty's best interest to make me nervous to see if I do anything stupid. Not sure what that would be, but I can be stupid. Plus, it would be smart of Flaherty to climb to the top on my shoulders. I have a good reputation in the community. And, my wife was murdered by bad coke. Maybe Flaherty thinks he has to shoot the best to be the best. Now why the heads up?"

"I think about you a great deal. And have done so since we first met in my father's office. I wanted to comfort you when Heather died. There was a small part of me that was almost glad that her negative life was no longer a burden to you. That you were free of a heavy millstone. I stayed a socially acceptable distance away. Sometimes, when I would see you at large parties or at one of the malls, my distance would be painful. You were hurting and it was obvious. I could not ease your pain. I had to stand on the sideline. Now, where were we about the excavation of the old case? I have heard even more about Flaherty's activities. He has recalled all the files with all the reports and all the depositions. He has assigned Assistant District Attorney Stuart Pennington to supervise the archeological dig. Flaherty has two others, devoting at least two hours a night to the project. That's a lot of muscle and expensive time being devoted to what appears on the surface to be a wild goose chase. I stress appears. Can you say aggressive? The word is that Flaherty knows something to justify this level of effort and money. Something that will stand up to the scrutiny of the grand jury. Nobody knows what Flaherty knows. But his ends have to justify his means or he is toast. One shot, one kill. One miss, one dead hunter."

"I asked Tory Covington to contact Flaherty. TC said he was stonewalled. Flaherty acted as if the re-investigation was on a very slow track and that his office was scheduling interviews at the convenience of those interviewed. TC is convinced that this response is proof that the investigation is being conducted in earnest. Maybe Flaherty wanted to act dumb and be read as smart. Who knows why? Tory and I agreed to say and do nothing until right before the real meeting. Now the big question. Who is your source?"

"A brief college roommate. She transferred to FSU after freshman year to be near her now husband. No one knows that we are friends. I think she handles some light administrative duties in the District Attorney's office. Her husband is well off. She doesn't need the money. She wants to feel useful."

"You mean she just called you up one day out of the multiple-year blue and started feeding you information. Why would she give you the information in the first place? I think she is casting bait."

"No, she didn't just call me out of the blue. I ran into her at the Eastshore Mall. As a matter of fact I see her there a few times a year. Briefly. And outside the malls, too. After shopping, we stopped for some coffee at the *Cafe Cafe*. We were just talking about jobs and such. And she mentioned the goings on at her office. She remembered how I feel about you. I had confided in her. She likes me. She is just being a friend."

"That kind of information leak would get her fired. And get you roasted as a conduit. Your job in Tallahassee could be in jeopardy. Because of its sensitivity and secrecy, the re-investigation is not something Flaherty's office would like to see in the paper or chewed over in the rumor mills before he is ready to step into the spot light. Nor does he want to spook anyone in to leaving town. I think your anonymous friend is taking a big risk for a long ago one-college-year friendship. I don't want to cast dispersions on her, but it would not be a complete shock to me if someone knows of your friendship with her and your feelings toward me and is using your friend to funnel information to me through the two of you. It's the why that I can't fathom. How about another beer?"

"Damn, Jake talk about a conspiracy theory. You sound way too paranoid."

"Someone once said, just because you're paranoid doesn't mean they aren't after you."

I would not mention my big question . . . is the source outsourcing the information to anyone else? My bet is she is. By now the beer is so cold and my mouth so dry, the nectar seems to burn my tongue. So cold it activates the nerves in my lower left molar. So cold it must be swallowed and not held in the mouth for flavor enjoyment, lest the chill produce a temporary headache. Beatrice takes four long pulls on the long neck and loosens the bath sheet of modesty. She doesn't open the wrap. Rather the butterfly is slowly emerging from its self-imposed cocoon. The sun's heat works with the beer and a half to soften the visual surroundings. Sweat has begun to seep onto my brow and my neck beneath my chin.

"This is nice. Thanks for inviting me. A struggling bachelor father luxuriates in this decadence. I must share my pool with hundreds of strangers, and who knows their bathing habits or how often they pee in the pool?"

"Where is Gene?"

"He and his buddies went to the beach with Alex's parents. Four teenage boys can be a real handful. Soon it's my turn to be the total parent. It's off to Adventure Island. The boys never get tired of the bragging rights when it comes to the rides. Arrive at opening. Ride our asses off for four hours. Leave. Get them back to my place. Order pizza. Leave them alone to disappear into the cyber-world of video games."

With that, I grab her hand and ease her off her throne. As I lead her to the pool, my towel and her sheet become path markers. I push her in and dive beside her. We are shoulder deep. I stare into her beautiful unique eyes, and am drawn by the basic natural magnet of he-she. She is receptive to the he. Kisses are short and sweet. Long and tender. On the lips and on the neck. Hands explore. I am aware I have not done this for years. I have not felt this way toward a woman for a long time. Too long.

"Wait . . . let's go back to the chaise. I want to make love there. I want to feel your entire body on top of mine."

"I want whatever you want."

Like teens, we hold hands during the ten steps back to the love plane.

She settles in and our bodies press the excess water away. Kissing assumes urgency. Kissing all over. Nose to toes. Shins, knees, thighs, hips, buttocks, back, and ribs. There is no place on either body that is not caressed by adoring lips. I am on top, but not the superior. I reach bliss too soon. I can tell by her eyes that she doesn't care that I am fulfilled and she is not. But, there is something in me that hurts; my inability to satisfy her. Male that I am. I touch her gently and commence delicate rubbing, while kissing her breasts. As she approaches completion, her hips buck and her back arches. Suddenly silent and motionless. The smile on her face tells me she is very happy. We rest. No reason to cover up. No one will see. I reach up and set the umbrella to an angle that will protect the white portions of my body from the sun's blister. Beatrice has a very small tan line at her mons and her breasts. She backs into me and we spoon. I can't remember why I disliked spooning with Heather. This is a pleasant experience. At full rest, I can feel Beatrice's heart beat. I can see the curves of her body and smell her perfume and her essence. I lean to kiss her tenderly on the cheek. She turns, raises her open mouth, and the entire pseudo-procreation process starts anew. This time I am better. I think I've got the hang of this thing. Swim. Dinner. Promises to meet again next week. Retrieve Gene. Home to bed. Sleep is deep. No dream.

Another Monday. Another Dr. Batt appointment. We probe my feelings about Beatrice. My sorrow and anger toward Heather. Particularly, my frustration at being unable to help her. Money didn't help. Moments of rage didn't help. Attempted control was ineffectual. Doing everything for her didn't help. Giving her everything didn't help. Enablement is a fruitless option. Not helping he get her illegal scripts didn't help. The concurrent conflict with my struggling business and the problems at home compounded my anxiety. Lack of funds fucked-up my family. She went through money like a piranha through a leg of lamb. Dr. Batt and I have gone over this road several times coming to the same terminus. Her destruction and ultimate demise of our relationship were her responsibilities. Since she chose this activity, there was nothing I could do to modify it or to stop it. The dreams will continue until I can see something new in them. They are just dreams and not forces of hurt. Beatrice is the bright light in my adult life. The Doctor and I schedule an appointment for three weeks hence.

Monday night treat . . . a movie. I submit to my son's desire to see a *teeny* flick. Something through which I will sleep.

My secure land line is blinking. A message from TC.

> *Jacob, I received a reply from DA Flaherty. He wants to meet with you in his office this week. I took the liberty of scheduling time on Thursday at 9AM. If that is a problem, call me right away and I'll reschedule. If I don't hear from you, I'll assume the day and time are acceptable. Let's plan to have breakfast at the Tower Club at 7:45 on Thursday to discuss the interview. My treat.*

* * * * * *

The Tower Club is a bastion of elitism. Judges, lawyers, bankers, stockbrokers, and all manner of the powerful have their special tables and meals. White linen and black staff. Heavy flatware appropriately monogrammed. Delicate off-white china with a royal blue and gold border and club crest in the middle. A small bouquet of freshly cut flowers highlights the center of each table. Chairs are solid and somewhat overstuffed. The subdued dining room lighting supplements the natural light, which floods through the twelve-foot windows. The windows look out onto the municipal building and vice versa. The carpet is deep and blue. The loudest noise is the striking of a fork on a plate or spoon in a coffee cup. Conversation is whispered. There are no menus for breakfast. Food is prepared as ordered. Breakfast is served from 6:30 to 8:00 AM. There are menus for lunch and dinner. Women, as guests, are allowed in the club for those two meals only. All orders are written by the diners and charged to a specific account via a numeric code. This is the club to which all young Turks aspire and few are recommended. Dues are steep, but worth every penny viewed in light of the socio-economic acceptance and perks derived.

The staff is male. Dressed in traditional uniforms, they are well compensated, but subservient nonetheless. The chefs and maitre de are at the top of the pecking order. Kitchen help is at the bottom. Everyone enters through the kitchen. Dishwasher, salad boy, and cook's assistant are the steps in the hierarchy. Knowing the particulars and routines permits upward mobility to the outside. Busboys, waiters in training, and finally waiters. Another hierarchy. After three plus years, these trainees have begun to garner a detailed understanding of the duties, the club members, and their peculiarities. At the appropriate time, promotion to waiter is offered and financial security of a modest level is assured. The entire process can take from five to eight years. Rarely is less time afforded the field hand to move to the big house. This is the old society of the new South.

"TC, how's Billie?"

"She's terrific. Keeps me younger than I deserve to be. The kids are great. Tom just completed law school and wants to practice with me. Not sure about that. I'd rather he cut his teeth at one of the very large sweat shops in the Northeast. You know, five or so years. Then, if he wants to come home to papa, I'll find a spot for him. Jenny is at Florida, majoring in Environmental Sciences. My biggest fear is that someday I'll have to defend some corporation against her allegations. Maybe I'll just hire her to help me defend the polluters. How's Gene?"

"He's fine. Getting stronger every day. As am I."

I write an order of biscuits and sausage patties with honey. Coffee and orange juice. A carbohydrate and cholesterol over-indulgence. Fine if you're a farmer and can burn up all the fats, sugars and starches by mid-morning. Lousy if you sit behind a desk.

"Jacob, I am not completely clear as to why you are being called in today. I was told that the DA's office wants to confirm some facts in your deposition in Heather's death. If that is the case and they introduce nothing new, their game will be to find inconsistencies in what you tell them. Then they can trip you up later. Why? I don't know. So, to the best of your ability, would you recount what you told them?"

"I was asleep in my room and my pager went off at 6:30 AM. It was Heather and Gene's number at home. I went to the pay phone at the Circle K and called. I never used my disposable cell phone so she could never call me. Gene was alternating between hysteria and stoic calmness. Heather was face down on the kitchen table and blood was everywhere. I raced over to 3301, notified security, and we entered the condo. Gene was right. Heather was dead. The hand mirror with two white lines, short straws, and the contents of the small plastic bag were testimony to her late-night activity. She had been fueled for a night of painting. My son was weeping and pacing. He wanted answers. He wanted reality. Building security called the police. They arrived in under ten minutes. The high profile high rise gets attention. I told the officers, who came to the condo, what I knew. They knew me or knew who I was. I had had brief verbal contact with Heather two nights before. The usual carping about fictitious money owed. Forty-eight hours later she is dead in a mess at the kitchen table. I was aware of some other deaths, and the similarities of each demise. I told the detectives about Heather's drug issues, both street and prescription. I had no idea where and from whom she purchased the cocaine. I knew she was seeing some guy named Peter Johnson. I thought he lived in St. Pete. Doubted he held a job. Knew he had a record and had done some time in Pinellas County Jail. My perception was that he was a low-life. Gene never spoke well of him. Gene never spoke ill of him either."

"I sat with Gene while they took his statement. Peter was a frequent sleep over guest at his home. Sometimes on the couch and sometimes in the big bed. Heather was not well. She needed lots of medicines. Peter and his mom argued often. Sometimes there were violent episodes. Pushing and such. But, Gene was never physically abused. Emotional abuse is another thing. His mom sometimes took Gene out at night. To the Projects to buy things and to drug stores to buy medicine. The drug stores were across the Bay and out in the farm country. Gene was very obviously shocked by the whole ordeal."

"Two days later, when the Silveras were found slaughtered, the police contacted me again. I told them I had never met the men. I had heard their names and read about their activities in some newspaper articles. They asked Gene. He told them he had never seen either Silvera. The case was closed shortly after that. That's what I can remember."

"I think we're OK, Jacob. Just stick with the facts. This may be mandatory housekeeping where you're concerned. When they go after the real bad guys, the DA's office has to reassure the courts that they spoke to everyone who had been involved initially. No favoritism or bias on their part."

V

The Office of the District Attorney is on the top floor of the municipal building, a twenty-three-story edifice to bureaucratic power. The protectors of the common good can survey their domain from four views. They can even look into the Tower Club. With a high-powered telescope and a lip reader, they might be able to learn a lot. I wonder if they were watching TC and me.

"Thank you for coming in today, Mr. Baker. And, Mr. Covington, how nice to see you, too. I think we'll be more comfortable in a conference room."

Flaherty and a female assistant named Bridgers lead us into a large corner room. A long and a short side are windowed. The table is a light-colored wood and the chairs are brown-fabric covered. Low-watt ceiling lights all around. Beige carpet completes the bright, yet non-threatening calming environment.

"First let me tell you that we have reopened the case involving the eight drug-related deaths and the murder of Hector and Osvaldo Silvera. We are reviewing all testimony and depositions. All the detectives' notes and all forensic reports. So, today we would like to review your statements to the detectives and this office. Just to touch all the bases, as it were."

"My client wishes to cooperate. But, he needs your assurance that his son will not suffer any further trauma as a result of this new investigation. In other words, the boy is not to be questioned. OK?"

"We have no interest in talking to Mr. Baker's son. We are fully cognizant of the sensitivity of this situation. We also do not wish to be viewed as ogres by the public."

"Fine, then let the game begin."

"Mr. Baker, did you ever buy street drugs for personal consumption?"

"Don't answer that Jacob. It's not germane to this investigation. If this line of grotesque interrogation is to continue, we will leave. Then, if you want to my client, you'll have to arrest him. And, since you have no specific charges, because you're fishing, you can't arrest him. So, back off this line of questioning. Or, grant Mr. Baker immunity from prosecution of any previous activity as it pertains to any use of recreational drugs."

"Agreed, let me rephrase that. During your marriage, did you ever meet or have any contact with Hector Silvera?"

"No."

"Osvaldo Silvera?"

"No."

"Did you have any contact with a male who looked like or resembled either Hector Silvera or Osvaldo Silvera?"

"No."

"To your knowledge, did your wife ever tell you of meeting Hector or Osvaldo Silvera?"

"No."

"Did you ever use drugs with your wife, Heather?"

"When you say drugs, exactly what do you mean?"

"By drugs, we mean cocaine, heroin, and marijuana. Illegal street drugs like that."

"Then the answer is yes."

"Which drugs?"

"Marijuana."

"Is that all?"

'Yes."

"How about cocaine?"

"Are you offering? If you are, that could be a violation of your oath of office and the police would have to arrest you?"

"Your attempt at gallows humor is in poor taste."

Tony was smiling broadly.

"Did you snort cocaine with your wife?"

"No."

"Who purchased the drugs, which were used by you and your wife?"

"My wife."

"Did she purchase cocaine for your use?"

"No."

"Did she purchase cocaine for only her use?"

"Yes."

"Did she tell you from whom she had purchased the drugs?"

"Yes."

"Do you recall from whom she purchased the drugs?"

"Yes, she said it was from her connection."

"Did she refer to the name or names of the connection?"

"No."

"Did she tell you where she purchased the drugs?"

"Yes, she told me she went to the Projects."

"Could you be more specific?"

"That's all she told me."

"Did you ever go with your wife when she went to the Projects to purchase drugs?"

"Yes."

"Were you in the proximity of the purchase?"

"Define proximity."

"Same room or hall."

"No, I waited for her in the car?"

"Approximately, when was the last time you went with your wife to purchase drugs?"

"Roughly eight years ago."

"Was this the last time you were in the Projects?"

"Yes."

"To what address did you and your wife go to purchase these drugs?"

"I believe it was somewhere around 22nd Street and M.L.K. Boulevard."

"Were the drugs purchased from a street vendor or did you enter a building?"

"<u>She</u> went into a building, <u>I</u> stayed in the car. I already told you that."

"Did you see her enter this building?"

"Yes."

"Do you remember the address?"

"The buildings all look alike up there. It was eight years ago. It was dark. The building's exterior lights were out. I can't recall."

"Can you describe the person or people from whom the drugs were purchased?"

"I was in the car. Heather went inside. I did not see from whom she scored."

"Asked and answered thrice. Move on Mr. Flaherty."

"Thank you for counting, Mr. Covington."

TC has my back.

"Did she purchase the drugs during the day or night?"

"I told you it was night."

"Do you remember the time of night?"

"Somewhere between nine PM and midnight."

TC nearly leaps from his chair.

"Stop! No more questioning. This was never part of Mr. Baker's statements to the police or to your office. You guys are on a fishing expedition and the river just dried up. What my client did eight years ago has nothing to do with his former wife's death and the murder of the Silveras. You would be better served if you talked to Peter Johnson. He is a known small-time dealer and associate of the former Mrs. Baker after her divorce from my client."

"Mr. Peter Johnson is on our list of people with whom we will be talking in the next few days, thank you. Mr. Covington, Mr. Baker told the detectives and this office that he had never met Hector or Osvaldo Silvera. We're just trying to confirm the veracity of that statement. Given his past drug activity, it is possible that he had met or seen the Silvera brothers."

"You asked that question and it was answered."

"Mr. Baker, have you ever seen the Silveras."

"Again, asked and answered. I suggest you move to a different line of questioning, or this so called interview is over. Tory's voice is very forceful."

"Now, your question was had I ever seen the Silveras? Only the photo in the newspaper, Mr. Flaherty."

"Well that ends this meeting, Mr. Baker. Thank you for your time, today. We'll let you know if there is anything else we need."

On the elevator down to the lobby. My pulse up to 80 bpm and pumping hard. Sweat had collected under my arms and on the back of my neck.

"Jacob, we got to Flaherty. He will not soon forget that you humiliated him in front of his office staff. He's fishing with dynamite. He didn't even know of Johnson until we gave them his name. I am convinced that Flaherty is going to use this investigation to further his career and he doesn't give a damn who he crucifies along the way. Talk to no one about this morning. I'm going to do some digging. I'll call you in a few days. Give Gene a big hug for me."

VI

My parking space is available. It better be. I paid for it with years of sweat equity and paying others to help. I took little or no reportable income until the business got off the ground. Then large chunks of the income were siphoned out of the company account by Heather. She could sign company checks during the initial years of the enterprise. That came to an acrimonious halt before divorce. I had to re-build both income and image. So I like my perks, like parking next to the front door beneath the shade trees. Inside the office, the telephones are ringing and people are answering. The noises of commerce. How soon before I have to add more lines or give everyone a cell phone? We have had a hectic year this year. Opportunities, some good and some that are a waste of time seemed that over the transom. Some looking for a freebie. Then there were the ice cream company and the orange juice processor. Both wanted to go from bulk distribution to consumer franchises. Both had they eyes opened by the cost of such a momentous move. Both agreed the venture would be worth it. They each had quiet capital and were willing to pay the hefty start up costs. When Heather was alive and spending like we owned the mint, I had to live cheap wherever I could. Now it is like I own the mint, and I can live well. It's also amazing how much happier I am now that she is no longer emotionally stalking me and telling me how to run my life.

Voice mail is uninspiring. Two people returned my calls. Since they knew why I had called, I can safely deduce they are interested in giving me what I want. Must call to set up meetings. Fourteen E-mail messages. The only one that matters is from *bconsolo*. I am apprehensive about opening it. We left it that unless we heard from each other . . . . Now I've heard from her. Will she cancel our date? Postpone it? The message is cryptic; *For Your Eyes Only*.

> *Jacob, let's go sailing this weekend. The two issues are . . . Do you get seasick? What to do with Gene? I propose a day sail on Sunday. Your call. I want another day with you.*

There is a photo attached. I am hesitant to open it, but very curious.

Pow! There she is in all her splendor, with nothing on but a smile . . . a tantalizing smile.

I e-mail a reply.

> *Love to go out on your boat. Gene will be with his pals on Sunday. He and I have a game on Saturday. Come and watch us perform. No I don't get seasick. Where and when shall I meet you? And, by the by, nice tan lines.*

Funny, when I want selfish time for myself, Gene becomes a second thought. When he wants time for himself, I feel cheated. This double standard may not be healthy, but it is how I feel. Dr. Batt and I try not to ascribe moral values to feelings. But they are attached nonetheless. I set up a luncheon status meeting with the ice cream team. Work is always backing up. Not late on anything . . . yet. But we don't get second chances to screw up. Sandwiches and sodas. No beer.

Back at my desk. *bconsolo* has sent another e-mail.

> *Sunday at 8 AM. Pier 3, slip 14 at the Yacht Club. I'll have lunch packed. We'll be back on dry land by 7 PM. See you then. Did your buns get burned?*

Follow-up calls to the two real people. One is looking to talk to me about some spec work. No thanks. One claims to have leads to business that he will steer my way for a fee. First the steer, then the revenue, then the fee. I don't trust him, but agree to meet him at his office. Take reading home for the night. Then a strange voice mail.

> *Mr. Baker, we hear the District Attorney has spoken to you about your wife's involvement in the deaths of Hector and Osvaldo Silvera. We know you know more than you told them. You know more than they know. You know the truth. Mr. Flaherty would like to know the truth. Would you like us to tell the DA the truth? Think about your options. We'll be in touch.*

"Gene, what are your plans for Sunday?"

"Matt asked if I could come over after the game on Saturday. The four of us are going to go *Balls Sports Pub* on Sunday to watch pro football games. Matt's brother, the one in college, and his dad are going to take us."

"OK. But, I'll give you money to pay for your food. When do you want me to pick you up on Sunday night?"

"About six."

"How about 7:30? Remember, somewhere between Friday and Monday morning, you've got to do your homework."

"7:30 is fine. Homework. I know."

"Also, since you are going to be away on Saturday night, it will be your job to do the laundry tonight."

"Slave driver."

The grin on his face is electric. The small chore or pre-penitence, as he calls it, is no big deal.

"And, while you're at it, you can do mine, too."

"Evil overlord."

I settle into my evening's homework. First I check my computer. There is the e-mail from Beatrice. Gawd, she is beautiful! The rest of the mail contains the usual pap and gibberish. The condo maintenance committee advises residents that they have contracted to have the water and waste pipes scraped and flushed. This is every-five-year-event and should cause only a temporary (four hours) disruption in normal water usage. The schedule by condo unit is attached. Our unit is scheduled for next Tuesday in the morning. A plumbing Dilation & Curettage. I can hardly wait.

"Wake up, Dad, it's time for bed."

"Thanks, Gene."

I unfold my legs, which are in deep painful sleep, and clear my lap of papers. Head to bed.

★ ★ ★ ★ ★ ★

Friday Mrs. Torres will pick-up Gene from school and feed him. I work a little longer than usual. I've got to get the company needs and budget projections ready. I must find a way to put away enough money for Gene's four years of college? Better count on him going to a private school. Ivy League. And, I must give a hard look at hiring one or two more people during the second quarter if the growth line holds for the first three months. Close the books. Head for home.

I access the message system at work and replay the strange message.

> *Mr. Baker, we hear the District Attorney has spoken to you about your wife's involvement in the deaths of Hector and Osvaldo Silvera. We know you know more than you told them. You know more than they know. You know the truth. Mr. Flaherty would like to know the truth. Would you like us to tell the DA the truth? Think about your options. We'll be in touch.*

I play the tape again. A flat male voice. Altered electronically. There is something vaguely familiar with the voice. The way some of the words are pronounced. No discernible background noises. Pull the tape. Do I want TC to hear this? Do I want to save it for a rainy day? For now I'll just keep this intrusion under wraps. Pour two big stiff drinks and gulp the first sip the second. Gene is asleep so I will follow.

I am in a slaughterhouse. Blood and the stench of death are everywhere. Lambs are bleating. Calves bellowing. Large men in black rubber aprons, boots and elbow length gloves populate the larger warehouse. Waist belts carry knives and cutters. Blood and guts coat the workers' gear. The men are muscular in build, yet fair of face. Almost childlike. The light through the widows creates a strobe effect as the human bodies walk through the shafts. Their prey awaits the conveyor belt trip from the pen, through the cutting room, and into the bleeding pit. They don't know their fate, but they are fearful. Some of the workers are hoisting the carcasses upside down and onto hooks to facilitate blood expulsion before the final cutting room. The carcasses on the hook line seem to dance in a macabre conga-line and pass through a plastic-curtained doorway into the. I can't see beyond the bloodied curtains. Before the hook line, the carcasses are sprayed with ice cold water to flush out the blood and internal remains. The mist and steam of the fluid is red brown. Dull fluorescent tubes overhead illuminate the red clouds as they settle over the workers and their work.

The grunting of the men melds with the cries of the pre-slaughter players in this macabre musical. All of this is punctuated by sporadic zapping of the stun gun. Used to knock out the beasts before their necks are automatically sliced and their bodies eviscerated, the stun gun is really two plates spiked with terminals. As the animals pass along the belt, they must pass through the stun gun. They don't fall down because large metal rods support their bellies. The rods help transmit the electric current through the beast's entire body, thereby relaxing all the muscles. Consequently the animals defecate and void their bladders. Water washes the waste into a sewage system beneath the belt. The belt is pressure-spray cleaned as it makes its turn and returns to the start of the process . . . the holding pen.

There is a strange fluidity in the herky-jerky motions of the animals, the belt and hook line, and the men. The overall process seems to be quite efficient. From beasts to large chunks of lifeless lamb, veal or beef in less than twenty minutes. The men who work this part of the process never smile, talk or look at me. They seem to understand their station. The animals know theirs. What is mine? Am I an overseer? A shift foreman? The owner of the plant?

Suddenly, the conveyor grinds to a stop. The animals are no longer fed into the system. The men stop their work patterns. The hook line is empty. A brilliant burst of light. An explosion? From the outside? Inside?

I sit up in bed. My surroundings, though different than a few seconds ago, are familiar. Pulse nearly audible. Breathing frantic. Pillow soaked with saliva and sweat. Bed linen strewn onto the floor. I have an erection. Is that a commentary on my recently improved sex life or a manifestation of emotional exertion? It's 1:34 and it's dark in the room. I need a drink to get back to sleep. Tomorrow is a big day. It comes all too soon.

* * * * * *

The defensive part of the game went as planned. Gene and the two tackles lived in the other team's backfield. The second team played the entire second half and did real well. A sack, two fumbles recovered and only 85 yards allowed.

Seven and zero. We are almost ready for the playoffs. After the he showers and packs, I take Gene to Matt's house.

★ ★ ★ ★ ★ ★

Pier 3, slip 14 is home for *Bea's Toy*. Thirty feet of expensive diversion. Very trim and quite appealing. Exactly like its owner. We motor onto the bay. Mainsail is hoisted. Off to the Gulf. Beatrice obviously knows what she is doing. She understands the minutia of the boat, the water, and the weather. I am along for the ride, as it were.

"Sit astern with me."

I am the mate, I must obey. Almost before I know it, she is heading into shore south of the Bay's mouth. We sail for about three hours. I can tell by the sun's position in the sky. It was time for lunch and a swim.

"Ready to drop anchor? Drop anchor."

In the small cove, our boat looked like a ship. The water was a clear light blue. The bottom of the cove is about eight feet below the boat. Ladder lowered. Beatrice dives overboard.

"Two mugs of Cuban coffee are about my limit before I have to pee."

She climbs back onto the stern, her well-maintained body glistening. The combination of suntan lotion, water and sun makes her beige skin glow. I dive in for bladder relief. Return for Cuban sandwiches from Wright's Deli and a Rolling Rock.

"I heard you were downtown talking to the DA. So, it's official, the case has been reopened. What did he want?"

"He wanted to confirm some aspect of my original statements. Who told you I was downtown?"

"My friend. She saw you and Tory Covington in the office."

"I don't mean to sound defensive, but again why the high level of interest about my involvement in the case?"

"Why do you think?"

"You're above idle gossip. So, it must be some level of interest in my well-being."

"Mister Obvious . . . or is that Mr. Oblivious . . . or Mr. Obtuse? I told you last weekend, I've thought about you and you and me for some time. I got tired waiting for you do to something about us. I screwed up the courage to do something about my feelings. I sent out signals. Nothing. So, I let you find me at the Grand Preview. You responded appropriately. You performed suitably last weekend. Now we are here. I don't know where this will go. But, if I didn't initiate it, it wouldn't go anywhere. That's why I am interested in what happens to you. Because in some small way it is also happening to me. Or at least my feelings. So there, asshole."

"Thank you and I'm sorry. I haven't felt cared for in a long time. I promise not to be so defensive. And, I'll try to be more forthcoming. That might be difficult since I have protected myself for a long time. But, if you forgive the occasional lapse, I'll work at being sensitive to you and your needs. Now, back to our tale of legal dirty work. Flaherty seems hell bent on connecting me to the Silveras immediately prior to their death. I'm not sure why. Tory says the DA is fishing. I'm interested to know if Flaherty is talking to others. And if so, who? Am I the only bum in the barrel?"

"I'll talk to my friend."

"Be cautious. Don't tip her that you and I are working together to get my dick out of the vise."

"Nice turn of phrase. She's my friend."

"Maybe, just maybe, she is being fed information, which she is supposed to give to you. Whoever is feeding her the information is fairly sure that it will go through you to me. Then, if I'm guilty of something or know something I shouldn't, I'll do something stupid. They can trip me up as a result of my reaction. Hell, they can even invent some semi-plausible reason to go after me with greater vigor. We need your friend to get information, however questionable.

We don't want someone to shut off the flow of information we are getting. So, we must be prepared to feed her information, which she will hopefully relay to those who initiated the information leak. Information that may not be totally reliable, but information that will lead others to behave as we want. Does all this make sense?"

"Of course. It's like the dog on the leash. The owner thinks he is in control. But, the reality is that the dog is in control. The dog works very hard to maintain that illusion. I will be judicious in dealing with my friend. But, why do we want to feed her information?"

"Just who is this friend?"

"Elizabeth Bridgers."

"Some woman named Bridgers was in the room when Flaherty grilled me the other day. I thought she was an Assistant DA. She did more than see me in the office. She sat at the tape recorder, took a few notes, and said nothing. You said she did some administrative work for Flaherty. The variance in her job functions may be our first piece of leverage. Can you do some digging via the Bar Association and the Court system? Also we should learn if she is happily married. Just what is her relationship with the DA.? Find out just who the mystery woman is. I am getting an uneasy feeling about her."

"Once we know who she really is, or her function in the DA's office, what then?"

"Then we'll test her reliability by feeding her some bogus information. Then we'll see how the DA reacts to new input. Enough work. It's swim time. By now the pee has dissipated."

The thrashing and splashing opens my head to more thinking and more paranoia. I am uneasy all right. Uneasy that I may be at the end of two conduits. Elizabeth Bridgers and Beatrice. How did Elizabeth know to reach out to Beatrice at the precise moment that Flaherty opened the case? Was she told to? Did Beatrice initiate the dialogue? Are they co-conspirators? Are they being used? By whom? Are they the ones who are using each other? Early afternoon top-deck loving culminates our stay in the cove. Beatrice allows me to captain the boat back to harbor with her hand on the tiller. Does she trust me or is she creating the illusion of trust?

The solace of and the strength infused by a child's love are wondrous. As we walk from Matt's house to the car, Gene leans on me and we proceed in lock step. In the car he is quiet, but reaches over and squeezes my hand twice. He knows I keep my promises. If I am to be somewhere at a certain time, I am there. And I am always early. I told him when he lived with his mother, that I would never be so far from him that I couldn't get to him and keep him out of harm's way. We joked that I was like the character in movies that was the silent protector. If the bodyguard is to be perceived by the audience as good, he is portrayed as an animal or a noble savage. If the bodyguard is to be perceived as evil, he is portrayed as a thug with a gun. Natural is good. Man-made is bad. Although I have the pistols my father gave me, Gene has never seen them. The matched pair of 25-caliber semi-automatics rests in their velvet formed impressions within a mahogany lock box. Clips by their side. Cartridges in a box. The deep blue steel guns with inlaid pearl handles have been lovingly cared for years. Dinner is Papa John's pizza. Bedtime is relatively early. Next Sunday is Adventure Island.

VII

There's something about careening down a 110-foot slide to crash into a three-foot deep pool that instantly kicks in adrenaline and testosterone. The flaunting of immortality in the face of destruction is a huge rush, whether one is 44 or 14 years old. I guess days like this keep me young . . . for the moment. If the boys can do something, so can I and vice versa. The objective to best one another is not the property of animals on the veldt. The competitive nature of the human male is universal. The difference is that the older beast is very sore the next day, while the younger beasts go off for another day of one-upmanship.

Monday. Call TC. Find out if he knows anything new since my fun-filled day at the DA's office.

"Jacob, I have reason to believe that someone wound up Flaherty and his attack dog, Pennington, and turned them loose. None of my contacts at state is taking any credit or pointing fingers. They could be keeping quiet to protect their men. Or it could be that our boys are federally or locally supported. My bet is federal. Local is too closely knit. No one shits without the power brokers smelling it. These are the real good old boys. Flaherty is a relative newcomer. He's been in Tampa only a few years. But, he has federal connections. Pennington has been here less time, but he has state connections. They make the ideal *Odd Couple*. I would not put it out of the realm of possibility that Flaherty was told by someone in the federal government to investigate the drug business and corresponding corruption. He is the ideal candidate for the job, because he could be perceived as a local. He acts as a deep plant . . . like the Russians after World War Two. I'll contact an old friend in Washington to confirm if I'm correct in my assessment."

"Excuse me. Drugs I knew about. But, corruption. What's that all about?"

"There've been rumors for years that the drug trade has been permitted to exist because the network pays tribute to community leaders. You may have noticed that no politician has ever run on the "Clean-up Tampa" slate. Just expansion. Expansion is progress. Progress is good. Progress means jobs. Jobs mean money and a solid constituency. No politician has spoken against the fetid underbelly of the city and county. Good and evil live and work side by side. Hell, the bad guys are even major donors to the hospital, culture, and the athletic venues. Who do you think paid for the new stadium? Give a little and get a lot has been their motto for nearly sixty years. So, in our drive to be a big league city like New York, Chicago, and Los Angeles, we have allowed crime to flourish below the surface. Like those cities did years ago. However, when the public is offended by multiple grisly deaths, and the local and national media make a big deal about the dangers of living in this tropical paradise, something has to be done. The streets have to be cleaned. That's when the feds put the pressure on. Either we do the cleaning or they will come into town like the vigilantes and turn the place upside down. Now we have the reopening of a case some people in power probably wanted kept closed. That's why I think Flaherty is taking his lead from the feds."

"Do you think the city and county governments are involved in the overall mess of the drug trade?"

"Only insofar as they know it exists and do little or nothing to stop it. I don't think that anyone on the City

Council or any of the County Commissioners is on the take. They just look the other way."

"By the way you and Beatrice Consolo were seen sailing last Sunday. While I can't tell you whom you can and cannot see, I would be cautious of being seen in public with someone, who has Beatrice's connections."

"What the hell does that mean?"

"She is the daughter of the mayor. The mayor has been in office for some time. He has been in politics and power for a longer time. I know she knows and has seen bad guys with her father. I am fairly confident that he is clean. I'm confident that she is clean. But, I'm only fairly confident. Just be careful what you tell her. Pillow talk can be a problem."

"I'll keep that in mind."

Fuck him.

VIII

Gene is great at practice. This is another rite of passage. He is the team leader. He is nearly revered. Leads the team in tackles and sacks. And he yells at slackers.

Over man-sized portions of black beans, yellow rice, and pork strips baked in sour oranges, Gene tells me of his goals for the year.

"I want us to go undefeated. I want no more TDs against us. And I want three sacks a game in the upcoming games. Most of all I want to crush the Jaguars."

"Good goals. Be careful that you don't look too hard into the future and stumble over the present."

"I have great team mates and an OK coach. We'll make it. I've got a ton of homework. Could you take care of clean up?"

He is up and headed for his room before I can respond. The trust between child and parent, on hiatus a few years ago, is being rebuilt one day at a time, one act at a time. Now I have to let Beatrice know of my fatherly feelings.

Beatrice suggests that we, as a couple, go to Gene's games. She will sit in the stands and berate the coach's dumb calls and cheer for the kids. She is unaware that her obvious appearance may send a strong message to Gene. A message he may not be ready to read. I should be the judge as to his ability to deal with such a message. She will trust my decision. I'll think about it.

Tory calls and wants me to come to his office to discuss what he has learned.

His personal office is huge and crammed with the accoutrements of success. Pictures of all the right political leaders, local, state, and federal. Men on fishing trips, hunting excursions, and golf outings. No women allowed. A huge portrait of Billie surveys the activity in the room. She stares at his every move.

"It's always interesting to learn what the police and prosecutors keep hidden from the public during an investigation. First, let me tell you that I believe we have only begun to know what they know. My job will be to put all the pieces together faster than they can, and to determine what pieces are missing. Ultimately I will have to have a complete picture so that I can be viable counsel to you. I was able to access the Medical Examiner and police reports. Not all of what I have is in the public domain, so don't ask how I acquired it."

"The ME's report reveals that all eight people died in the same manner. Death was a result of blood loss and the poison they ingested. The blood poured from the nose and mouth of each victim. The cause of the blood loss and the poison were in the substance they had snorted. While it was sold as cocaine, the powder was, in fact, a mixture of coke, Italian baby laxative, PPC, ground glass, and rat poison. The first two ingredients are standard street fare, I am told. The second three were the agents of death. The objective of the mixture was to kill. Why? I do not know. Was some individual the specific target, and the others just collateral damage? I don't know. When we learn the 'why', we will know who. The same mixture was found in all eight victims and in street bags at the Silveras' apartment. Maybe they owed money or were about to rat somebody out for a bigger territory. Something triggered the vicious assault. And the Silveras' deaths ended the carnage."

Now, the killer dope could have been planted there, but I don't believe that's a viable avenue. At least four of the victims were known to have frequented Silveras' place to buy drugs. Heather was one of them. There are witnesses to these comings and goings. Therefore, it is logical to make the direct connection between the Silveras and the eight. That leaves someone or some ones, who caused the death of the others. That is frightening."

"The PPC gave Heather a feeling of great strength. Almost as if she could do anything. The ground glass, in a minute quantity, etched through the walls, the membranes, of the sinuses. Heather didn't care if she was bleeding, because of the combination of coke and PPC. A nose bleed had, no doubt, happened before. She probably shrugged it off as just part of the whole process. A small leak that would heal. A small hole that would permit the coke to work faster and harder is good to a user. After a few hits the glass went further up into the brain. The PPC was the agent that now worked even faster and harder. She wanted more powder. The blood was no longer trickling. It was flowing. But, the drugs were working on the brain. More was needed. The rat poison entered her blood stream and went directly to the nervous system. After snorting three short lines, the bleeding could not be stanched. The glass had cut direct passages from the nostrils to the brain. But, she was too far-gone to care. The bump from the coke and the push from the PPC drove Heather to snort herself to death. Sorry for all the gore, but it's all here in the report."

"That's OK. I saw the results. I'm over the loss. It's hard to get over the damage she did to our child, though. Could I have some iced tea? And could we take a break?"

"Sure. Ms. Waters, could you bring us some iced tea?"

The recess is over in fifteen minutes.

"What else were you able to find?"

"Well, back to the killer drugs. I am not positive that either of the Silveras knew the stuff was deadly. There are two possibilities: They bought coke from someone other than their usual supplier or they got it from their usual supplier . . . the up line in the multi-level marketing of drugs.

In either instance, they did not test the merchandise before they resold it, because they trusted the source or they wanted to move it instantly before the regular source found out they were buying from a new seller. If they got the bad stuff from a new source, the source may have planted the killer dope to discredit the Silveras and their regular supply chain. The new source could then take over their regular customer base. If they got the dope from his regular source, it may have been tainted to discredit the brothers. They may have done something bad. Something that required they be taught a severe lesson. Show all street vendors what happens to dealers who don't toe the mark. Like buying from a second source. It could have been the initial killings in a territorial drug war that stopped before it got rolling. Then who killed the Silveras? Regardless of the different scenarios, my suspicion is that their regular drug supplier killed them. Understand that all of this is speculation."

"TC, for an old fart of a lawyer, you paint such a rosy picture of the workings of the netherworld."

"There's more. But this stuff is very, very preliminary. There were eight victims of the Silveras' poison drug . . . your former wife; Pamela Ortiz, a sales clerk at Brooks Brothers; Bob Merritt, an insurance salesman; two gay schoolteachers; Billy Lord, a city cop; Ted Gervin, an Assistant Vice President at Florida Banks; and Jean Belloi, a third stringer for the Bolts."

"If the Silveras' murders were not gang related, we could speculate that it was a revenge killing by someone left behind by the victims. I feel strongly that this is a very weak premise. Although it might be used to justify the reopening of the case. It certainly would explain why the DA wanted to review your statements. If they are fishing in this river, let's examine the possibilities."

"You. Since you were divorced from Heather for a few years, and there were, certainly, no emotional or physical attachments, seeking revenge is not reasonable. Forgive my personal comment, but among other emotions related to Heather's death, I suspect you felt some measure of relief."

"Pamela Ortiz was single and her family lived in Puerto Rico. They left the island to retrieve their daughter's body and went home immediately. She had no other relatives in Tampa. I doubt if there is any other connection between Pamela and the boys' deaths."

"Bob Merritt lived in Jacksonville. He was here for a sales convention. His wife and two daughters have since moved back to Duluth, Minnesota. He bought the wrong dope at the wrong time. No connection for revenge."

"The two gay schoolteachers . . . or roommates as the paper noted . . . were not known to frequent the meat racks. They were both in their 40's and had been a couple for over twelve years. They kept to themselves. No relatives claimed the bodies. That's gives a strong indication that no one would revenge their deaths."

"Billy Lord was a major loss to his family. His father had deserted his mother when Billy was sixteen. The boy helped raise two sisters. Worked to support the household. Graduated in the top ten percent at Hillsborough High. Went to UF on a baseball scholarship, and graduated third in his class at the police academy. Three years on the force. Single and giving his mother money every month. He had uncles and cousins on the force and with the fire department. His funeral was a huge show. Two churches and lots of wailing, gnashing of teeth, and beating of breasts. Preachers spoke out against the drugs and the crimes they bring. Here are two strong possibilities for revenge. Cops don't like cops being killed regardless of the circumstances. They would be willing to overlook Billy's of addiction to exact revenge. Or, did Billy's family and extended family . . . the Black community . . . find Billy a martyr worthy of revenge."

"Ted Gervin, the banker, frequented the singles bar. And there is some indication he liked the rough trade. That would explain the purchase of street drugs. He had no significant other, male or female. His parents are in their eighties and are active in the Methodist Church. Ted's brother and sister live in California. It would be a real stretch to see revenge coming from that direction. But, I'm sure the DA will pursue every possibility."

"The goalie for the Bolts was new to the area. His family, like the Ortiz's, claimed the body and retreated to the safety of their native land."

"There you have my take on the victims and the possibility of revenge from loved ones. Plus, the factor of timing. The Silveras were killed four days after the first victim was found and two days after the last victim, Heather. Those whom the victims left behind would have spent more than four days just finding the boys. All of those except you and the police, that is. My guess is that the beat cops knew exactly where the Silveras lived. You were not sure. You had been to his neighborhood, but not his apartment. The cops could be motivated to avenge one of their own and maintain their prestige of power in the community. They can't let some street dealer get away with murder. It tarnishes the illusion that they are in control. With Heather dead, you have Gene to care for. You would be a fool to risk losing him as a result of an act of revenge. In my book, there is some layer of the force that is deep in the weeds on this one."

"What about Peter Johnson, Heather's druggie, low-life lover?"

"There is no record that the police talked to him. His name was a real surprise to Flaherty. Did you notice his expression when we mentioned Johnson? How his eyes widened? And, Miss Bridgers wrote down the name. It was the fourth entry she made in her notebook. The fact that there is no record of the police talking to Johnson doesn't mean they didn't. It's just not in the records that Flaherty had seen or that I can access. What about him?"

"He has a minor record. Heather once intimated he had been indicted for murder, but the charges were dropped. He was a fisherman of sorts. Day boats for tourists. I think he bought drugs for use with Heather. I'll bet he went with her to buy drugs from the Silveras. He used to live in St. Pete. Near Alternate 19 about 54th Avenue. This was years ago. I have no idea where he is now. But, since you're digging and I'm paying, Peter Johnson is someone about whom we should know more."

"I'll get my people digging into Mr. Johnson. By the way, we have never discussed my fees and expenses. Because I am intrigued with all of this and am convinced I can get some benefit from it beyond my stipend, my fee will be halved. My expenses cannot be altered. They are outside my immediate realm."

"Let me know when you reach $5,000. I'll pay at those increments. I believe that is the equivalent of 100 pints of blood. OK?"

"OK, but don't forget the sperm bank. They pay handsomely."

Billy Lord and the long blue line of the police force. A viable choice for the revenge angle. It would also explain why the investigation ended with the Silveras' deaths.

Stop by the office. Nothing that requires my immediate attention. Show and tell with the ice cream company next week. I want to see all the material two days before the presentation. I go home for a swim. I can connect to the office network with my home computer.

Afternoons like this are rare and I always have to pay with night work. Shower and check my e-mail. *bconsolo: Heard from Liz Bridgers. Flaherty is going public with the investigation. Seems he feels confident he is on the right trail. There is even some pressure from somewhere inside the government to 'cleanse this festering sore with the bleach of public awareness'. This is not my quote. The caca will hit the rotary very soon. Guard, keep and protect Gene from the intrusion. Hugs and kisses.*

The evening news is right on cue. A breaking story centered on the DA press conference. A background story during the second hour gives the viewers a plethora or non-information. Names, occupations, situations. NewsBreaker 11 promises further details during the late news. Stay tuned. The door bursts open.

"I'm famished. I wanna eat. Why are you home?"

"Steak, brown rice and beets OK?"

"Dad, road kill would be fine if cooked long enough."

"I took the afternoon off and so I gave Mrs. Torres the afternoon off. Is that OK with you? Now shower and change. Dinner will be ready in half an hour. How did you get home?"

"Mrs. Torres called the school, and I got a ride with Ben."

After the first few feral bites, he eats very slowly. Extracting the flavor and texture from every bite. This makes the meal last almost an hour.

"Gene, the District Attorney announced today he is reopening the murder case of Hector and Osvaldo Silvera and the deaths of your mother and the other seven people. There is nothing to fear and nothing we can do. I have spoken to Mr. Flaherty of the DA's office and he has assured me that they have no need to talk to you. I have hired Tory Covington to represent us . . . you and me . . . in this matter, although I doubt our involvement will be great. I know this is like picking at old ringworm sores. I want you to know you will be protected. We haven't talked about your mom's death in great detail. I have stayed away from the subject. I had hoped you could work all garbage out of your system with Dr. Yager. I think it's time we talk about it now."

"OK, I was here in the house when she died. I woke up for school. I found her at the kitchen table where she often painted. I called you. You came. The police came. We went on a two-week vacation. The place was cleaned up. We came back. You moved in. I go to school. You go to work. I guess we're a family."

"What are your feelings about mom's death?"

"I was sad. Sometimes even now, I am sad. At first I felt there was something I could have, or should have done to protect her. She was very sick. She took a lot of medications. I realize now she was probably taking too many pills. But, it was her life and there was nothing I could do. She cared for me in her own way. As best she could. Sometimes she tried to convince me that I was not well and that I would feel better if I took "happy pills". I tried that for about three weeks. I flushed the pills down the toilet. One of us had to be strong. It had to be me. I don't feel guilty or abandoned. I wish she were alive and healthy. But, that can never be."

"You have made some terrific progress according to Dr. Yager. I want you to know that I never get into details with him. He won't let me. I do get an outline status report every three months. He has told me, and I'm sure you know this, you can stop seeing him when you feel comfortable with going solo."

"Soon I'll be there. I've got some things I want to understand."

"Thanks. You sound very grown up. Maybe more than me. I'm sure the news has reached your buddies at school. There may even be some talk about it. If you need help, call me. I can be at school in a heartbeat. Now off to study and sleep. I'll take a hug."

His embraces me with solidarity from neck to knee and he squeezes me.

I turn my attention to clean up; the after-meal exercise that wastes time. He sounds very grown up. Too grown up. Very cool. Very collected. Maybe too controlled, like a watch spring. May be wound too tight. This makes me think.

This is another step away from me. Gene is expanding his universe and I am not in it.

Very early morning at the office. Before sunrise. After two hours I must go back home and waken Gene for school. E-mail Beatrice and thank her for the advanced warning. She replies:

> *I can get away from Tallahassee and come to 'Pa town to be with you on Saturday night, if you want. Tell me the motel and I'll be there by six. If it's OK?*

I reply:

> *I am honored and excited. It will be like a college date. Motel room for two. No chaperones. I have made reservations at the Embassy Suites on Lawton Childs Parkway. Can you make the game . . . it starts at 4:30. I'll send directions. I'll call the motel and tell them that you will be staying there also. Thanks for taking the initiative.*

I better tell Gene at dinner tonight. Tory calls. He informed the DA's office that they best be very careful in their proclamations. His clients, Mr. Baker and his son, Gene, don't take kindly to the public looking through their windows. Any intrusion into the sanctity of their lives may result in a very nasty lawsuit. Sometimes, Tory gets a touch to folksy. Particularly when he threatens.

"Peter Johnson is not to be found at any of his old haunts. His neighbors think he moved over to the beach a few years ago. His former employer hasn't heard about that, and I quote, 'worthless piece of fish gut' for six months. But, the owner of a fishing boat gave us some leads. My people are on it. And, here is the best part. I took the liberty of leaking to our friend, Mr. Flaherty that I thought it strange that Mr. Johnson's name was not mentioned during the press conference. Flaherty was cool. He didn't miss a beat. Told me they were trying to contact Mr. Johnson to see if he could shed any light on the investigation. Flaherty acted as if Johnson had been on the interview list all along. Hell that dumb Yankee never even knew who Johnson was until I told him. Better two coon dogs on the trail than just one."

"Tory, you're too much. I am going off radar after the Saturday game . . . around six-thirty. If you need me, call before then. I will not be taking my cell phone on the trip."

"Hell no. Have a good time. I'll talk to you Monday. By then I will have located Mr. Johnson. Then you and I will have to decide what to do with him. Safe trip off the radar."

Dinner. Laundry. Sleep while the dryer is running.

* * * * * *

The game goes as practiced. The second team started and played three quarters. They were great. We held the Seahawks to 65 total yards. Eight wins. No losses. Gene and I head for home. He showers and heads downstairs to be picked by Jon and his mom.

* * * * * *

I begin to think of Beatrice. Is she pursuing me? Why? She could have any number of men. Some more successful. Some with greater potential. Some younger. Most better looking. And while the analogy of looking the gift horse in the mouth demeans Beatrice's beauty, I can't help but ask why me? Why now? Suspicions are terrible. They play with your mind. Suspicions about love eat at your soul.

I was suspicious of Heather. Her all-nighters without me. Coming home as I was leaving to go to work. I remember the night she came home wearing the unmistakable aroma of Polo. She claimed she was at a party and they were spritzing each other with the host's colognes. I wanted to believe her. I could not. I didn't make love with her for four weeks. I couldn't. I was so hurt, I was furious. That night was a test of our relationship and she failed. My unearthing of her failure ate at me for years. I treated her differently for the next few years. Sex was, on most occasions, alcohol induced. I didn't want to love my wife I wanted to abuse a stranger. I attempted to brutalize her whenever I could. I would do things and make her do things that were outside my world of enjoyment. Lotions, instruments, apertures. Nothing was off limits. Our bed life became couch life, bathtub life. It was frenetic. I would take her with no emotion other than the drive for my release. Fast and violent became my style. If she enjoyed it, fine. I didn't care. Finally, she stopped coming to bed. She was afraid of the violence and hated the absence of her fulfillment. Tough shit. She started it.

The Embassy Suites is a pleasant chain. I register and pay. As I unpack, the telephone rings.

"Are you naked?"

"No."

"Well, you better be naked when I arrive."

"And when would that be?"

"When you hear the knock on the door."

Immediately there is a knock on the door. I am behind the door peeking out at the hall. She is standing in the doorway cell phone in one hand and unbuttoning her blouse with the other.

"How far is the restaurant from here and what are you doing with your clothes on?"

"Five miles and I'll take them off if you close the door."

On Sunday, my date heads back to the state capitol. The guys meet at home.

IX

We played the first game of the day. Twice each season the Varsity and JV teams play in the morning and the two younger squads, Midgets and Super Midgets, play in the afternoon. The Varsity has to arrive at the field by 7 AM sharp to dress and walk through their assignments. Getting 13 and 14 year old boys up and out of the house by 6:30 on a Saturday is a Herculean task for any parent. Young teenage boys look and act like zombies at that hour. It is the coaches' job to instill excitement in the souls of the players. No easy task. The boys know the importance of each game. They also love to complain. The league officials and the coaches know there will no beer drinking and very little gambling in the stands at this hour. The playoffs are a different story because they are held in the late afternoon. The coolers and the odds makers will be visible throughout the stadium. Once the morning game is underway, the boys will perform up to their level of excellence.

The game goes well. Despite sluggish starts on both sides of the ball, the offense scores five times and the defense shuts down the Bucs. The second team defense plays two and one-half quarters. They are maturing nicely. We are nine and zero. Now all of us have the afternoon and evening off.

Saturday afternoon at the mayor's manse. Beatrice, me, and 100 of the mayor's closest and dearest friends. I am not a political invitee. I have been invited to be scrutinized by *mami* and *papi*. I am the man who has been seen in public with their only daughter. It is now time to step in to the lion's lair and be sniffed. Approaching the wrought iron gate,

I am more nervous than when I was a teen on my first date. The electronic system has been deactivated and the gate is manned by two uniformed cops. Two older guys who have been rewarded with this tough overtime duty.

"Jacob Baker."

"Thanks. Pull your car up to the house someone will park it for you. Have a great time."

Their smirks told me they knew exactly who I was and why I was on the short, family list. Not the long, business list. The valets were also cops. The cars on the side yard ran the gamut from utilitarian to ostentatious. My 320i, with its modifications, pales in comparison to the other male toys. Some say the bigger the car the smaller the penis of the driver, and the smaller the car, the larger the penis. How I wish that were true. Beatrice is waiting in the double door entrance to the house.

"I was slightly concerned you were going to be a no-show. And, I think I would have understood it if you hadn't shown. But, you're here."

I have never been in a house of three generations of Tampa wealth and power. The house certainly manifests its status. The heavy and ornate furniture, sconces, carpeting, and floor lamps speak of the turn of late 19th Century Spanish culture. The designs, color schemes, and art reflect international trade. My Scottish heritage, grounded in the rudiments of household décor, was almost disoriented by this environment.

"Jacob, you know my father."

"It's nice to see you, sir. Thank you for inviting me."

"Jacob, it's good to see you. I hope you and your son are standing up under the magnifying glass of public scrutiny. The DA's office hasn't got to him have they?"

"No sir. Mr. Flaherty, Mr. Pennington, and Mr. Tory Covington have an agreement to leave Gene out of all this nonsense."

"Antonio, don't monopolize Mr. Baker."

"Mrs. Consolo, it's nice to meet you. I believe we met very briefly once before. A Grand Preview at the Museum about a few years ago."

"Jacob, please call me Marguerite. Why yes, I believe you're correct. *Photography* of *the Fifties* was the show. It was before the tragedies. Let's not dwell on the past. Let's look to the present and the future."

Marguerite glanced at Beatrice and smiled a motherly, wishful smile.

"Be comfortable in our home. Did you bring a swimming suit? We have a big pool."

"Beatrice told me about the pool and I came prepared to swim later."

A small lie to keep up pretenses.

"Please excuse us. We must attend to other guests. Stay after the party. I'd like to have some real time to talk."

The mayor disappears through a sliding oak door into his den. There are four men waiting for him. I have never seen them before. Two short and thin. Two bulky . . . like body guards. They do not smile or acknowledge the mayor's entrance. The door slides shut and is locked.

Beatrice takes my hand firmly and leads me to the sun porch. From the dark red, black, and gold entry toward the sun and flowers of Eden. The first phase of paradise. A few couples are seated in the expensive pillowed wicker furniture. The three sets of small paned double doors open to the patio, which looks over the flower-bedecked lawn. The long-stemmed flowers nestled in tall blue or purple glass vases on the tables sway in the breeze. Wicker furniture and flowers to match the print of the pillows. Slightly different floral arrangements. Nature's breezes do the work of ceiling fans. Twos and fours. The women seated. Men hovering. All very brightly dressed in tropical finery. There are no charcoal, brown, or olive colors. Shoes are pastel or white. Servers mingle, distributing drinks and canapés. No shouting. Muffled laughter. A lot of whispering.

There seems to be no cross-pollination of clusters. No ebb and flow. The societal pods have been established and are stet. Only Beatrice, her parents, and her aunt and uncle can interject themselves into the tightly knit sets. Hell, it's their party. And, in that I am a guest of Beatrice, I am afforded the privilege to interrupt, introduce, interject, and move on. Two hours of this is more than my quarterly quota of mingling. I am not a social animal among strangers. I begin to think of Gene. The simple days of doting father and adoring baby. His look. Hair. Stature. Demeanor. My reverie is broken.

"You look like you could use a swim."

"Is it time to cleanse the social dust of the Wonderful One Hundred from my body?"

"In about thirty minutes, the pool will be ours. *Mami* and *papi* will join us. You can change in the cabana. You remember where that is, don't you?"

"I think I can find it. I'll get my suit from my car. Excuse me will you?"

I can maintain the charade as long as necessary.

No need for the valet to retrieve my trusty steed. I find the key and stroll casually to my car. My suit is wrapped in a towel on the passenger seat. Beneath the towel there is an envelope. Something added to my car while I was inside. I am careful to open the envelope by holding it with towel covered fingers. Must protect any fingerprints. In the envelope is an audiocassette. This, too, I handle carefully. I go to the driver's side, open the door and sit. Turn on the ignition and insert the tape in the player.

Jacob Baker, what the hell are you doing? Talking to the DA? Hiring that fat cat shyster, Covington? What the fuck are you afraid of? We know don't we? Running with the Consolo bitch won't protect you any more than Covington, the big condo with all its security, or your goody two shoes public persona. Silence is golden. Our silence is worth about $50,000. We'll be in touch.

With all the cops around, how could any low-life have gotten the keys off the valet rack, entered my car, and put the keys back without arousing suspicion. Unless the low-life was a cop or part of the catering group. I doubt he is a cop. More likely the scum is a part timer working for Cortez. I put the tape in the envelope. Keys in my pocket. I will be leaving well after the valets and gate guards.

Rush to Beatrice for protection. She won't let anything bad happen to me. She is already in the pool on the inflatable raft. Not the appropriate time for a rerun of the first swim.

"Jacob, hurry and change."

I do. Diving into the deep end, I swim with measured strength to the raft and hold on for dear life. She cannot know of the gift of sound in the car.

"Look out here comes *mam*i."

"Jacob, I watched you this afternoon. You handled yourself well in among the sharks and backbiters. Some of this crowd can be rough. But, they love Antonio. They should. He has made most of them rich beyond their childhood dreams. Now come over here and visit with me."

"Yes Marguerite."

I replayed my life's history in the abridged version. Just the extremes. Highs and lows. Where I was, am, and hope to be soon. My audience of one absorbed every word and nuance. I was auditioning for the leading role in her daughter's life and, beneath the façade of maternal graciousness, *mami* was an exacting critic. Her eyes bore into me. Her smile was warm, but constant, and, therefore, somewhat cosmetic. The interrogation lasted about three quarters of an hour. I am saved by the mayor's arrival.

"Marguerite, you're going to frighten Jacob away. He will think your police-style Q&A is how we treat all of Beatrice's male friends. Jacob, would you like a Scotch? I have some 21-year old single malt. A name I can't even pronounce, but I'm told it has the taste of heaven. Not my version of the promised land, though. Join me in the cabana."

Antonio has provided a genuine excuse to leave the world of the thumbscrew and bamboo shoot.

"It's pronounced Balvenie. And, you're correct. It is a soul-warming balance of peat smoke, malt richness, the spike of heather, and the sweetness of honey. Aged in casks, which are never reused, but destroyed by fire. The ashes are used to filter the next batch before it enters the casks. I'll have mine with an equal part of water and no ice, thank you."

"That's damned amazing. I can't drink the stuff. You romance it. We don't have much time here to talk like men, so listen. I know you're getting heat from the DA's office about the deaths a couple of years ago. Beatrice asked if I could help take some of the pressure off you. Unfortunately, there is nothing I can do to protect you and your son from the public scrutiny. That would be interference. And I'm a politician. I didn't get elected to three terms by interfering with police investigations. That would look very bad. But, be aware that I am aware, and if I hear anything I will tell Beatrice. Now let's go to the ladies."

What the hell was all that about? I never asked for his help or the help of his office. Why is he even involved? Now the whole family has their noses in my business. Who else?

The day drifts into twilight. Gene is with Alex. A good bond. Among the many things a parent can hope for his child are good friends. As I examine this concept, I realize how inane it really is. A child's first friends are his parents, then siblings. If these relationships are healthy, the child will associate with similar healthy people as he grows. When Gene was a tot, he had parents who were his good friends. As he grew, his mother drifted in to self-pity and self-indulgence. I tried to fill the void. I was not completely capable, because one cannot take the place of two, and I had become very angry. His parochial school gave him the environment he needed as his home life endured early tremors. He met kids, who would be his friends for the next twelve to fifteen years. Maybe for life. He joined a healthy new family. Ruminations like these always lead to self-flagellation. Was I a bad parent? Why didn't I do more? Where did I fail? Ad nausea. It is so easy to slip into that slime pit. Stop.

"Earth to Jacob. Earth to Jacob."

"Sorry."

"You had the look of someone who was not here. Where did you go? Was it fun? Can I come along next time?"

"Just thinking about Gene. And I guess the alcohol and the pressure of the day got to me."

"What pressure?"

"The party. Your parents. Be honest Beatrice. Your mother must have learned her questioning skills in a former life. Handed down from the Spanish Inquisition. From Torquemada. Don't get me wrong. I appreciate that she is concerned about who is seeing her daughter. And, I'll bet there is no small interest on her part about your long-range plans. I was not offended. I am honored."

"*Mami* and I argue about control. She wants control over my life and I won't to give up any control. So, her way of inserting herself into my life is to know and be known by my friends. She has scared-off a few of the weaker ones over the years. She and I have had hell to pay. But, we get over it. I knew she would confront you. I hoped you would be strong enough and sympathetic enough to handle her. You are and were. *Papi* was next. But, his discussion is more direct. Remember I am their baby daughter. Are you hungry?"

"God no. I ate all afternoon. But, I will avail myself of another tip of your father's scotch. Can I get you anything?"

"A cold beer. This one is almost hot."

✱ ✱ ✱ ✱ ✱ ✱

On my way home I replay the tape. Blackmail. Who the hell would blackmail me? Why? I have very little money. I bought the condo with the meager amount left by my mother. For all anybody knows, I live month to month as my business grows. I should take the two tapes to Ross's Studio. Reggie can dissect the recordings. Like reading entrails. He'll be able to tell me who the voice is. I'll call Reggie on Monday morning before he goes out on the boat. See if I can get into the studio with him alone before noon.

I reach him on his personal cell. He is not pleased to come to the studio on Monday. When he moved here from Michigan and set up the studio, he let it be known, he would work only four days a week, and never on Monday. But, we go way back. I have to tell him some of the details. He knows most of the rumors. I provide a few threads of texture for his head only. He sets up both tapes so that the electronic pattern of the voice can be displayed on side-by-side monitors.

The vowel "e" is not quite same in each. The word pacing is not quite the same. The breathing is not quite the same. Reggie plays the tapes over and over and over. He tweaks this dial and that button. More fade. More balance. More bass. Less treble. He tries to override the distortion. Find something in the background. A hint. Anything.

"These are definitely not the same voices. The voices are both males. Tape one has the flatness of the Midwest. Tape two has a slight drawl of the South. Tape one is in a hurry. Tape two is calm, cool, and collected. And the tracks were not even recorded in the same place. In tape one I can hear what may be traffic noises. In tape two there is nothing. Also, the tapes have different timbers and reverbs. So, Jacob, me boy, you have two friends. And, I'll bet they each has their own set of buddies. I am not going to ask about the message content. As a good friend, I would never presume. I have done my analytical best. Now, if you'll excuse me, I have a boat to sail."

* * * * * *

Are they really sequential? Did someone else hear the first tape and decide to join in the blackmail game? Who? Who owns the first voice? Someone I consider a friend? Who would do such a thing? Did the second voice know of the first message? I want to set a trap. Call TC on my office phone tomorrow and relay the horror of the tape, all the details, and my suspicions. Make sure people in the office know I am calling Tory. My guess is that a third tape, and there will be a third, will reveal the general area of the leak. Then Reggie can analyze the voice and I'll know if it was caller number one or caller number two. I can go from there. I have time. If caller number two is serious about the money, the third call will be within a few days.

I am now bait. Just what I've always wanted to be is a lamb in a shark tank. My parents did not spent tons of money for a very good Ivy League education so I could be bait for a blackmailer. I'm sure they would not be happy their money was so badly invested.

Wednesday, the message light on the home phone is blinking.

> *We reconsidered our offer of serenity. You are trying to fuck with us so your peace of mind will cost you $100,000. One simple payment and you'll never hear from us again. Start collecting the money. We know you can find it. We'll call you tomorrow with delivery instructions. Do not involve the police. We have ways of making you very sorry for your stupidity.*

To Ross Studios. He excuses all the staff. He needs thirty minutes. Compares tape three with tape one. Not the same. Tape two is the match. Could it be someone in my office? Someone who heard the first tape, tried to replicate the voice, and almost succeeded. Thought he could profit. Why does he hate me? I call TC and tell what I know. He tells me to give all the right signals. Without publicly announcing my task, make sure people in my office are aware that I am busy collecting a substantial amount of money and doing so under duress. Then wait for the next call.

Thursday evening.

> *We know you have done as you have been told. You're not foolish. Just evil. Tomorrow at 6:05 AM drop the money in a green trash bag in the third basket from the south end of Palm Ridge Boulevard. That's real close to your home. No cops before, during or after. Then you are free. If you don't follow our instructions precisely, we will take drastic and very painful steps to reprimand you.*

Tory delivers the monopoly money in tightly wrapped packages inside a sealed green bag that night.

"Just do as he said. Take the bag out to the basket, drop it in, and leave. I'll take it from there."

"I feel stupid asking this now, but shouldn't we involve the police?"

"You are being extorted for a crime in which you have no involvement. But in which the DA thinks you are deeply involved. The criminal thinks he has some information about the death of your wife and the murder of the Silveras you wish would never come to light. We know there is no connection between you and the crimes two years ago. But, our friend Flaherty would be very interested in making something out of nothing. To build his reputation. It's his job. We want this tempest to blow away with no damage to you. And, there might be a connection between this caller and Peter Johnson. Maybe the caller can lead us to Mr. Johnson. Let me take care of this matter. Once we have the caller in our possession, I'll call you. Then we can get on with our lives."

✶ ✶ ✶ ✶ ✶ ✶

The sun is hinting at rising. There are few runners on the boulevard. I drop the bag in the basket and go home. In the midst of my post-shower toweling, the phone rings. TC, the trapper, has the extorter and the bag of funny money at a warehouse in West Tampa. I am there after getting Gene up for breakfast and his ride to school with Ben.

"Jimmy English, you rotten fuck. Why?"

The upper half of Jimmy's body—from his hair to his waist—is covered with bright yellow powder. He is wearing running clothes. His wrist is cuffed to an eyebolt in the wall. He's not running anywhere now. He looks stupid. Not a threat.

"Easy money, man. You had it. I knew you had the money. I wanted it. I heard about the first call and just expanded on the concept. I figured you would cough up the money to hide something. Hell, we all have evil in our closets. The first caller thought you did something bad. What are you going to do about it?"

"I gave you a good job. You made good money. You had security. And you tossed it all away. You are a real dumb fuck. Tory, what am I going to do about it?"

"Mr. English is going to make a statement, audio and written, sign the written copy and quietly leave town. Never to return. We'll even help him pack and buy him a one-way plane ticket to the city of his choice. If he ever attempts to make anything of this affair, I will have Mayan, my friend here, make still his tongue. The entire process should take less than two hours. You needn't stay. I call you by noon."

Tory hands me an envelope. His bill for time and expenses—$5,250. And a note: *One down and one to go.* I'm not sure what happened except I have been extricated from a very awkward situation. Am I out of the woods?

* * * * * *

Back at the office. E-mail from Beatrice:

You passed the test. When can we get together for special tutoring? How about a Sunday trip to our lagoon?

My reply:

You're the captain. I must follow your orders. See you at 8. Same pier. Same slip.

Gene and I are beginning to spend less time together on weekends. Partly his choosing. Partly mine. The process of leaving the nest is done in small, and somewhat painful, steps. I know Beatrice relieves my discomfort. I'm sure his buddies relieve Gene's, if he even thinks about it. This Sunday, Jon's dad is taking the boys horseback riding and target shooting at his farm near Brooksville.

Friday night we clean the condo. A task neither of us relish. Not a task for Mrs. Torres. She made that crystal clear when I hired her. But, we get closer as peers doing this pain-in-the-ass chore. Complete dusting and polishing. Scour the bathrooms with very strong disinfectant. Wash the kitchen and all the appliances. The project takes two hours. The two TVs are constantly blaring Friday night High School games. Next year Gene may even be on the game of the week broadcast. We shower and head to a neighborhood sports bar for wings and burgers. Three beers; one too many. Sleep is calling. Gene will be picked up by Jon's dad after the game on Saturday. He is excited. I am excited about a day on the water with Beatrice.

Saturday's game was sloppy. We gave up too many yards and two TDs. The second team was outplayed. Hell, they were spanked. But we are nine and zero. We are in the red meat of our schedule. No easy games as we get closer to the playoffs. Every team wants to play down in the elimination process. We always want to play a team that finished below us, so we can move on to the tougher games.

Three hours to our cove. No other boats in sight. Beatrice sheds her oversized T-shirt revealing breasts and a thong. I am out of my swimming suit in half a heartbeat. She is very orally active. I am her indulgence. It is a good thing.

X

Nine pumpkins are resting on a red Formica-topped, Aluminum-tube legged, two-winged table. This was the table my parents bought after WWII. It was a showpiece of economic prosperity and relief that the war was over. They had the table at both houses, in which I was raised. When we moved to the big house in the country, the table was relegated to the laundry room. Before the dump, I saved it like a stray puppy. The fluorescent lights are buzzing and dimly flickering. Their ragged luminescence is reflected in the pots, pans, and prep knives strewn on the counters. Despite the two walls of windows, there is no light coming from the outside. The floor is slimy with the strings, meat, and seeds of pumpkins. I have to steel myself from slipping. There are no supports. No chairs on which I can sit to perform the pre-Halloween ritual of creating Jack 'o Lantern from a candle stub and a face carved in the pumpkin. The evil spirits of All Hallows Eve are deflected from entering the home by placing the Jack 'o Lanterns by the front door and at the windows. Tonight I must carve while standing in the muck and slime of previous endeavors.

Cautiously I slide-step to the counter and take two pearl-handled knives. One has a wide blade of eight inches and will be used to make the initial, broad incisions. The blade of the second knife is narrow and three inches long. This will be the instrument of artistic creation. All the anthropomorphic details . . . eyeballs, eyebrows, teeth, curvature of the smile, and ears. Next I find a long-handled spoon for scraping and scooping the life from the pumpkins.

Once a lid is cut around the stem and lifted out, I dig the spoon into the meat, and remove the entrails of strings and seeds. Then I must dig an inset for the candle stub. Varying the length of candle as well as the height and size of the mouth produces differing countenances and light sources.

I survey the first trying to see the appropriate face for the Jack 'o Lantern. Each gourd has its own personality based on size and shape, and that specific personality must be manifested as the face of the finished product. The size and slant of the eyes. The distance from each other. Eyeballs or not. Big toothy grin or twisted snarl. Small nose or no nose at all. Before I can properly portray the psyche, I must study the pumpkin from all angles. Before I can cut, I must have a good idea how it will all turn out. Carpenters measure twice and cut once. For this all-important task, I must visualize numerous times and can cut only once.

I take the pumpkin in my hands to view all possible angles. It moves. I twist clockwise, it turns counter clockwise. I grip it firmly and try to twist again. Again it counters my turn. I can't lift it from the table. The vegetable appears to be firmly affixed to the Formica. It's on a swivel of some type. I stare at the side it wants me to see. Facial features appear. A human face, vaguely familiar, is emerging from the orange outer skin. Eyes, nose, and mouth. No hair. It as if it were projected by an outside light source. Eyes open. Lips begin to move ever so slightly. Am I seeing the flickering fluorescent light cast shadows off the ridges of the pumpkin? Or, is there true movement? The eyes look hollow. The lips display human sadness. There is some substance oozing from the nose. Dark mucus runs down the upper lip, around the mouth, and onto the chin. Tears appear in the corners of the eyes. They, too, flow to the chin. Now strings and seed begin to slide from the mouth of the human face on the pumpkin.

No noise. Just the emerging clarity of the face and the slow outpouring of glop. I look at the other pumpkins and they have acquired faces. Each different. Some male. Some *female. I'm not sure if they are trying to talk or if they are opening their mouths to let the goo pour out. They seem to be swaying. Not bouncing. They are moving in unison. There is a rhythm to their movement. I reach for the larger knife, but am powerless to grip it. All empty eyes now turn toward me. The mouths form words, but there is no noise.*

My gasp for air shatters the noiseless transformation from dream to reality. I sit up in bed unsure of my surroundings. I squeeze the pillow and reach for the bedside table lamp. The light is reassuring.

Three squad cars arrive simultaneously. One is forty-five degrees to the right; one is forty-five degrees to the left, and one parallel in front of the 1,000 square foot bungalow. It is not yet light and the nine uniformed policemen go to their assigned stations. Weapons drawn, the detectives bang on the door.

"Peter Johnson, open the door. It's the police and we have a warrant for your arrest in connection with the murder of Hector and Osvaldo Silvera. You have five seconds to respond or we will break down the door and enter the premises."

There is prescribed wait and one of the uniforms slams the door with a battering ram. It folds in and splinters as if it were made of balsa wood. Instantly, through the doorway cram four armed protectors of the populace and collectors of the corrupt. In less than ten seconds they pounce on the groggy, skinny body prone on the living room couch. Handcuffs are affixed. Rights are read. The fugitive is lead to squad car #3478. The entire process from arrival to departure consumes fewer than three minutes. The search of the dwelling takes several hours. In the fishing tackle, beneath the tarpaulin on the ground of the storage bin, Patrolman Rodgers comes across the second objective of the raid, a 25-caliber semi-automatic hand gun.

Peter Johnson is taken to the Hillsborough County jail on Orient Road. No preliminaries at a precinct station. All the paperwork is completed and he is given a chance to call an attorney. The public defender probably won't get there until 9 AM. Time for the Detectives and Assistant District Attorney Pennington to start their probe without the bother of legal niceties.

My voice mail light is blinking. Tory.

> *Jacob, the police found Peter Johnson. He is now at the Orient Road facility. I think his capture will heal this reopened wound. The police feel confident they have their man for Silveras' murders. Where they go with it is anybody's guess. Mine is that, if Johnson is the killer, Flaherty will not be happy until he pushes up the ladder and connects Johnson with the drug distribution in town. He'll get Johnson to roll on the big guys. This is the reason the DA's office opened the investigation to begin with. The fun for them is just beginning. Talk to your soon.*

At the facility on Orient Road, the Public Defender Sarah Stewart, her client, the police, and Assistant DA Pennington fill one of the small interrogation rooms. Johnson looks stunned. Hair unkempt. Face unshaven and dirty. Eyes glassy. Motions slow. He has yet to come to grips with the reality of the situation. A gram of coke, a dab of PPC and a lot of rum the night before make the morning after really tough. The PD is familiarizing herself with the charges. Her expression confirms the confused nature of the situation.

"Ms. Stewart, we'll have the ballistics report in a few hours. Once we confirm the 25-caliber hand gun found at your client's residence is the same gun that was used to murder Hector and Osvaldo Silvera, our case is a lock. We have two witnesses that put Mr. Johnson at the crime scene at the time of the murder. We know Johnson is a user and small-time street vendor. Here's what we surmise occurred. Johnson goes to the Silvera place to buy a load to deal. He and the Silveras get into it. Price, quantity, or quality. We don't care. A struggle ensues. We have photos to confirm that the place was a wreck. Neither Hector nor Osvaldo can get to their respective guns before Johnson pops them. Then Johnson continues the popping. Does a little surgical embellishment, because he is crazy or very angry or simply high on coke. He is used to gutting fish. So disfiguring the Silvers was not a stretch. Then he casually leaves. We have witnesses who heard the ruckus and gun fire. We have witnesses who put Johnson in the neighborhood before the Silveras' death and witnesses who see Johnson running from their building sometime later, after the shooting. Counselor, your client may not realize it now, but he has just begun a journey that will end when the state takes his life."

"Mr. Pennington, Mr. Johnson and I are not prepared, at this time, to discuss the merits or lack thereof of your case. He is obviously not well and requires medical attention. I have called the facility's staff and they will attend to Mr. Johnson. After which, he and I will confer. Then and only then will we discuss the situation. Until then, this camp fire is over. Mr. Johnson, say not a word."

"Miss Stewart, take all the time you need. We are proceeding to indictment, then trial, then conviction, then the death penalty. The public demands that this case be closed. It has remained open too long. Like a festering boil, it has caused the good people of Tampa great anxiety and unrest. It is the duty of the District Attorney's office to see that the guilty man is punished for this most heinous and brutal crime so that the people of the community can move on."

"The fact that the case has been open for so long is the result of shoddy police work and the flawed approach of your precious District Attorney's office. The DA's office simply closed down the case, because alleged bad guys were the victims. Now the new DA decides it is in his own best interest to reopen the case, find a scapegoat and grab a bunch of headlines. Save the speeches for the press conference. Nothing substantial will happen until I am ready. One thing you can't do is railroad my client. Your predecessor tried to ignore the murder as if it were just a couple of bullies fighting in the alley. Now you're trying to hang Mr. Johnson without a complete understanding of the situation of that night. Do they give you guys in the DA's office expediency training? You know, do what's best to ensure the sanctity of the office. But, don't let the truth get in the way. Well, the game has always been to do what the law intended. Facts and process. So, there will be no railroading. Not today. Not here. I'm sure even you understand that concept."

The knock at the door signals the two male nurses and a guard, who will take Johnson to the infirmary for a check-up.

"Mr. Pennington, I'll call you after I have had the opportunity to talk to my client. Say, sometime tomorrow. Until then, I want you to think self-defense. As in my client's reaction to the threat on his life made by two hopped up drug dealers. It was self-defense. Or, you could try to explain to me and a jury why you don't have the knife that did all the cutting. And, most likely cannot match the gun found to the gun fired. In other words, you have bupkus. Have a pleasant day, and stay away from my client."

"So what you are saying is that he is innocent of murder. But if he is guilty of something it is self-defense. A weak, transparent defense. Have a nice day."

✳ ✳ ✳ ✳ ✳ ✳

The ballistic report indicates only a very similarity of the LANs and grooves on the slugs from the Silveras and the test firing of the gun found at Peter Johnson's bungalow. No match. It would have been a greater percentage but for the fact that the slugs extracted from Silveras' skulls had flattened. They had ricocheted around the cranial cavity. Pennington must keep the damaging evidence out of the files until the last possible moment. Stewart would have a field day with a no match situation. No match of the slugs. No match of the gun. No murder weapon. She would say that it was simply uncorroborated circumstantial evidence. Add this to the absence of the cutting tool and the DA could have no murder tools at all. Not a good situation for Pennington. But, DA Flaherty goes public anyway.

"We have arrested the murderer of Hector and Osvaldo Silvera. Mr. Peter Johnson was arrested this morning at his home. After many weeks of sifting through the evidence, this office concluded that Mr. Johnson was the murderer. And after many hours of excellent police work, he was found cowering in his home, apprehended and taken to jail."

The usual inane questions are dealt with in the usually vague manner. Except three questions from Bill Stott from the *Weekly Inquirer*, a tabloid, voice-of-the-people type of newspaper.

"Mr. Flaherty, do you think Mr. Johnson acted alone or at the order of his bosses in the drug syndicate in this community?"

"At this time, we have every reason to believe Mr. Johnson acted on his own and not in concert with or at the command of others. However, we will keep an open mind to any facts, which may lead to further indictments."

"Mr. Flaherty, how deep into the political and social fabric of this community are you willing to go to unravel the drug money and influence, which has plagued this community for decades?"

"I believe you're getting too far afield. We have apprehended a murderer. And, although the crime was particularly brutal, Mr. Johnson is, as far as we know, just a murderer. We will ascertain if he acted alone or was contracted to assassinate the Silvera brothers. That determination may lead us to others."

"One more question; do you have the knife and the gun used in the butchery?"

"Thank you all for coming here this morning. That concludes the news conference. We have to get back to our jobs."

The newspaper of the establishment carries lots of background. Not Mr. Stitt's questions. Once again the eight victims of the Silveras' killer coke are displayed before the public. The DA's office pushed the newspaper coverage, because Flaherty wants public support for his work. Dragging out the long-since-dead victims is the easiest way to garner public sympathy. It also doesn't hurt that, at the same time, the average men and women of the community hate the arrested criminal. The theory goes, obviously, the police would not have arrested him, if he were not guilty. The lemming thinking process is clouded by sympathy and guilt. Sympathy for the victims. Guilt, because the common man is egotistically convinced he could have or should have done something to prevent a heinous crime. This all makes it easier to get a conviction. The seeds of righteous revenge are planted now. When the twelve good and true peers are seated in judgment, they don't even know they have been pre-conditioned to find the poor bastard guilty. Revenge sprouts upon the reintroduction of some, but not all the, facts. And it grows like kudzu, which chokes the jurors' objective, rational process. If the DA is really good at his job of influencing public opinion and reaction, he is assured of a conviction. The same can be said for the defense attorney. If she gets to the public quickly and with gusto, and paints a picture of pawn, dupe, frame up, or some other malady, she can keep her client on the street before, during and after the trial. The question is who is the more effective. Gene and I can finally put this ordeal to rest. The police have Johnson and enough evidence to convict him. Maybe even fry him.

"Good afternoon, Mr. Flaherty. Would it be convenient for you to take time from your hectic schedule of public appearances and spend a few moments with me this afternoon? You can even invite your toady, Mr. Pennington."

"Miss Stewart. How convenient. It appears that I have an open half-hour at 4 today. See you then."

Click. The game is afoot in earnest. The PD is going up the chain of command in an attempt to belittle the Assistant DA. Perhaps, Miss Stewart is a worthier adversary than Flaherty had assumed. Perhaps, she is schooled in the arts of brinkmanship, bluffing, and innuendo. Never know what they teach in law schools today. Flaherty grins with anticipation. He loves a battle of wits, when he has a bigger weapon. Size matters. He calls Pennington and listens to the conversation Pennington had at the jail.

* * * * * *

"Mr. Flaherty, my client is innocent of Murder One. That said, I'll give you some of the details to substantiate my statement. Mr. Johnson was in the Silveras' apartment the night the brothers were murdered. We acknowledge that. Mr. Johnson did not go there to buy drugs. Mr. Johnson went to the apartment to confront the brothers about the deaths their drugs had caused. Mr. Johnson was under great mental stress, because the drugs the Silveras sold had killed Mr. Johnson's lover, Heather Baker. Mr. Johnson was consumed by grief.

But, murder was not in his heart. He simply wanted the Silveras to understand the consequences of their actions, and to find out who had supplied the dope to the brothers."

"Mr. Johnson was not a violent man then and is not one now. I can produce character witnesses to that point. I will introduce testimony from his psychiatrist to that fact. And, I will allow that a state-appointed psychiatrist examine Mr. Johnson. I am confident your psychiatrist will corroborate the findings and opinion of the psychiatrist of the Public Defender's office. I am confident that the state-appointed psychiatrist will conclude that Mr. Johnson is not a violent man and could not have killed either or both Silvera."

"When my client arrived at the apartment, the Silveras were already dead. Blood was everywhere. Mr. Johnson panicked. And he had every reason to panic. He was standing over men who had just been slaughtered. A gruesome and heinous butchery. He was aware of the implications of his situation. Yes, Mr. Johnson was a customer of the Silveras. Yes, he was a street drug dealer. Yes, this is not a worthy profession and not a good business relationship in the public's eyes. But, he is not a killer. Then my client did something very stupid. He ran. I chalk it up to the fast acting combination of panic and stupidity."

"Wow! What a fascinating story. A fast acting combination of Gulliver's Travels and Alice in Wonderland. Drug induced fantasies. We have witnesses, the gun, and motive. SSSSSSSSSSSSSSSSSS. That's the noise of the electric pump forcing poison into Mr. Johnson's artery. Or would he prefer ZZCHCHCHRZ. That's Old Sparky's last word and testament as thousands of volts run from Mr. Johnson's head to toes."

"You are a sadistic Neanderthal."

"Your client is a butcher and a murderer. And he will pay for his evil deed."

"Not in your life time, sir. Good day."

Hell, she's not good at the game at all. She lifted her skirt and Flaherty saw she had no weapon of attack. This is going to be too easy. Caller ID tells him it's his friend from Atlanta.

"What did the Stewart woman have to say?"

"Nothing of substance. Just some fairy tale about Johnson being a softie and arriving at the scene after the murder. Johnson was grief stricken that the Silveras' bad dope had killed Johnson's lover. Now get this; his lover was Heather Baker. But, according to the good counselor, Johnson just wanted to talk to the brothers. To find out who had supplied the bad dope to them. He did not murder the suppliers out of anger and revenge. Seeing the corpse, he panicked and ran. What a crock of shit."

"Slow down. Do you think you can use Johnson in any way without jeopardizing the case against him? Does he have any information, which he would like to trade for a lighter sentence? We can afford to stop here only if this is truly the end of the line. Let's not stop too soon, like your predecessor. I agree the story has the smell of crap. But, if he had been to the Silveras' apartment before that night, he might have seen other people. People your predecessor did not want exposed. People, who could lead to people of influence and power in the drug trafficking business. I don't want to hurt the beast by cutting off an ear when I can kill the beast by lopping off its head. So, go slowly, don't let your hormones interfere with your judgment. Extract more from Miss Stewart and Mr. Johnson. And, while you're pursuing that path, I'll keep the national public happy with snippets of sound dealing with truth, justice, the American way, and your good work in Tampa. Stay in touch."

Flaherty stares at the cartons of folders that make up the police work on the case. Depositions and testimony. Medical reports. Evidence reports. Why does he have to do the dirty work? Because, his mentor has let it be known that he wants to ride this one all the way to Washington. And if the mentor goes to Washington, he will take Flaherty along as a faithful and trustworthy companion. Flaherty has to work so as not to be the horse, but rather a fellow traveler. So, he will be sure Pennington does all the heavy lifting. He looks briefly at the witness reports. Questionable veracity. The three men gave identical testimony. A description of Johnson. The time of his arrival. His car, color and make. The first three digits of the license plate. Even their vagueness was precise. Obviously they were coached. The police must have seen this. Maybe they were the coaches. If the former DA saw this conspiratorial consistency and did nothing, he was culpable of dereliction of duty. If he did not see it, either he was stupid, because he never asked, or it was kept from him by the police. Who paid him to not ask? If this evidence was kept from him, the police who conducted the evidence were in on the murder. And, its cover up. Who paid them? Well the new District Attorney has new squeaky-clean cops on his investigative team. Flaherty made sure clean cops were part of the arrangement that preceded the investigation. They will re-contact the witnesses. Call them in separately. Scare the shit out of them. Get one or more to contradict his statement. All the while the Pennington will be pouring over medical and evidence reports for inconsistencies.

The evidence report details fifty grams of the killer coke found in the apartment. Already in street bags. The ingredients of the stuff in the apartment matched that found by each victim. Four of the vics were regular customers of the Silveras. Again, testimony from the late night sidewalk superintendents. Different people. A mixed bag of men, women, and kids. So the stuff came from the Silveras. Where did they get it? The bags at their place were stashed behind the bed inside a wall panel. There was no cutting equipment or material in the apartment. It is safe to assume the brothers bought the stuff, already bagged, and were moving it out the door as quickly as possible. Who was their regular source? How can Flaherty find out?

XI

While Pennington sifts through the sand pile of documents, Flaherty turns up nothing spectacular . . . and that maybe something. It all appears to be too smooth. No major glitches. In fact, too many carbon copy similarities. This is a small and very often overlooked detail discovered by a fresh set of power-seeking eyes. The smallest details can tell the biggest story. One of the witnesses died of cancer shortly after the murder. His widow is now living much more comfortably in his death than when he was alive. Three-bedroom house with an in-ground pool and a new car in an upper-middle class neighborhood far away from the projects. Her situation is interesting. One witness left town to parts unknown. Left about three weeks after the murder. How convenient. The third witness owns a string of prosperous bodegas. When questioned twice, the storeowner stuck to his story. His memory was a little foggy on some of the facts, but he was consistent. He's the weak link. But, before sweating him out, Flaherty digs into the finances of the widow.

She receives a pension from the Seamen's union. Nice, but not enough for the cash that bought the house and cars. Records indicate that her two children, Paco and Anita, paid for the house. The house had been abandoned. The bank, which had foreclosed, was very interested in getting someone into the house. Why was a $250,000 house available for three-fifths of the assessed value? Motivated seller met people with cash. Deal done. Too neat. Too sweet. What about the children? How did a part-time sales clerk and a supervisor for the Parks Department come up with $150,000 in cash? On their incomes and with normal household expenses, they would have had to scrimp for at least 15 years. Yah, sure, like that could happen. Were they given the money by someone who wanted to reward their father's loyalty? Who?

The bodega properties were purchased as distressed merchandise from the same bank that held the mortgage on the house. Tampa Bank. Convenient distressed merchandise. It just so happened that this witness was looking to leave the sanitation department. Trade a cushy civil servant job for the long hours, stress, and uncertainty of the retail trade makes no sense to Flaherty. Makes sense that someone with very deep pockets financed purchases for statements that fingered Johnson as the murderer. Financed the statements to have the investigation stop with the murder of the Silvera brothers. But, why didn't the cops arrest Johnson. If they had their man and they could have convicted him then, why stop short of victory? The former DA stopped short of victory, because he was told to. The police stopped short of victory, because they were told to. The puppeteer has his hand in the pants of the DA and the cops holding all the Johnsons. Pete Johnson must know something. Something the puppeteer did not and does not want written in the newspapers and said on TV. How did Johnson protect himself? That question will have to wait? Flaherty knows to always follow the money. Go to the source of the money; the bank.

Tampa Bank, locally owned and very independent. Started about fifty years ago by the citrus grove owners, ranchers, and steamboat line families. They got their money from fathers and grandfathers who also owned land in the Caribbean islands and Central America. Shipping to and from. Distributing produce and livestock throughout Florida, the near Southeast, and then the South. The bank was a logical extension of the empires that were related through marriages. Rather like the kingdoms of Europe from the 13th to the 19th centuries. The bank had one office. It occupied a city block dead smack in downtown. The original building had been razed a decade ago to accommodate growth of commerce and services. Ever expanding its influence, the corporation simply acquired land, and added wings, then floors. Twenty of them to be exact. A commanding view of land and sea. And the Tower Club was just one flight up from the executive suite. Rumor has it that there is even a private, locked stairway connecting the top two floors . . . bank and club.

Professional bankers brought in from all over the world ran the day-to-day operations. But, the power of the money was controlled by the board of directors. Seats on the board were assigned to the eldest males of the founding families. There were no outside directors. Fathers and sons. Uncles and brothers. No women. Ever. It was the duty of the seventeen men to make damned sure that their empires ran smoothly and profitably. No glitches. When the empires ran smoothly so did the city and county. When the city and county ran smoothly, the citizens were happy. Hell the state was happy. No one from anywhere had ever questioned the integrity of the men. No one had ever doubted their loyalty to the area or their vision of a prosperous and growing future. Simply, the bank was in everyone's best interests. And everyone knew it.

The bank's annual report is sent to holders of voting and non-voting stock. There are twenty-seven non-voting share holders. It is rumored that these are the partners in the law firm, owned by the bank. A bio of each board member is standard for the report. The resume also covers business interests. E-commerce and software are the newest additions to the potpourri of businesses. The other businesses have been on the list for decades. The mayor's name is on the list of board members, but he is not permitted to be active while he serves in office. So his son, Alberto Consolo, fills the seat on an interim basis. How long is interim? Alberto, the son, has been invisible for years. Never seen at social events. Rarely visits his parents. The word on the street is that he lives in

Costa Rica and manages his family's international business from there.

Flaherty doesn't see a red flag of suspicion on the board. But, he knows there has to be some undertow of negative influence. The bank is too big not to be involved in everything that happens in Tampa. Good and evil. The bank was involved in the widow's new house and the bodegas. If it facilitated the dispersal of money, the money had to come from somewhere. Maybe it was on deposit. Maybe it belonged to the bank in a secret cash reserve and they just diverted it to keep customers happy. Hopefully, transactions necessary to buy-off witnesses would be visible on the bank's books. Hopefully, but doubtful. The transactions motivated by the board probably were never seen by a lowly bank officer. How does Flaherty get the bank's books without alerting everybody? If the board of directors smells an investigation, they will close the books and throw up the smoke screens of powerful legal delays. They have some of the best, most wired lawyers in the state. Hell, they own them. Flaherty cannot dig now. Not yet. He is like a peeping tom. He knows all the facts are within eye sight he just can't touch them or let anyone know he is looking. He will go after Johnson and the bank, while Pennington is assigned the job of attacking the bodega operator and the daughter of the other witness, one Anita Winny. These tasks will keep him buried in a less-than-fruitful exercise.

Pennington orders the police question Ms. Winny. Also a widow, she had given part of her late husband's insurance to her mother. A gift for all the money *mami* had spent raising her daughter. The daughter also could afford to send two children to private college. They lived away from home the four years while at school. She had expenses, yet she was able to come up with a big dollar gift for her mom. More digging is required. At the same time, Flaherty orders an excavation of the son's finances. Where did he come up with $75,000 on a Parks Department salary?

The Assistant DA learns that the owner of the bodegas, Ralph Sweat, is somewhat confused about the details of the night in question. He thinks he remembers a car. Not sure of the license. When he's supplied a phony description of Johnson, Sweat swears to it. The Assistant DA orders the cops to bring the lying bastard in to his office for some real tough questioning. Pennington wants him brought in after six PM. Night time questioning normally produces the best results. The interrogators are cranky, and the people being questioned are scared. Pennington will ask the questions and be sure that no one gets physical. The guy will be mind fucked.

"Mr. Sweat, we need to confirm a few details of your statement to the police about the night of Hector and Osvaldo Silveras' murders. Are you OK with that?"

"Sure. But, I gave the same information to the police a couple of times before. Why do you need me here now? I think I should call my lawyer."

"As I said, we just want to confirm a few very minor details. If you think you need a lawyer, please feel free to call one. As of now you're not under arrest. You're a witness, who is doing his civic duty by being helpful. And we are hoping this information gathering goes smoothly. Just a few questions. Just a few very minor details. You could be a big help in finally closing this case. Then you can go home with the thanks of this office and the citizens of Tampa. But, if you would feel more comfortable with your lawyer present, we can wait for the lawyer to show up. If we have to charge you with obstruction of justice, he can arrange bail. Is that what you want, Mr. Sweat?"

"No, I want cooperate. I want this to be over quickly."

"Great. Then let's begin."

"Do you remember where you were on the night the Silvera brothers were murdered?"

"Yeah, I was at the corner of 23rd and MLK. Hangin' with some of my buds."

"Who were the buds with you at the time?"

"I'm not sure of their names, just some guys I know from the 'hood."

"Are you sure you can't remember anybody's name?"

"Yeah, I'm sure."

"Were you drinking while standing on the corner?"

"Sure. Some Olde English and BB's. That's shots of blackberry brandy."

"You were drinking malt liquor and shots of blackberry brandy."

"Uh huh."

"Approximately how much malt liquor and blackberry brandy did you drink that night?"

"A quart and a pint."

"Did you get drunk that night?"

"Nah, I got a buzz, that's all."

"While you were at the corner of 23rd and Martin Luther King Boulevard did you notice any cars drive up and stop?"

"Lots of cars."

"Did you notice any cars containing white men?"

"Sure did. Just one. Damned few white guys come to that neighborhood at that time of night."

"Do you remember what the white man looked like?"

"Yep. He was about five seven or so. He had long dark hair and a black chin beard. He was a bit on the chunky side. No, more like he was built solid."

"Do you remember the car he drove?"

"Gray or light blue. Four door. Chrysler product. Pinellas County plate. First three digits were HDZ. The other numbers had mud on them."

"Do you remember what the white man wore?"

"Bright yellow short-sleeve shirt and tan pants. He had very clean white sneakers."

"Did you see where the white man went after he left the car?"

"He went into building 2309."

"Did you see the white man after that . . . later that night?"

"Yeah. He came runnin' out the building, jumped into his car, and raced off down the boulevard."

"How soon after he left his car to enter the building did he return?"

"About thirty minutes, I think. I wasn't payin' much attention to his comin' and goin'. I didn't keep a stop watch on him.'."

"Thank you, Mr. Sweat you have been very helpful."

"Can I go now?"

"Not fucking likely, you lying sack of shit."

"On the police report of two years ago, you described the man as tall with light hair. You said he wore a red shirt and dark pants. Which description is the truth, Mr. Sweat?"

"Maybe I'm confused. Maybe I was confused then. The booze and all. The darkness. I don't know. I better call my lawyer."

"Yes, you better call your lawyer. Mr. Sweat you're under arrest for hindering an investigation, obstruction of justice, perjury, and conspiracy to commit murder. You have the right to an attorney . . ."

The police take Sweat to a holding cell to await his lawyer.

Pennington is smug. He has out done Flaherty. He has pierced the armor of misdirection and obfuscation. He calls the big boss at state. No sense in going through Flaherty to earn points.

"So, you got something from an old man who admitted he had been drinking that night. His defense will stress the quantity of booze. Get him off as being just a drunk asshole, who craved the publicity. Better push him hard and fast. Get him to turn on the source of his money. Who got to him? Who paid him? Also, dig into the finances of Anita Winny's brother, Paco. On his limited salary, he had to be a conduit for someone's money. We need two legs on the ladder. Not bad so far. While you're devoting your time to that, I'll help you with the Johnson issue. Send me copies of this file. Somewhere among the den of liars, drunks and junkies, we'll find what we need."

The boss from state was cutting Pennington no slack. The boss maintained his lofty position, while Pennington did all the shit work for Flaherty. But, grabbing headlines and sound bytes was another story. Flaherty was the face to the public, because, as he had said numerous times, that was his job. And Pennington's job was to make Flaherty successful.

Paco's finances were clean. On the surface. Salary, $42,500. Normal deductions. Pension. He had moved up to Supervisor. Commanded twenty-two people. How in God's name could he accumulate $75,000 for his mother's house? Where did he keep it before he gave it to his mother? Records from his accounts at Tampa Bank showed that approximately three months after Paco's father died there was a deposit of $75,000 into Paco's savings account. Two months later, he gave the 75 to his mother. He probably conned his sister into paying the balance. Guilt is a powerful weapon. Get Paco to the police station to discuss the source of the 75. Pennington orders the police to pull Paco off the job during the day so everyone knows what is happening.

"Paco, we are investigating the death of the Silvera brothers and we'd like to ask you a few questions about your father."

"Not before I call my lawyer."

"You can call your lawyer, but it probably is a waste of time and your money. He'll charge you for wasting his time."

"So?"

"We just want to clear up a few minor details. We need your help to clear up these few minor details. If you help us, you will win the appreciation of the District Attorney's office and the citizens of Tampa. Just a few questions. This would be a big help, and you would be doing your civic duty. The citizens of Tampa, and the District Attorney's office would be very grateful. OK? Is that too much to ask?"

"No and no. I want my lawyer."

"OK, we'll wait. In the meantime, would you like some coffee or a soda?"

"Nah. Hey, what about my time lost on the job? Who's gonna pay me for that?"

"We'll clear it with the Parks Department. You're just doing your civic duty. Like jury duty. Unless you lie to us. Then we will have to arrest you and you will be away for a while."

"OK. I can't afford to be docked any pay."

The lawyer, his uncle on his mother's side arrives in thirty minutes. Obviously not too busy.

"As we have told your client we are trying to confirm a few minor details as background for our investigation into the murder of Hector and Osvaldo Silvera."

"My client had nothing to do with the murder or the investigation. His father, my brother, God rest his soul, gave a statement to the police. How can you expect my nephew to add anything to his dead father's story? He wasn't there."

"Well, we were reviewing Paco's bank records and we noticed a very large deposit into his savings account around the time of the murders, his father's death, and the purchase of his mother's house. We were wondering where he got the money."

"Why were you illegally examining my client's bank account records? What in the world would they have to do with the statement my brother made to the police about the murder?"

"His bank records are germane to our investigation. We have a duty to follow all leads. We find it very intriguing that such a large sum of money was deposited into Paco's account. Out of the blue, as it were, $75,000 mysteriously drops into his account. We know he is not a gambler, he does not play the ponies or the dogs, he didn't win the lottery, and he didn't sell any kind of illegal substance. Plus, he has been making bi-weekly deposits into the savings account of $100 over the years. Therefore, we were surprised by the size and timing of the deposit."

"My client's personal finances are not for public scrutiny. His personal finances have nothing to do with a closed murder case."

"They may have a great deal to do if they are illegally gained. They are important if he received the money as a payoff for his father lying to the police. For his father providing false testimony as to the identity of the man, who he claimed murdered the Silvera brothers. If your client took money as a bribe or as a payoff, we will prosecute him for hindering and conspiracy. And, we'll take his mother's house and throw her out on the street, because it was purchased will illegally acquired funds. But, if he cooperates and provides us the source of the windfall and we find it satisfactory to our needs, we'll let him go back to his life. We'll let his mother stay in the house."

"This is bizarre. May I have a few minutes with my client?"

Pennington and the two detectives leave the room. Stretch, pee, and coffee break. There is something exhilarating about the feeling a prosecutor gets when he has the bad guy by the nuts and there is nowhere to squirm. The bad guy has to remain still and do as he is told or suffer excruciating pain. Pennington feels this power now and he wants to savor it for a long time, but the lawyer calls.

"My client wants to be sure what he gets if he tells you the source of the money? How will that affect his mother's house? And, if the information he gives you helps in your investigation, will he be protected from reprisals, both legal and otherwise?"

"We don't think Paco is involved in the real issue of the investigation. We just need his help. If the information aids us in convicting the top bad guys, we will waive all prosecution of Paco. This meeting and the details he provides will not exist after the conviction. His mother's house will be safe. The bad guys will be put away, so there will be no retribution from them. We can't and won't be responsible for what happens on the job or from anyone not associated with the case."

The stare between stool pigeon and advisor tell all. Paco will give it up.

"OK, but I need your promise in writing."

"I'll have the document of potential immunity on your lawyer's desk by tomorrow noon."

"I get this call one day. Have no idea who the guy is. He tells me there has been a special deposit made into my savings account. The money is a gift from a friend, who appreciates what my father had done. I can do whatever I want with the money. Then he hangs up."

"Did he tell you how the money got into your account?"

"No."

"Did anyone, other than you and your wife have access to the savings account?"

"No."

"Did anyone outside the bank and your family know the account number?"

"No."

"What did he mean about what your father had done?"

"On his deathbed, *papi* gave me a key to a safety deposit box. I thought it was weird that the box was not at his usual bank. That's Tampa Bank. The box was at West Coast

Savings. He told me to look inside the box. Read what he had left and use it only if I was in serious trouble. Trouble I couldn't get out of without a lot of help. I never looked in the box."

"You mean that some guy, for no reason at all, gives you $75,000. You never wondered why. You never went to the safety deposit box to learn what your father had left you. Can you say bull shit? How stupid do you think I am?"

"OK, OK. The day after the funeral, I looked in the box, and read *papi's* diary. I saw what he had told the police about the night of the murder, and what he really saw. I saw where I should contact Jimmy Jimenez or Roberto Pena if I got into trouble. They would make sure I got money for what *papi* told the authorities. It was all in his hand writing."

"So it was Jimenez or Pena who called you to tell you the money was in your savings account?"

"No, I told you I didn't recognize the voice. But, the guy was not Jimmy or Roberto. I know that for sure."

"Do you still have the key to the safety deposit box?"

"Yeah, it's at home in my jewelry box."

"We'll need to get the key and get the diary from the box. In the meantime, you will be safe in jail."

★ ★ ★ ★ ★

Miss Stewart has been summoned to the District Attorney's office.

"Thank you for coming on such short notice."

"Where is Mr. Pennington?"

"His talents are needed elsewhere."

"Good he was a pompous schmuck. Besides, he was not very smart. Rather like your go-fer. I am happy to deal with the decision maker."

"Well, I'm sure you'll find our working relationship more to your liking. The District Attorney's office wants to keep the Public Defender's office happy."

"Allow me to repeat for the record. I had informed your office that Mr. Johnson had been at the scene of the murder, but that he had arrived after the Silvera brothers had been shot and mutilated. Mr. Johnson was grief stricken that the Silveras' drugs had killed Heather Baker, who had been Mr. Johnson's lover. Mr. Johnson panicked and fled."

"Why is it that Mr. Johnson never came forward with this testimony before now?"

"The police never came after him. So he just remained quiet. He didn't want the publicity. He is known to have frequented the Silveras' apartment. And he most assuredly doesn't trust the police or the legal system."

"Is there any other reason Mr. Johnson sat on this incredible information. Was he influenced to do so?"

"I can't say, because I don't know."

"If he is innocent, as he protests, how can he prove it?"

"Without a confession from the real murderer, Mr. Johnson cannot provide an iron clad lock that would prove his innocence. But, then you can't prove his guilt without the gun and the knife. And I doubt that you have either weapon. Oh, you have a gun, but since there has been no ballistic report made available to me, I doubt the hand gun found at Mr. Johnson's home is the weapon that killed the Silveras. Let me get back to a previous point. If there were involvement in this murder by parties, high profile parties, would this have a bearing on the prosecution of my client?"

"In the abstract, yes. In reality, maybe. The extent of involvement by other parties and their position in the community could influence this office to offer some type of lesser sentence to Mr. Johnson."

"Suppose my client had been encouraged to keep his mouth shut. Not about the murders, but about whom he saw at the Silveras apartment before the murders. About the Silveras' drug source. Not only the direct connection, but also people levels above the connection. Hypothetically, if Mr.

Johnson had this information and was forthcoming, would that influence your prosecution of him for murder?"

"Hypothetically, this office is always interested in landing larger fish and letting the minnows swim away. Tell your client it's better to be a witness than a defendant."

"Let me talk to Mr. Johnson. I'll get back to you."

"Make it snappy. The second hand is moving."

"You're almost as big a putz as Pennington."

"Well, I'll have to work at raising my standards, now won't I?"

XII

These weekends are getting to be regular. Regular is good. On Sunday, I'm with Beatrice and Gene is with his buddies. Dinner and a movie with my son are not possible when Gene has decided to take this other step away from me. It's tough to encourage his progress, when I want him to stay close. I know he can never grow up unless he does most of it on his own. I am the safety net. He always knows how to reach me. Years ago, when I was a kid, I called home. Today, Gene calls my cell phone. This Sunday he is with Alex. Movies and the mall. I have no idea what the big attraction is with the mall. I suspect it is female in nature.

Beatrice has promised to cook for me. Strange that she didn't say "cook for us". It's as if I was a lab rat for her culinary experiment. She has promised shrimp, lobster, and grouper in a light cream sauce. The rest she will make up on the fly. I bought two bottles of dry Chardonnay for the festive occasion. Poolside at the mansion and drinks are the order of the day. The meal is working. No sense in being in the kitchen until it is absolutely necessary.

"Where are your folks?"

"They flew to Costa Rica to visit Alberto. It's his birthday next week. Plus, *papi* wants to talk business face-to-face. I think there is a group of *papi's* business associates on the trip. Very boring way to spend time."

"Beatrice, I have to tell you what has been going on in my life these past weeks, hell, months."

"It's not life threatening is it?"

"No, but in concerns Heather's death."

"I have had these terrible nightmares. They all relate to her death. They started when you came into my life. I think I'm trying to shed the old baggage, which I have held onto for these past two years. I found you and it's time for me to move on to a better place. Except there is a part of my psyche or soul that won't let me move on until I let go of what has held me back. Does that make sense?"

"Yes. I'm sorry you're going through nightmares, but it's clear that I triggered them."

"I've been torn by so many forces. First the divorce and my humiliation of Heather's affairs, the damage Heather did to Gene, her death, my reconciliation with my son, my struggles with the business as it mushrooms, while I help rebuild Gene. Now you are here with me and Gene's growing away from me. All of these things. All of these important things. Sometimes it's too damned much. Sometimes I want to scream or hide. I don't know which."

"You are going through a lot. Maybe more than you can handle alone. Are you seeing someone? Beyond me. I mean are you getting professional help?"

"I see Dr. Sam Batt once a month and it helps. What I need to do is to talk like this to you on a regular basis. Not someone like you. You."

"If you want me to be a listener, I will be the best. If you want me to give you advice, I won't even try. My attachment to you is too strong for me to be objective. My advice would be colored by my feelings toward you. And, you know what they are."

"Maybe this is the beginning of the necessary process."

"Come here."

I slide to her chaise and we embrace. No kisses. She transfers her love to me. I am stronger now.

"Now rest here while I get dinner."

"What can I do?"

"Nada. I'm just going to put everything on the serving cart and bring it out to the pool. Sort of a meal on wheels.

Except we are much too young and healthy for that. We can eat on the table in the cabana. It's been set for two. Oh, I almost forgot, there is something you can do. Open the wine and light the candles."

In the flickering orange and yellow, Beatrice is beyond beautiful. Her eyes, those different colored beacons, transfix me. I am the deer immobilized by her headlights.

"Have you heard anything new about Liz Bridgers?"

"Yes, I was duped. She is working in the DA's office, but not as an admin as she told me. You were right. She was feeding me information, which Flaherty hoped would get to you. Why, I don't know. I'm angry, but there is nothing I can do about it."

"Sure there is. How would you like to get even for the dirty trick? Really mind fuck her and her boss. Do you think she knows that you know who she really is?"

"I'd love to get even. There is no way she knows that I know. I found out by looking at records. Not talking to anyone."

"OK, then. Let's feed her some bogus information, which she will take to Flaherty. Flaherty and maybe even Pennington who will follow the lead, and most likely, ask her to get more. Once we know they have been hooked, we'll let them know they have been had. This little diversion could also create a chasm between Flaherty and Pennington as the both struggle to be the one who solves the case."

"Is that safe?"

"Mostly, but that's the allure of it. You, know . . . risk and reward in a twisted game of quid pro quo. Besides, they started it. We're just ending the game. I'm sure you've heard they arrested Peter Johnson for the murder of the Silveras. This is their big break in the two-year old case. Johnson was given to them by Tory Covington, my lawyer. The DA's office didn't even know he existed before Tory told them. He matches the description of the murderer given to the police during the original investigation. But, the police and the previous DA never pursued Johnson. Then Flaherty, based on what he has been fed, will press Johnson's name and face all over the paper and the TV. He will be portrayed as a low-life drug addict. The ideal candidate for murderer. Now what we have to do is to give them another candidate. Someone who they think is as real as Johnson. Only he's not guilty."

"We could get in trouble for this."

"Not really. Or maybe not much real trouble. I feel like a kid again. Investigators and prosecutors go down blind alleys all the time. It's part of their job. They have to explore every avenue to be sure they have the right one. And they fight with each other behind closed doors . . . out of the public's eyes to best the other. The goal is to come to the a right conclusion before the other guy. We're just pointing out another possibility."

"But, I heard they found the gun used to murder the Silveras."

"They can't be sure that this other person didn't plant the gun to set-up Johnson. Maybe he was pissed at Johnson. What if we find someone, who had access to Johnson's house, and was . . . say, Johnson's homosexual lover? He was furious that Johnson was in love with Heather. As if he had gone over to the dark side. If the spurned gay lover couldn't have Johnson, no one would. So he kills the Silveras, who are Johnson's drug suppliers, to frame Johnson and destroy Johnson's life."

"Too warped. Too convoluted. Too intriguing. You're fiendish. I love it."

"I'll have to find someone who could fit our description. I'll do this while you're in Tallahassee. When I get the guy, you can leak it to Ms. Bridgers."

"OK, but be careful."

"Now let's talk about us. I love these weekends, but I want more of you. More time for us to be together."

"What are you proposing?"

"Let's not use the word proposing for now. What I'm suggesting is that instead of you commuting between your apartment in the capitol and your parent's home, why not use my condo as your home in Tampa. Let's find out if we are compatible more as lovers than daters."

"That's a bold step. One I'll have to think about. Can you give some time or do you have to have an answer now."

"I have to work this all out with Gene. Don't be silly. What kind of a lover would I be if I asked you to make a life-changing decision and didn't give you time to think it over? I'd be someone with whom I wouldn't want to live. So take your time and be sure you are comfortable. OK. Time's up."

"Thanks", she giggles a young girl's giggle.

"And now for the washer-dryer combination filled with dirty men's clothes, a sink filled with pots and pans, two unmade beds, and no food in the pantry, your answer please."

Her laughter was raucous. A real belly laugh. She had to put her wineglass down to keep for dropping it. Her body curled in convulsions of chortling.

"That's a side . . . of you . . . I had only heard . . . about. Off-the-wall humor. Comedy of the very weird. What a great find. A man I can trust to say outrageous things when they are most inappropriate. Sort of like a whoopee cushion in the Senate. Now to something serious. If you clear the table, wheel the cart to the kitchen, and put the food in the fridge and the service in the dishwasher, I'll uncover the Jacuzzi and get it warmed up."

"Yes'am, Miss Beatrice. But, I needs a kiss befoe' ma' choes. And I'll need ta fine ma swim suit."

"Don't waste time looking for something that may get ripped. Now hurry about your business. And no kisses 'til you're done."

She left a mess in the kitchen. It seems that she may move in with me just to have someone to clean up after her sorties in the kitchen. Plastic containers to the left of the fridge are for leftovers. Plates, glasses and flatware loaded in the dishwasher. I notice a pot scrubber cycle. Scrape the pots and pans. Load them. Less work. Back at poolside. No Beatrice.

"Where is the Jacuzzi?"

I am speaking to the night air.

"To the left behind the cabana. Take the three steps and turn."

The voice mysteriously leads me. I can hear the water jets and smell gardenia and jasmine. There are four fat candles on the deck surrounding the bubbling cauldron. Beatrice is up to her neck in the roiling water. Her clothes are heaped at the last step. Towels beside the clothes.

"If you are done with your chores, I command you to take off your clothes and come into the Jacuzzi."

"Yes ma'm. Holy shit the water is hot! Why didn't you warn me?"

"Did the water hurt the big man? Or the little man? What a pity. Bee-bee is sorry."

"Bee-bee? Who gave you that name?"

"My brother, Alberto. His nickname is Bay-Bay. What's yours?"

"Well, I guess real trust starts here. My nickname is Cookie. I got it from my father, who thought I was so cute and sweet that I was edible like candy. Remember it's Cookie, like Cookie Lavagetto the baseball player for the Brooklyn Dodgers."

"Who? What team?"

"Never mind the details, just accept the name."

"OK, Cookie, Bee-bee owes you a kiss for your chores. If you come closer I'll give you your dessert."

The night rolls into passion. Passion that is all consuming. I want to be inside Beatrice. I want to become her. I want her to become me. A melding of bodies like in some Sci-fi movie. I take her. She controls me. Apogees are achieved and nadirs endured to reach other apogees. Exhaustion is never a possibility. We are greedy. Greed stemming from years of unemotional passion. Tonight, we sampled everything on the menu of hunger.

"Gene, do have any time for the old timer, today."

"Want to go to a movie? Something mindless and brutal. Lots of explosions and blood. Check out the Cinema 24 at Hillsborough. Maybe we can even see a couple of movies."

Done deal. We will buy tickets for the 2:00 showing of *Cell* and stay to catch the 4:45 showing of *Saw VII*. Break for a meal consisting of hot dogs, nachos, Raisenettes, and Dr. Pepper. Finally, we ease our weary butts in front of the third screen . . . *Art of War*. Three movies for the price of one. Our Sunday together ends at 9. We are exhausted, proud we have gotten the most for our money, and yet embarrassed we have devoured so much junk food. We have over-indulged in fantasy and food. The latter will stay with me longer than it will stay with Gene. He'll lose most of the junk food by Monday evening. The weight room and sauna at the condo will complete his exorcism. I will stretch out on the couch and plan my attack on Flaherty's snitch.

"Gene, we need to talk."

"OK, what about?"

"Nothing ominous. Something I need you to understand. I want Beatrice to be a regular guest in our home. When she is not in Tallahassee, I have asked her to live here. I want you to be cool with this. If you are not, she and I will make other arrangements. Waddaya think?"

"I think it is a good idea that you have someone your own age to play with. Face it, dad, our time together is fine, but I want more time without you and you need more time without me. So, if you and Beatrice want to shack up, that's OK with me."

"Somewhere in your honesty is a maturity beyond your age. Thanks for being so candid."

"And, besides, I like her. Plus, it will be cool when the guys learn you are not dead from the waist down."

"Now that's a tad crass. Go to bed after you give me a hug."

XIII

The first step is to go to the gay bars near Johnson's home and work place. Ask if they've ever seen Johnson. See if there is anybody who might resemble Johnson. Monday night I begin *Operation Back Door*. E-mail Beatrice with the code name and steps to be taken. I'll let her know my progress by Wednesday.

Monday is a good day. The work for the ice cream client is first rate. A little cutting edge, but not too risky. Certainly worth our fee. Gene knows he must fend for himself on Monday night. Mrs. Torres will prepare his dinner and I will be out of the house on business for the evening.

The Parrot. The bartender and few regulars have no idea who the guy in the picture is. Two more saloons, each raunchier than the last, same results. *Big Bridge Sports Bar* is inhabited by the neighborhood regulars. Most live in one of the three trailer parks that surround the joint. Some working class. Hard workers. Some live off Social Security. Hard drinkers. Night in and night out, the pub populace pours in and fills up. Hoping to find Mr. or Miss right, they find each other. Then back to some flat surface. Sweat, grab, and exchange body fluids. A newcomer is greeted with apprehension and interest. Fear of exposure to the outside world is real among the denizens of the dive. But, they are always interested in the possibility of a fresh participant in the after hours, mindless pleasure. I just wanted some information. I knew it would cost me beers. Drink from the bottles.

"Have you ever seen this guy?"

"Not sure. Lots of guys come in here."

My eyes finally adjust to the smoky darkness. I now see that all the clientele is male. The dart tossers. The dancers. The couples huddled in booths. I circulate and ask each group.

"Yeah, that's Pete Johnson. He used to come in here a lot. Haven't seen him for some time. Two years maybe. His picture was in the newspaper and on the TV. Arrested for the murder of the drug dealers. Why, what do want with him? You'd be better off talking to the cops. They got him."

"What do you know about him?"

"What do you mean?"

"What kind of a guy was he?"

"Kept to himself a lot. Came in here drank and shot pool or darts. Then he left."

"Did he come in here alone?"

"Why? What's it to you?"

"I'm trying to help him. Get information the police wouldn't bother seeking."

I slide a fifty to the man.

"Why didn't you say so?"

"Sometimes he came in alone. Sometimes he was with Sammy."

"What is Sammy's last name?"

"Ahl. Sammy Ahl."

"Was Sammy a regular?"

"Nah. Just came with Pete."

"So Pete left with Sammy?"

"Yeah. They would spend the evening drinking rum. Then stagger out of here arm-in-arm."

"Have you seen Sammy or Pete lately?"

"Hell, no. Not for two years. And that's a good thing. The bastard, Sammy, owes money to just about everybody in the place. He's a mooch. And a bad-tempered mooch at that. If you reminded him that he owed you money, he'd threaten to pop you a good one. Pete covered a lot of Sammy's debts.

He was so gentle. Strange that he was tight with an angry guy like Sammy."

"What does this Sammy look like?"

"A lot like Pete. That's weird ain't it? The two of them looked like brothers. Same build. Same coloring. Faces almost had the same structure. They gave new meaning to the phrase, brotherly love. Too weird for me."

I just got lucky, as it were. For fifty bucks I learned enough for my little game. Exited the saloon and raced home to shower and sleep. E-mail the pertinent facts to Beatrice to be relayed to Ms. Bridgers. Flaherty will learn about our little ruse on Friday after he has devoted resources to the new confidential information. Ms. Bridgers will be chastised, and he will know that I know,

Miss Stewart arrives at DA Flaherty's office ten minutes early.

"Please come in. I assume you've had a chance to talk to your client."

"Yes. And we want to know what kind of consideration he could expect if he gave you information that would help you expand on the Silvera investigation?"

"Consideration? We have Mr. Johnson cold for the murders."

"You and I know the murders are just the tip of the iceberg. And, beside we both know your case against Mr. Johnson is shaky, at best. What you really want is to follow the Silveras up the chain of command and to nail the entire drug ring in West Central Florida. Suppose my client could help you on your quest. Names, dates, amounts. Information like that. What could he expect to get from you in exchange for his cooperation?"

"Not much."

"Not much. You must not think much of your career."

"I have an obligation to the people of this city to ferret out and prosecute the bad guys. To protect the citizenry from the bad guys. Mr. Johnson is a bad guy. By convicting him, I can bring closure to murders that have haunted this town for two years."

"Do you get a nose bleed sitting atop that high horse? Assuming you can convict my client, which I doubt, your career as a crusader will come to an end. You will be known as a local yokel with no juice outside the county. Or, at the very least, your career will take a seriously long pause. So long, you will retire before you move up. You are being offered the opportunity to go beyond the murder of petty dealers. An opportunity to earn real stripes in the war on crime. Get you name published in law journals and newspapers. Picture looking up from your big file-covered desk and everything."

"I'd need to know precisely what he has to offer, before I can agree to anything."

"We'll accept no less than a total walk for the information."

"You must think me a fool."

"Most often, but not now. Rather, today you are someone who has a great ambition and can see the benefits gained from understanding and exchange."

"Murder Two."

"A total walk."

"Give me some indication of Mr. Johnson's information."

"My client had been to the Silveras' apartment on numerous occasions. Mostly to buy merchandise for himself. Sometimes to buy for others. When he was at the apartment, Mr. Johnson saw and was introduced to several different people, who were there as part of the enterprise of sale and distribution. Two of these people Mr. Johnson saw on several occasions. These two people were paid substantial amounts of cash by Hector and Osvaldo Silvera for delivering merchandise, a small portion of which was subsequently purchased by my client. I am confident you would enhance your efforts to clean up the drug trade and further your career by apprehending these two people. Therefore, my client would be willing to testify as to the dates he saw these two people, as well as their names and descriptions, as well as other details such as amounts of money. For this information, I would accept a total walk on the bogus murder charge. Hell, pin it on one of the two scum bags you get from Johnson. You can do that, ya' know."

"Give me some time to think about your offer."

"Make it snappy. The second hand is moving."

"Why, Miss Stewart, how putz-like. I'll call you tomorrow."

Flaherty's intercom buzzes as Miss Stewart leaves.

"Put him on. Stuart, what have you to report?"

"I think we have a huge opening in the drug dealing business in this town as it relates to the murder of the Silveras."

"Slow down. You have just made no sense."

"Jack, I think we can prove that the witnesses who fingered Johnson were lying. I think we can prove that they were paid to lie. I think we can get two guys to turn on the people who created the lie. And I think the people who orchestrated the whole scheme are big in the drug business."

"Tell me more."

Pennington tells Flaherty of the statements of the Ralph Sweat and Paco Winny. The Assistant DA is very proud of his plotting, interrogation, and theorizing skills. He simply fails to mention that this information has been provided the boss at state.

"Why would someone get Mr. Sweat and Paco's father to lie unless they knew they had a patsy? That would mean they knew who the real killer was or they figured that the former DA was interested in not finding the killer and not pursing the matter beyond the blood and gore. If this latter is true, they probably acted in concert with the police and the DA. Maybe others in the community knew what was happening.

Someone was pulling the strings of the DA and the police. If Johnson was the designated fall guy, why didn't the police arrest him? Why was he allowed to remain free these past two years? Maybe he knew too much. The police had to be told not arrest him, because he knew some bad things that would come out during a trial. They kept him in limbo. I'll bet he let them know he knew the score. He bought insurance. So the case ended with the mystery murderer. A Mexican stand-off. Sir, I want to follow the trail of money. We'll get names and dates. Move up the food chain. What do you think Johnson could tell us?"

"I have a meeting with his lawyer tomorrow. I'll begin to probe Mr. Johnson's willingness to cooperate. In the meantime tell no one what you have learned. Let's keep this under wraps until it is advantageous to let the public know. Call me when you learn anything."

XIV

"Sarah, may I call you Sarah, thank for returning to my office on such short notice. I apologize for putting a strain on your day."

The honey of insincerity dripped from Jack Flaherty's lips. Sarah Stewart could almost see the golden droplets on his shirt and tie.

"Why no, Jack, resolving this matter to everyone's satisfaction is my goal."

She removed the jacket to her suit. The white blouse was tight against her. She knew it and she knew Jack Flaherty saw it. Her nipples were outlined in silk. She even fluttered her eyelashes. Two can play the con game.

"I assume you've come to your senses and are ready to drop the charges against my client."

"I have given it some hard consideration. Before we open up the doors of Orient Road for Mr. Johnson, I will need more details."

"Do I have your word and the promise of this office in writing that my client can walk free, if he provides you names and dates of people in the drug trade? Information he will be willing to testify to in court."

"You have my word."

"Then, I'll give you time to draft the agreement, while I get some coffee from your break room. OK?"

"OK. Then my driver can take us to the facility."

After coffee, a perusal of the agreement, and two signatures, they gather their papers and Sarah her jacket to leave. The intercom buzzes.

"Sir, it's Mr. Pennington and he says its important."

"Tell Mr. Pennington, I'll call him back. I'm sure it is important. My work is important, also. Tell him to just sit on it."

On the way to the jail, Flaherty has the driver call to make sure Johnson is waiting in the interview room. Stop. Pass security. Pass security. Walk a labyrinth of halls. Enter room.

"Now, Mr. Johnson what information do you have that might interest me?"

"Not yet, Peter."

"Mr. Flaherty, I want you to tell Mr. Johnson that he gets a walk on all charges, before he tells you anything."

Flaherty bristles at being asked or ordered. His response is curt.

"These are the conditions as spelled out in the agreement: His information must help us in our efforts to crush the drug trade. Make convictions, not just headlines. From his information we must be able to make arrests at levels far higher than the Silveras. For that, he is a free man. If he partially meets the condition, he loses his freedom forever."

"If he partially meets the conditions, that is, if you indict but cannot convict for whatever reason, he gets Man Two, 3-6.?"

"We'll see."

"Yes or no deal."

"Yes. I'll add that addendum by hand that to the agreement, we can initial it."

"OK."

The guys you want are Roberto Pena and Jimmy Jimenez. I seen both these guys at the Silvera pad a couple of times. Hector was paying them big time. Looked like at least 30 large both times. I was at the pad to make a buy. The merchandise was fresh. I got it right from the big bags Pena and Jimenez had delivered. It was already bagged for the street. Osvaldo didn't have time to step on it or re-bag it."

"What do Pena and Jimenez look like?"

"Bobby is real thin. About five six. Shaves his head. He's dark skinned. Two gold earrings. The three times I saw him there he wore nice long-sleeved shirts. Tailored and pressed. Expensive looking shoes. He never smiles. I cracked a joke one night. Ya' know 'We've got to stop meetin' like this.' Jimmy and Hector laughed. Bobby never reacted. Jimmy is taller. Five ten or maybe six foot. Built like a jock. Wears tight T-shirts to show his muscle. Yeah, he wears those warm-up pants. Nike or Adidas. I'm not sure. Short hair in a flat top. Military style. No jewelry. He twitches a lot. And he sweats. Like he is on somethin'. 'Roids would be my guess."

"Why do you point to these guys for the murder?"

"I parked near Bobby's car when I went to see the Silvera boys that night. It was gone when I came down from the apartment."

"How do you know it was Bobby's car?"

"The license. It said *Bobby P.* I don't think you'll find too many tricked out chocolate black big BMWs with that license."

"How do you know it is chocolate black?"

"I seen it one day out at the pier where I worked."

"So far all you've given us are two of your possible accomplices to your murder. Did the three of you kill Hector and Osvaldo Silvera?"

"No man. I didn't do nothing except be at the wrong place at the wrong time."

"The 25-caliber pistol was found at your home. You had a viable motive. And you were there. Hell, without breaking a sweat, just on those facts I can put you away for 15 years, maybe 25."

"Jack, that's not our deal. You do not have the murder weapon or the knife and we both know that. So cut the crap. You said that if my client helped you in the on-going investigation of the drug business, you would give Mr.

Johnson a walk on the murder. He just threw in the killers. You ought to reward him."

"Miss Stewart, your client has not given me what you had promised."

"OK, OK, OK, there's more. When I saw these guys at the pier, there was a big group. Three SUVs, a van, three pick-up trucks, and a white limo. The rear window of the limo was down so that somebody could see better what was going on. I didn't recognize the guy. But, I heard Bobby call him Mr. G. It seemed to me that this Mr. G was the man. The guy that was running the operation."

"What operation is that?"

"Bobby and Jimmy and a bunch of other guys were taking baskets and crates from the pier and putting them in the pickups. The baskets and crates seemed to be loaded with iced down fish. The truck doors had signs on them. The signs said Gutierez Fresh Seafood. It seemed strange to me that they needed guys in nice clean clothes to off-load fish from the trawler to the trucks."

"So, buying fish dockside and transporting the goods to a business is not a crime. There is still no connection to your alleged drug enterprise of Mr. Pena and Mr. Jimenez."

"Wait, that's not all. On both the nights I seen Bobby and Jimmy deliverin' the goods to the Silveras, they mentioned Mr. G. They talked like businessmen. Mr. G. doesn't like you steppin' on the merchandise so much. It gives his merchandise a bad rep. He's losing' market share to other people. Outsiders even. Once they talked about Mr. G. havin' to raise the price of the merchandise to cover increased costs like delivery and protection. And that this was no excuse for the brothers to step on the merchandise. Once they mentioned a couple of guys who didn't pay attention to what Mr. G. wanted. And Bobby couldn't remember what happened to the two guys, except they lost their heads over the mistake they made. Jimmy sneered at that one. Hector and Osvaldo looked scared."

"Well, Jack. That's our side of the bargain. Now it's your turn."

"To show my good faith, I'll get the courts to lift the bail requirements so that Mr. Johnson can get out of jail . . . for the time being. I will note his cooperation as a corroborating witness. Thus voiding the charges. If his information proves valuable, leading to indictments and convictions, I will follow the agreement. While we are investigating his allegations, I strongly suggest that Mr. Johnson not leave town. I also suggest he remain invisible. And that you, counselor, are the only one who knows his whereabouts every day. I'm going out on a very thin limb for your client and I'll hold you personally responsible if he gets a sudden urge to take a long-term vacation."

"Not a problem."

"Before we leave here, I will make two copies of the final agreement. Then I'll have the typed paperwork before the court by two this afternoon. You can go with my Administrative Assistant and wait for a copy signed by the judge. Bring the signed order back here to the jail and they will release Mr. Johnson."

Sarah thought that even in a loss, Jack had to maintain the image of superiority. He wanted her to run around like a secretary. Well, what the hell, she won. The limo was waiting. It was a very quiet ride back to downtown. Before she returned to her office, Sarah stopped at an ice cream shop. A double scoop cone of Pralines and Crème. Her reward for the victory. Jack Flaherty starts the agreed to legal process and leaves his office. He has a racket ball game after a late lunch at the Tower Club. Then he will call Pennington.

✶ ✶ ✶ ✶ ✶ ✶

"Can you get Stu Pennington on the line?"

The gloat of the conquering hero resonates over the intercom.

"Stu, now, what is that you had to tell me?"

"Two amazing turns of events. Remember I told you I thought we could prove the eyewitnesses were lying about who was at the Silveras' when they were murdered? Paco Winny and Ralph Sweat independently gave us the names, Robert Pena and Jimmy Jimenez, as two guys involved in the false statements. These guys wanted Johnson fingered as the murderer. They never told Paco's father and Sweat why they wanted the descriptions given to the police. They just did. And it was worth a bunch of money. Unfortunately Paco's father died. But, Paco's father did leave him some very valuable information about the real events of that night and whom to call for the reward. Plus, Paco found out that Sweat had received money to buy the bodegas. At first Sweat claimed that he got the money anonymously. Then he admitted he initiated the conversation with Bobby. Paco claimed he got some information written by his father before he died. The information was kept in a safety deposit box. Paco claimed to us he memorized some of the writing and recited it to Bobby. Two days later 75 K finds its way into Paco's savings account. Now here is the really strange part. Paco never gave anybody any information about that account. No bank name. No account name. No account number. But, the cash fairy knew where to deposit the money. We checked and there is no paper trail. Just *poof* and the money is there. Very, very strange."

"You mentioned two amazing events."

"Yes. A well-informed source has told me that Johnson may have been set up by a jealous lover. A guy named Sammy Ahl. Word is that this Sammy was furious because Johnson was seriously exploring his straight side with Heather Baker. Johnson had moved out of the pad he shared with Sammy and was making noises about setting up a love nest with the former Mrs. Baker. I have learned that the spurned lover looks much like Johnson. They look almost like brothers. Sammy goes to the Silveras, who he knows are the dealers of choice for Johnson and Heather, and he wastes the dealers. Sammy makes sure that people see him. The witnesses give the description. Everybody thinks its Johnson. We arrest the wrong guy."

"Whoa. Stop. Do you realize you have just put forth two separate and contradictory theories as to the identity of the murder?"

"Yes, I do. That's why I said these were amazing. And there's more."

Flaherty's expression mocks surprise. Pennington can't see it over the phone.

"Ralph Sweat gave a totally different description of the individual he saw arriving by car and leaving the neighborhood of the brothers' apartment. His new description contradicts the one he gave the police during the initial investigation. Now he says the guy's short and solidly built with dark hair. We both know that Sweat is a juicer, so there may not be any credibility to either of his descriptions. Except, he was able to recall the car and a partial license plate, where it was parked, and how long it was parked. He just failed the perpetrator description test."

"What does all this mean to you, Stu?"

"I have to pursue this Sammy Ahl and simultaneously dig deeper into the possibility that the new description is the accurate one. Plus, I have to find out who Bobby and Jimmy are. And see what their connection is to this whole mess. How the money got into Paco's account at Tampa Bank. And, now that you have Johnson in jail, you can squeeze him for corroboration. Particularly about Sammy. More options, but less certainty. What does it mean to you, Jack?"

"More work for the overworked DA's office. Sorry, that's my other line. I'm expecting a call from out of town. Let's talk tomorrow."

Jack just let a fish out of the net. And there was no way to retrieve him without looking very stupid to the court. A lie to a PD doesn't bother him. That's part of his job description. But, looking stupid in front of the court and the public is a career damaging event. Jack's heart sank. He was fucked.

XV

"Jacob, I've known you for years. You have many great character traits. You also have a flaw or two that can harm you. Self-righteous indignation is one of those flaws. I hope you know your actions might lead to some form of reprisal by the District Attorney."

"Tory, whatever do you mean?"

"I mean feeding the DA's office bogus information and sending them off on a wild goose chase. Costing them time and money, not to mention the possibility of a delay in their speedy indictment and trial of Peter Johnson. That could be considered obstruction. Have I noted the possible public humiliation? If Flaherty didn't have his plate over flowing, he might consider filing an obstruction charge against you. One that I would be hard pressed to properly defend, because I would be grinning too much."

"How could you accuse me of doing such a heinous thing?"

"Easily. I have my ear to the ground and hear all. Plus, I put myself in your shoes. You're concerned that Flaherty dredged up this old mess. You're pissed that he questioned you and went beyond the scope of his investigation to cast dispersions on your character. So you decide to get back at him."

"Between client and lawyer, that's not quite what happened."

"Just in case I need to know the truth to schmooze Flaherty, tell me your side of the story."

"As you know I am dating Beatrice Consolo. Quite by accident . . . wink, wink, wink . . . she meets a brief acquaintance from college, who claims to be an administrative assistant in the DA's office. This alleged admin begins providing information to Beatrice, her old friend, about the investigation. Nothing serious, but confidential information nonetheless. I learn that this old friend is the same Elizabeth Bridgers. She is the woman who sat in on my interview. She's a damned Attorney in the office and she's been feeding Beatrice information to get to me. Information from Flaherty and/or Pennington. Well, we just ran backward up that street. Beatrice was only the conduit. I dug up the information, fed it to her, and she passed it along to Bridgers. Bridgers told Pennington, who saw an opportunity to one-up his boss and curry favor with the higher-ups at state. And, because everybody in the office is so blindly ambitious, Pennington dedicated people to chase the phantom. Some anonymous caller informed Mr. Flaherty that his office had been had. Egg on Pennington's shirt. Oh well, oh well."

"Flaherty is the butt of the daily jokes in the courts and every law firm that ever dealt with the putz. And, he is wet-hen angry at whoever played this prank on his office. Guys in his position don't like to be laughed at in the halls of justice, the media or at cocktail parties. Be careful, you have made a powerful and vindictive enemy if he ever finds out it was you. By the way, you'll be interested to know that Pete Johnson was released from jail and all charges have been held in abeyance until he testifies. He is basically a free man. Now Flaherty has no one on which he can pin the blame for the murders. Back to square one."

"Fuck him."

* * * * * *

Beatrice is coming to town for the Sunday. On Monday, she has a meeting with a grower's coop in Lakeland to discuss laborer rights and needs. She will be with me the day before. A dinner date at the condo.

"Gene, Beatrice is coming over on Sunday."

"Do you want me to let you two alone?"

"Don't be ridiculous. We're going downtown to the museum. Then I thought the three of us would have dinner together."

"Sure, what time?"

"About 7:00 ish. OK?"

"Fine, but don't you love birds vant to be alon'. I assume Beatrice will be spending the night."

"Does that bother you?"

"Not at all. I was wondering when you were going to come clean about you and her. I think it's great. If you're happy that is. I mean you never seemed to date anyone. You'd go out to big functions. But, never a one-on-one that I was aware of. Now Beatrice. She's nice. As far as I know."

"Thanks. That's very grown up. I guess one of my problems is that in my eyes your growth stopped when your mother and I split. When you and I began living together, I thought our relationship would pick up where it left off . . . two years prior. Before you hit puberty. But, in the years apart, you grew up. And I missed it. Now I may do and say dumb things because I think you are a pre-teen. Sorry."

"No need to be sorry. I'm glad we're together. I'm trying to understand you, too. I guess if I could tell you anything it would be to get a life outside of me. Making me the sole purpose of your life puts too much pressure on you and me. And I can feel the pressure. Sometimes you watch me like a hawk. Cut me some slack. You can't protect me from making mistakes. And some mistakes are good for my growth. I know you will always be there for me if I really fall on my ass. That's important. I want to grow. And it could be difficult if you don't let me make mistakes. Other than that, keep the moaning and groaning to a minimum on Sunday night. I'm a light sleeper."

My boy had become a young man. And, is asking me to let go.

✱ ✱ ✱ ✱ ✱ ✱

Saturday's game is more difficult as we strive to be ranked at the top for the playoffs. We gave up too many yards and two touchdowns. Fortunately the offense was on fire and scored five. We are now ten and zero. The first team seems to have lost a focus and sharpness. Missed assignments, shoddy tackling. The second team played the half the second quarter and the entire fourth quarter. They did OK. Maybe the season is too long for their minds and bodies. Maybe I make too many demands on them. I have to re-think my approach this week in practice. I'll introduce a new wrinkle or two to keep their minds fresh

✱ ✱ ✱ ✱ ✱ ✱

"Sammy, what are you doing here?"

"I came back to find out what you had done to me, Pete. First you leave me for some gash. I'm devastated, but I got over it. Then years later, out of the blue, the cops are banging on my door. I get dragged down to the station and questioned about my whereabouts the night that drug dealers you used to know were killed. They think I did it as some form of revenge for you leaving me. They accuse me of killing kill the dealers, but you take the hit. I win and you lose. I'm angry that you left me, but not stupid. The next morning, they release me saying it was all a mistake. They claim they checked out my alibi. What the fuck did you do to me? You humiliated me."

"Calm down. I had nothing to do with your arrest. I just got out of jail on the same charge two days ago. Somebody is trying to fuck us both. And with no kisses. I'll bet the person who fingered us did so because we look alike. The police said they were looking for a murderer based on my description. I was arrested first. Then you. Maybe we should try to find out who would do such a thing and why."

"Where should we start?"

"Where we both were known. *Big Bridge Sports Bar.*"

XVI

Gutierez Fresh Seafood occupies two warehouses on Mariner Place. The small retail operation in the front of one building satisfies the desires of the discriminating non-professionals. The store is open six days a week from 8 AM to noon. The wholesale operation runs from 5AM to noon serving the best restaurants in the five-county area. Recently, the operation has been shipping seafood to the major inland Southern cities. To restaurants who can charge a premium for premium food. Romero Gutierez is a fourth generation fisherman. He hasn't been out on a boat since he was a boy and went with his grandfather. Romero's two sons harvest the catches offered up for purchase by the local fleets, large and small. It is no secret that Gutierez Fresh Seafood will purchase only the best and freshest fish and crustaceans. The family requires each boat crew pour over each catch to be sure they are selling only the best. Then the two boys, Antonio and Pedro, scour the baskets and crates to make sure their company and its customers don't get screwed. Reputation for superior quality is vital to long term success. Any slip in quality would do irreparable damage to business. They profit from their reputation of providing only superior quality food. The company employs eighteen people outside the family. Mostly sorters and stock boys, who prep the deliveries. Six drivers, an office manger, who is also an expediter, and two at retail. Roberto Pena and Jimmy Jimenez are listed as delivery supervisors.

The police, at the direction of the DA's office, run detailed background checks on everyone. Calls are made to the Feds to access their data banks. The DA gets a judge to authorize phone taps and bugs throughout the seafood company buildings. Recently the DA planted a few other phone taps without a judge's authorization. Used a private plumbing contractor. These taps supplied the DA with information at the re-opening of the murder investigation. Information on how the suspects reacted to being part of the investigation. Information that could lead to truth, but never could be used in court.

This is an old family in an old family town. The legal taps have to be by the book and done in absolute silence. If the authorities are right, the old guard will crumble. If the authorities are wrong, two will be banished to Guam or Anchorage.

"Jack, when do you want the cops to pick-up Bobby and Jimmy?"

"Two days. Make them very upset. Send them crying to whomever. But don't have them arrested at the market. Do it at their homes with all their neighbors looking on. I want a public perp walk. I want deep humiliation. I want their kids to see them taken away in a wagon, not a squad car. And, for good measure, let the TV stations know what's going to happen and when the perps will arrive at Orient Road. In other words, stage an event."

"So we only have to say this once. Listen up and listen good. Roberto Pena and Jimmy Jimenez, you are charged with murder in the first degree, conspiracy to commit murder, bribery, obstruction of justice, and witness tampering in the mutilation deaths of Hector and Osvaldo Silvera. Arraignment will be as fast as we can get into the courtroom. Tomorrow morning at 9 AM."

Flaherty hopes bail will set at $1,000,000 each along with revocation of their passports. The risk of flight is great. None of the Gutierez money will be visible, but Flaherty knows it will be at work. The money for bail, or for the lawyers, and for the appeals, which are a foregone conclusion, must be not traced back to the Gutierez organization. The two fine, hard-working, and upstanding pillars of the community would not be free to deliver the merchandise for Gutierez Fresh Seafood or drugs for Mr. G. tomorrow or any day in the near future. But somehow, money would become available through anonymous third parties. The funds will appear as if by magic in the personal bank accounts of the two miscreants.

Pena's lawyer is James Tidmore, an out-of-towner from parts unknown with a reputation of working for persecuted family organizations in Miami, Atlanta, Nashville, and New Orleans. Everything about his demeanor speaks of money and flamboyance. He is his own firm with a sea of resources. Well-versed in the intricacies of criminal law, precedents, and the latitude of the justice system, Mr. Tidmore knows his job is to gain the freedom of the accused. A reduced charge will not to be pursued.

Jimenez was represented by Bailey Biche, a local. Bailey was long in the tooth, but his bite is much worse than his bark. He shares office space with Solomon Tuggs. In fact, the two of them first shared space in college, and through law school, as well as before and after Solomon's tenure on the bench. Bailey's basic strategy is to lull his opponent into a false sense of advantage, then cut-off the other lawyer's nuts with some exceptionally well-reasoned, multi-precedent argument. Everybody thinks Bailey uses Solomon as a consultant. Rumor has it that recently Bailey has suffered a minor stroke and that his mental capacity is diminished. So Solomon may be the real brains behind the man. Rumors can be started by anyone.

"Mr. Tidmore and Mr. Biche I appreciate the opportunity to meet with you both. I can see that Mr. Pena and Mr. Jimenez are very well represented. And, I'm sure that within the scope of this indictment, we can reach a satisfactory conclusion."

"As you both know, we have statements that Mr. Pena and Mr. Jimenez were at the scene of the murder. The two gentlemen were known to be business associates of the Silveras. They were drug dealers. Prior to the night of the murders, their business dealings had become fractious. That night was the culmination of the rancor. Something about merchandise sold by the Silveras that was not sold to them by their usual source, i.e. Messrs. Pena and Jimenez. And by selling this merchandise, the Silveras had deprived the two suppliers of revenue and profits. Your clients went to the apartment of Hector and Osvaldo to explain the precise nature of the business relationship. And, how sacred was the trust they placed in the brothers."

"We also have testimony that Mr. Pena and Mr. Jimenez paid certain individuals to make false statements to the police so that the police would not pursue them. We also know that certain police were paid to write up their reports in way that would keep your clients' identities hidden. These police officers have been very cooperative in an effort to avoid jail time. That is the sum and substance of the case against your clients. We have witnesses and documentation. We have them cold."

"Thank you for your edification, Mr. Flaherty. I'm sure that you and Mr. Pennington realize I am still gathering information about the crime and my client's alleged involvement in it. So if you will bear with me, I would like to study your indictment and the laws of Florida, which govern your actions.

"Mr. Tidmore, normally in deference to your persona, I would say please take all the time you need. However, given the solid nature of the case against Mr. Pena and Mr. Jimenez, as well as the public outcry against drugs and murder on our streets, I am compelled to seek a speedy trial. Say thirty weekdays. That's six weeks for anyone who is counting. I have been fortunate to get on the court's calendar for six weeks from yesterday. The only other date was nine months from now and that was just too far in the future. Besides that it is dangerously close to violating the speedy trial concept."

"Mr. Flaherty, I am appalled you are trying to railroad my client by this rush to judgment. You are not providing me adequate time to develop a familiarity with the case and to prepare a proper defense. I will have to divert my energies to prevent this excessively, obviously biased, speedy trial of yours."

"Go ahead and file your motions. But, the court in this circuit and the courts of appeals throughout the state are under a mandate to accelerate the entire indictment-to-trial process. Something about saving taxpayers' money and eliminating crime by sending a message about public scrutiny. I believe the real underlying reason has to do with reducing the hourly charges the lawyers have been collecting. But that would be petty on the part of civil servants, would it not? So, as they say on the street, knock yourself out."

"Well, Mr. Flaherty, it seems that you have done your homework. Or at least part of it. I have a lot of work before me. I just hope that given the time constraints and my health, I will be able to mount an adequate defense. Can I assume that I am free to discuss this matter with either you or Mr. Pennington?"

"Mr. Biche, please free to call this office at anytime. Now, if you gentlemen will excuse us, we, too, have much work."

The two bullies had been called before the principal, and been warned.

"Who do think will want to deal first?"

"Stu, dealing is not in Tidmore's nature. Biche, on the other hand, wants us to think he will deal. Then, just as we slow down our attack to work out the deal, he springs something. So, we have got to press . . . constantly press. Set up interview time with Pena for 1 o'clock and with Jimenez at 3. This should keep their lawyers busy."

* * * * * *

Cookie, I'll be at your place Saturday at 6. If the weather is nice, let's go out on the boat all day Sunday. Would Gene like to join us? Sunday. Nothing to do but lounge around heaven all day.

Bee-bee, Sunday looks great for you and me. We have the final game before the playoffs on Saturday. The game will be over by 4:30. I suspect Gene will have other plans for Sunday. He is happy for me and for us.

* * * * * *

The first team has taken to the new wrinkles admirably. Stunts by the interior line and in-and-out blitzes. These are pro moves and the kids revel in them. Stunt A involves the right tackle looping behind the center, who slants to his right and pushes the pile into the spot vacated by the tackle. This leaves a gaping hole for the tackle to swoop into the backfield, while jamming any attempt at a run off tackle. Stunt B involves the left tackle looping behind the center who slants to his left. It is just a mirror of Stunt A. Blitz A involves the left inside linebacker and the right outside linebacker. Blitz B involves the right inside linebacker and the left outside linebacker. These two blitzes give us seven on seven and a great chance of sacking the QB or hitting the runner as he is handed the ball. The game is nearly a walk over. We hold the Patriots to 95 yards. They never get into our territory. We are undefeated. The second team has mastered the basics. In practice next week they will get the new wrinkles. Next week the Jaguars. They are also undefeated. Beatrice and I are not part of Gene's Sunday. We are all of ours.

Beatrice and I will spend a day at the museum rather than risk my certain stomach discomfort on the Gulf. The latest exhibit is called *Beaches*. The material ranges from 18th century paintings to photography from two centuries. The show is in the main gallery. The staff has constructed a labyrinth from wall panels with sections by era and not medium. The labyrinth is as tricky as a European hedge maze. It is fun. Lots of false trails and dead ends. There are benches every so often so that the weary travelers can rest and contemplate the art. But we stand to rest. Beatrice and I are alone.

"I hope the trick we played on the District Attorney's office won't backfire."

"Relax. It's ancient history. TC informed me that our ruse had its desired impact. That part of the game is over. We tied and tie goes to the runner, me. Flaherty and Pennington are now moving up the drug corporation ladder. They're after bigger fish than Johnson or his lover could have ever been."

"You never told me how you knew Johnson was gay. Or that you could find a spurned lover."

"I always had my suspicion about Johnson. I met him twice and he just seemed to fit a stereotype. You know angry, nervous, and shifty-eyed. Very phony macho. Besides by simply saying it, some people will believe it. They always want to believe what they consider to be the worst in people. More importantly, Liz Bridgers was conditioned to be a conduit of information, real or bogus. And, who's easier to con than a con? It was almost too easy, but I'll take it."

Beatrice is not ready for all the truth.

"I don't think I'll be talking to Liz again for quite a while."

"No loss.

"One more thing. How do you know what is going on downtown?"

"Tory has a legitimate friend in the County Clerk's office. He knows all the judges, the bailiffs, and all the legal assistants. He knows who is sleeping with whom. I'm sure Tory is not the only one he talks to. But, he is a truthful source, because he has nothing to gain."

"Jacob, I've been thinking a lot about our discussion the other weekend. Moving in, commitment, and all the attendant work and benefits. And I keep coming to the same conclusion. I'm sorry if the next few statements are brutally honest, but there is no better way to be than honest. I'll never know about us if I don't try to grow the relationship. I tried once and it was a painful failure. We were both too young. You and I are not too young now. Also the previous arrangement was stifling. Neither of us had a life outside of the one we shared. We lived and worked together. Last. Outside of the physical moments, we talked little or communicated in any other way. Because of the previous failure, I have kept to myself. Devoted my energies to work. Political work can consume every waking moment of one's life. So, I let it. My social life was, on the surface, pleasant, but empty. Now I don't have those negative feelings. I'm aware of them as in my past, not my future. I am optimistic about me. I want to continue on that path. So, I am willing to make the beginnings of a commitment to you and your life. Is that OK?"

"It's more than OK, it's terrific. I'm hesitant, too. Hell, I am scared. I have been wrestling with past. Holding on and struggling to free myself at the same time. I know I have to let go. I am now at the point that I want a chance to try with you. If I could promise that all would be wonderful and there would never be a screw up, I would. Unfortunately, that would not be the whole truth, because I can't predict the future. But, I want to try to be a good friend and lover to you."

We kiss. We hug for minutes. Then she turns her back to me and slowly grinds her hips against my crotch. I kiss her neck and she settles back into me completely. My hands slide from her waist and cup her breasts. Her breathing is measured and deep. The pelvic grinding intensifies. Her right hand finds the zipper to my pants. I slowly raise her skirt. No under wear. She leans forward onto the bench to ease entry. The undulations are in synch. She has control of me. The event is precious.

Here are two adults making love in a public place. Making love beneath the stares of the famous and infamous, the dead and the still living, men, women and children. Eyes look, but do not see. Expressions never change. To the wall hangings, are we performers? Lovers on a stage. Like some sleazy act in some sleazy theater in the Combat Zone. Very pornographic. Any minute some museum visitor could wander around the corner of the warren and catch us. Would he or she be surprised? Absolutely. Run in terror? Or stay and watch? Wishing to join us. We care not. We are locked in the moment.

The moment ends for me, but I am still aroused. My partner, the place, and the forbidden act. She must clench her teeth so as not to moan. Silence is a shield. I can feel her contractions. She is finished. We sit on the bench. The eyes of the wall hangings seem to be staring in disapproval at us. From every age, from every angle, the eyes stare. None are happy for us. Some are shocked. Some condemn. Some don't care a bit. We don't care what they think.

XVII

"Mr. Jimenez, we know you were at the murder scene. The deathbed diary of Paco Winny's father and the testimony of Ralph Sweat are all the court will need to nail you for murder. The murder planned and executed in street gangsta style. Then there is the little matter of the bribery of two witnesses. That's tampering and obstruction of justice. In case you can't be scheduled for an execution, the tampering and obstruction convictions will add years to your sentence. You will never get out of jail. You are in jail to stay. No bail now. No bail during the appeals process. And no freedom for at least 75 years, which is FOREVER! Very soon your friends will forget you. Your wife will forget you. She'll change back to her maiden name. She'll even change your children's names. Hell, she'll probably settle in with one of the guys you protected. If you're lucky, you will live a long life in prison. If you're not lucky you'll be gang raped and stabbed at the request of the guy who is then fucking your wife. This is the same guy who sold your daughters into the hooking trade. I understand some sick bastards are willing to pay a lot for a pre-teen."

"Easy Mr. Flaherty. That's the stick now show my client the carrot."

"What carrot, Mr. Biche? There is no carrot. I want to convict Mr. Jimenez, send him away forever . . . maybe send him to Starke so he can visit Sparky. Then this sordid mess will be closed once and for all. I want him to suffer for his crimes."

"What if I could tell you things?"

"Be quiet Jimmy."

"Let Jimmy talk. What could you tell me that would be of interest?"

"I might tell you things that could help you get bigger guys."

"If you mean by bigger guys, the Gutierez brothers, forget it. We know what they have been up to and we know where to find them. They're next. After you have been found guilty and are sentenced to life, we will get Antonio and Pedro for conspiracy to commit murder, because they ordered the slaughter. So there's nothing you can give us on them that will help you."

"What about guys bigger than the brothers? Guys like the old man and his cronies. I maybe could help you there."

"Maybe could help is not help enough. For sure help is help enough. We know that Antonio and Pedro wouldn't do much without the father's approval. We know Romero Gutierez runs the show. What we'd like to know is with whom he works."

"Stop right there Jimmy. Don't say another word. If Mr. Flaherty wants you to help, he must be prepared to offer you a reward. We're listening, Mr. Flaherty."

"I have grave concerns about us even talking about this in front of you, Mr. Biche. You see, I believe Mr. Gutierez pays for your services to help Mr. Jimenez. He has the funds, which he supplies to someone, who supplies them to you. And he has a vested interest in knowing exactly what is going on. He would like to stop the investigation and incarceration with Jimmy, here, and no further. I would not be surprised if you will report to Romero on this meeting today. Once Mr. Gutierez hears that Mr. Jimenez is being cooperative or even considering cooperation, Romero will take action. And, most likely, that action will help Mr. Jimenez to understand the folly in cooperating with me. Action that may include Mr. Jimenez being shanked in jail before trial. Or maybe a member of his family is killed in a car accident or drowns accidently in the bath tub. So, counselor, I think Mr. Jimenez would be wise man if he fired you and sought legal help from a truly independent party. I can recommend a public defender. She is very good."

"Mr. Flaherty that is utter rot. I have an obligation to my client to give him the best counsel. Counsel, which is designed to get all the charges against him dismissed. How my fees are paid has no influence over how I conduct myself."

"Now what you say is utter rot. You can't serve two masters. You can't serve your client and your patron if the wishes of those two conflict. And I think the wishes of Mr. Gutierez and Jimmy Jimenez do conflict. If Mr. Jimenez, as he has indicated, is willing to tell my office many things about Mr. Gutierez, I think Mr. Gutierez would find that detrimental to his life style. Maybe his life. Maybe the lives of his sons. I further think that by stepping forward, Mr. Jimenez has already started Mr. Gutierez's retaliatory process. In other words, Mr. Jimenez, the safety of you and your family is in serious question at this very moment."

"Everybody shut up. Mr. Biche, is what he says true?"

"Mr. Jimenez, you are my client. I am sworn to defend you."

"That's not the answer to my question. When I go back to my cell, do you go back to Mr. G. and tell him the DA has offered me a deal if I roll on him, his sons, and his pals? And that I am thinking about the deal? Am I a dead man already?"

The silence in the small room is palpable.

"No."

"I think it's too late to for me to turn back. I'm fucked if I don't cooperate, and I'm fucked if I do. Mr. Biche, you're fired. That you can tell Mr. G. So now it's up to you to protect me, Mr. Flaherty. What are you offering?"

"When Mr. Biche leaves and goes back to report to Mr. Gutierez, we will protect you from those who wish you or your family harm. We'll take your statement, and immediately thereafter you will be held in the safety of isolation."

As Biche leaves, the slam of the iron door reverberates through the entire floor. It rattles the mirrored glass and it stirs the souls of the men remaining in the room. Flaherty holds his finger to his pursed lips. Jimenez is quiet for three minutes. When both Flaherty and Jimenez feel comfortable that Biche is gone, the statement begins.

"First of all I don't care about my old lady and the kids. None of them are mine. They were brought here from Colombia. They are part of the good-guy costume I wear. Mr. G. thought it would be a good thing to have a family. So if he kills them, it's no worse than they could have expected in their homeland. At least they had some good times in this country before they got capped. What do I get?"

"I appreciate your deep concern for your family. I can contact my federal friends and hide you where no one can reach you. Get you into the witness protection program. After the trial during which you must testify. Maybe plastic surgery, new papers, different place, decent job. You will be out from under all of this crap. A free man with no past and only a bright future. All of this when your testimony proves worthwhile. Worthwhile as in indictment and conviction. Agreed."

"Agreed."

"Remember, we need a confession of all your deeds. The murder, bribery, and your drug involvement with Romero Gutierez. The more you confess to, the stronger the case, and the more likely the feds will agree to hide you. Remember, Sammy "The Bull" got almost nothing for seventeen murders, because he gave up the bosses. He knew it was better to be a witness than a defendant. Plus, he earned great street creds for the fact that he got away with his crimes. You can earn street creds like Sammy's by taking the whole weight for the murders. I want a complete slate of information against your bosses and their bosses and their bosses. We'll arrange the protection program for you tomorrow. You can start your life over and get out from under this mess. A little confession and a lot of trial testimony. You will be free and safe. How does New Mexico sound?"

The offer was too tempting. The tape recorder is turned on.

"My name is Jimmy Jimenez. The statement I am about to give, I give at my own free will without coercion by any member of the Tampa District Attorney's office. Two years ago, I went to the Silveras' apartment to teach them a lesson. They had bought coke from another dealer. And it was a bad quality dope. The new dealer was trying to muscle into Mr. G's territory. Mr. G is Mr. Romero Gutierez. Mr. G. didn't take kindly to that. Hector and Osvaldo Silvera had to be taught a lesson. A lesson all the other street dealers would understand. Antonio Gutierez ordered the hit. He said to make it brutal. Real ugly so the other guys would understand not to fuck with Mr. G. After the murders, Roberto Gutierez gave us some money to throw around to people who could influence the investigation in a favorable way. Get witnesses to make sure the dumb cops would have a suspect they could find. Then pay the cops not to look. I know that Mr. G. and his boys threw more money than we got."

Jimmy looks up at Flaherty like a dog seeking reassurance that he has done the right thing. Flaherty nods encouragement for Jimmy to continue.

"Mr. G. and his boys could not do the business they do without a lot of help. Help from all sides. I've never met the people who help Mr. G., but I do know the Tampa Bank is deep into this. Every other day, I would make cash deliveries to the bank when it looked like I was making fish deliveries to the Tower Club. Supposedly I was going to the Tower Club. Up the freight elevator with fish. Then I went down the private stairs to the executive floor of the bank. I would deliver envelopes, not the letter size envelopes. But, big brown or yellow envelopes. A couple of times I opened an envelope and saw a big stash of 100's. At least five hundred, maybe more. All for a Ms. Brown at Mail Drop W-1935-74. Never met the lady. I have overheard conversations between Mr. G. and someone named Connie. Never heard her voice or saw her. Connie might be Ms. Brown . . . ."

His confession takes nearly three hours with water and pee breaks. The retelling of his facts is not linear, but bounces around in time a space. It contains many pertinent and damaging facts. He spews forth dates and people as if he were a fire hose. Occasionally, he has to stop and take a breath and drink some water. His saga makes him out to be less of a bad guy and more as a messenger. Clearly he wants to just go away free from any connection to the hydra-headed syndicate. Jimmy is trying to please his new master. Hopeful for a lifetime treat. Flaherty periodically nods approval and more information is forthcoming. The DA had his break. The gold star would be placed on his file . . . next to his name. The tape will be transcribed for Jimmy' signature tomorrow. The meeting with Mr. Tidmore and Mr. Pena had to be pushed to 10:30 AM the next day.

Pennington was toiling over the tapes collected from the Gutierez place. The police already had edited the weeks of listening to two hours. Peoples' nicknames, as well as amounts of money. Kilos of merchandise. Ships names. Dates of delivery. Weight for each sub-contractor. Payoffs for the captains. Payoffs for the cops. A judge. But, no real names of his cronies. Code names: Foxy, Connie, Baby, Candy, and Choo-choo.

In all the excitement, Pennington and Flaherty lost sight of the eight bloody deaths. They had become footnotes to greater crimes. Footnotes to ambition. Heather Baker had been relegated to death number 6. The sixth death from drugs sold by men, who were subsequently killed by those, who normally sold the men drugs. Who will remember the innocent?

XVIII

The sun is at that nanno second where it is about to dive into the Gulf. Long red fingers seem to be reaching out; grasping at the earth to hold the sun's body above the horizon for a little while longer. The breeze is cool. The sand still warm from the day. The water turning colder in the sun's absence. Gene is running. He is about one hundred yards ahead of me. His gait is strong and graceful. Mine is plodding. Briefly he's beside me. Then he's in front. Then he's beside me again. When he's beside me, he is small. When he is in front he is larger. The farther away he is, the larger he becomes.

When he is beside me he touches my side. As he pulls away in this faux race, he reaches out as if to take me along. But, I can't reach him. His hand is fully grown and well developed. Mine has fought the ravages of time and lost. His body is firm and it moves in a unified and graceful manner. My flesh flops and jiggles as if it were not part of my body. Beside me he gazes. When he looks back, his eyes pierce. And the color is different. Close they are hazel. Far away they are chocolate black.

And his running gear changes with distance. When beside me or even nearby, his T-shirt is white and his baggy shorts are light blue. As he runs ahead, I notice a running shirt replaces the T-shirt and shorts are tighter fitting and shorter. The running shirt is a maroon color and the shorts are black. His shoes have made a transition from sneakers to what look to be high-tech running shoes. My shirt, pants and shoes are gray, dirty, and worn.

The sun's last light backlights Gene. He evolves to featureless black and stops. As I approach, I can't distinguish his face, nose, ears, fore head. Now his size looms larger. More muscular. I look into his face and can see nothing save two black eyes. Like a shark's, they appear lifeless.

I am struggling to run and breathe. My legs and chest feel as if they are encased in lead. Every ounce of energy is needed to reach him. He is standing on a mound. A huge clump of seaweed. From out of the clump hundreds of crabs, large and small, are scurrying. It's as if his weight were pressing the crabs from their home. Like pressing water from a towel. The crabs are red and have bits of flesh in their claws. They've been dining on something. I can't distinguish a form other than a clump. Gene begins to look smaller. He is shrinking. His legs are disappearing. The crabs are eating my son. My voice is soundless. My motion stilled. I can't help him. Just watch him be devoured.

My eyes pop open. The reality of my bedroom is brief solace. I need light. Out of bed. Get a drink of water. Take a pee. Sneak into Gene's room. He is safe. Sleeping like a stone. Walk to the living room and peer out the window to lawn and trees. Palms swaying in the night breeze. No scurrying of Palmetto bugs, crabs, or any other creatures. The house is safe. Add some scotch to my water. Three gulps. Back to bed.

✸ ✸ ✸ ✸ ✸ ✸

The call to Jack Flaherty's home came at 6:14 AM. It was the Captain of the Guards at the Orient Road Jail.

"Mr. Flaherty, Jimmy Jimenez was found hanging in his cell when the shift changed. He was hanging from the top section of the door. A bed sheet was the noose around his neck."

"How the hell could that have happened? Jimenez was in isolation and under a twenty-four hour watch. I want to see the tapes. I'll be there in thirty minutes. Also, I want to talk to the officers on the graveyard shift and those who came on at six AM and found the body. There's going to be hell to pay for this screw up."

Flaherty calls his driver, showers, and rushes to the front door of his condominium waiting for his ride. At this time of day, the trip to the Orient Road facility takes twenty minutes. He is late. Captain Miranda is waiting, with his men, in the ready room.

"Gentlemen, I need a very good explanation as to how the primary witness in the biggest investigation in the city's history could hang himself while he was in your care."

"Mr. Flaherty, the shift Sergeant has told me that his men saw nothing unusual as they were observing the monitors in Jimenez's cell. There are six inmates in the isolation wing. Each cell has two cameras . . . one at each end of the cell . . . so that the inmate is under complete observation. The officer responsible for monitoring it all is given a break every two hours. He takes a five-minute break to stretch and visit the restroom, if necessary. He eats his meal at his post."

"I'll take it from here, Captain. Who was the officer on duty last night?"

"Gil Darwin, here sir."

"Who relieved you, Officer Darwin?"

"Officer Melton."

"Thank you, Captain. Officer Melton, did you give Officer Darwin a break every two hours?"

"Yes sir. I relieved Officer Darwin at midnight, 2 AM and 4 AM."

"And did you notice any irregularities in any of the six cells?"

"No sir. No irregularities. All the men in the cells were asleep."

"Thank you. Who has the first shift of the day at that post?"

"Officer Crecco, sir."

"Officer Crecco, when did you relieve Officer Darwin?"

"Sir, I relieved Officer Darwin at 6 AM sharp."

"And what did you observe in Mr. Jimenez's cell."

"I observed the inmate, Jimenez, hanging from the gated door. A bed sheet was around his neck and attached to the uppermost rung in the gate."

"What did you do then, Officer?"

"I activated the alarm and notified the shift Sergeant. Other Officers went to Mr. Jimenez's cell and cut him down. I observed the event from my post."

"Captain, please excuse your people. I need to talk to you alone."

The walk to the Captain's office takes three minutes. Enough time for Jack to calm down just a little. He had just lost his key witness. The taped statement may be enough without a signed copy. But, a signed confession would be much better. The tape seems to sound as if Jimmy is disoriented, but all the facts are there. Without a black and white signed statement the taped version may not enough. A tough defense attorney like Solomon Tuggs, Biche's puppeteer, or Tidmore could wiggle a client out of the charge, like a camel through the eye of a needle. Tidmore has gotten a lot of evidence thrown out during other trials. He and Solomon could do it here. Then Flaherty would be screwed.

"Captain, it seems to me that someone on your force really dropped the ball. Or, worse, was involved in helping Jimenez kill himself. See, I'm not completely convinced it was suicide."

"What the hell are you saying? My people are clean. I vouch for them myself."

"Then I have doubts about you, sir."

"Watch what you're saying, Mr. Flaherty. Don't walk in here and start accusing me and my people of murder. I will devote all my attention to finding out exactly how the incident was missed."

"I suggest you also find out why. For now the hot potato is in your hand. Hopefully it is burning your flesh. I expect to hear from you before I go to your superiors by three this afternoon. I expect you'll have all the answers I need. If not, your pension will be in jeopardy."

On the ride to his office, Flaherty makes two calls. One to Bailey Biche to advise him that his client was dead and to make sure he understands the death is on Biche's head. Jack had to remind the old man that he couldn't serve two masters: the law and Romero Gutierez. Bailey got the message. The second call is to Bill Stitt, the pesky reporter. Give him the leak about the suicide, as the police are calling it. Retaliation and subterfuge in the twenty minutes riding to his office. Ah, the benefits of a car phone.

The call at 9AM to Jack Flaherty's office is from Police Commander Asher. A traveling companion on Flaherty's mission to clear up the drug trade and corruption in the city.

"Good morning, Jack. I'd like to give you an update in our investigation of Mr. Jimenez's suicide. We have reviewed the videos. It seems that there was about forty-five seconds of static on the screen and video from Mr. Jimenez's cell. In fact the static appears on all the videos from all the cells. Remember, we had a big storm last night. So, static caused by a hiccup in the power delivery would not be thought of as out of the ordinary by the men on watch. The static occurred just before Officer Darwin left his post and Officer Melton relieved him at 4 AM. The static cleared up and the videos showed that Mr. Jimenez was asleep in his bed. As you know we switch the discs every two hours. Remove the old discs and insert fresh ones. Then we download the discs to ultra big thumb drives for storage and we re-use the discs after they have been cleaned. The transfer of old discs for new discs coincides with the relief. When Officer Darwin was relieved at 6 AM, a new disc was inserted. That's when we discovered the hanging."

"So, you're telling me the hanging took place between 4 and 6 AM and was not seen by any of the cameras. Who has access to the area where the discs are off loaded and stored?"

"Anyone who is not on post."

"So anyone could have gone to the tech room, and inserted an old disc of Jimenez's cell. One showing him asleep. Say asleep between midnight and 2 AM. This disc could have been repeated for the two hours between 4 and 6 and the person on monitoring duty would have been none the wiser. Once the old disc was in, anyone could have gone to Jimenez's cell and hanged him. I'm on the path of police conspiracy and it could be very bumpy for you."

"Not so fast, Jack. Remember these men are responsible for watching twelve monitors. Occasionally, they take their eyes from one cell and watch for details of motion in another. I'm not defending the men, just trying to put their vulnerability into perspective. I think conspiracy may be too broad a term. The third shift has been sent home. We re-contacted them to ask them about the goings on during 4AM and 6 AM. We can locate everybody but Officer Melton. No answer at his home. No response to pages or his cell phone. I am concerned about the safety and whereabouts of Officer Melton. We sent two of my detectives to his house. I expect to have their report shortly. I'll call you then."

He is late for his 10:30 meeting with Mr. Tidmore and his client. A return engagement on Orient Road. Before he leaves, Flaherty calls Pennington to discuss protection for Paco and Sweat. They must be stashed out of the city after his meeting with Tidmore. They agree that Miami is suitable for the time being. The transfer must be done in secret using plain clothes' detectives. Not regular force. Contact

Commander Asher for men he can trust with silence. Asher will make arrangements with Miami-Dade corrections.

"Well, Mr. Flaherty, you and the police certainly have established a strong negative precedent for maintaining the safety of individuals you have in your care. Immediately upon hearing of Mr. Jimenez's very unfortunate death, I rushed over here to protect my client."

"Mr. Tidmore, since the police surmise that Mr. Jimenez committed suicide, from whom would your client need protection? On the other hand, if Mr. Jimenez met his death at the hands of someone other than himself, did you assume that this person would attempt to kill your client? Perhaps? If that is the situation, do you have any idea who might have killed or ordered the killing of Mr. Jimenez?"

"I need to protect my client, because we both know Mr. Jimenez was murdered. The police were the murderers. They did it to close ranks. Protect their own from your witch hunt. They are guilty of cover-up in the murder of the Silveras. They chose not to pursue the case."

"If Mr. Jimenez were murdered, I think I know why. He could have been murdered because he wanted to tell my office everything he knew about his employer and this employer's involvement in the drug trade. He was about to talk about his employer's business associates. Today was to be his big day. He was going to be a star. The life of this shooting star is short and unfulfilled."

"So which is it, Mr. Flaherty . . . murder or suicide?"

Tidmore doesn't blink or smile, he knows he has won the verbal jousting. But this is just the undercard for the main event.

"What I'd like to know is how long you plan to continue this charade?"

"What charade would that be, Mr. Tidmore?"

"My client's alleged involvement in the series of fabricated charges."

"Well, we have witness testimonies on the murder, on bribery and obstruction. These witnesses are hidden away so no harm can befall them before the trial. And they will disappear after the trial."

"Given your most recent example of protection, if I were one of the witnesses, I would be very afraid."

"Since we don't have Mr. Jimenez to accuse of the murder and bribery, Mr. Pena will take the full weight of all the charges. My estimate is that he will spend a long time in jail, if his former friends don't get him first. Given your talents for obfuscation and minutia examination, the death penalty might be out of the question. But, the sentence of a long time behind bars is a reality. And there is no room to deal down, because I want to end this mess, now. Before you or your client say anything, let me play the little scenario of last night."

Flaherty replayed the offer he made to Jimenez in the presence of Biche. And how Jimenez knew he was screwed either way he went. He chose to go the right way and he died at the order of his lawyer's employer.

"If I were to offer you a deal, Mr. Pena, Mr. Tidmore would have to tell Mr. Gutierez of the offer. Mr. Gutierez would become worried that Mr. Pena would tell many bad things about him, his operation, and his associates. If he gets worried enough, he will take some form of drastic action to ease his worry. In my recent history, like the history of the last four hours, I've seen drastic men do drastic things. But, you know Mr. Gutierez better than I do. You know he would protect you at all costs. Wouldn't he? Not fucking likely. So, to protect your life, I won't offer you a deal for information about Mr. G. I can make the case against you and him without your rolling over. Plus, I want the public display of my victory in solving the murder of Hector and Osvaldo Silvera. I want the public to see that I have done what the previous DA had not done. Head on the shield and all that entails. Find guilty murderers. Without a trial, there can be no victory. So, I guess all I can do is say see you in a few weeks."

"You are certainly full of yourself, Mr. Flaherty."

"And a good day to you, Sir."

XIX

Flaherty hands Commander Asher's detectives the warrants for the arrest of Antonio and Pedro Gutierez. The media have not been alerted, yet. They're still chasing Jimenez's death. The arraignment of the boys is set for the next morning. Romero's office and home are strangely silent. Nothing to record. Tidmore can't represent the boys. And, Biche has been hospitalized with a stroke. Or, is he hiding in a room at Tampa General? Maybe he fears for his life, given he could not prevent Jimenez from talking and being murdered. No one is talking.

Thirty minutes later, Commander Asher calls.

"There is no trace of Melton. Not at his home, health club, or neighborhood. He is gone. My guess is that he took whatever money was offered and ran. He's vanished. His house looks lived in. Yet lots of clothes in the closet. He was in a hurry. We checked the airlines, trains and busses. Because, his car is also gone, we also checked Orlando and Miami airports for possible flights. Nothing. We have alerted security in Atlanta and New Orleans. We contacted his credit card company. Don't ask how we knew. When he uses it, they'll notify us."

"So you lost him."

Displeasure, though inaudible, was audible in spirit.

"We didn't lose him. He is temporarily out of sight. I firmly believe he is the only bad apple. My guess he took money from someone who wanted Mr. Jimenez to remain quiet. I am sorry, if this slammed your case. But, we'll get him. And soon. Then he'll talk."

"My case is not slammed. It just got bumped. I have a lot of evidence against Pena. And, he'll take to full load. Call me when you have Melton in custody."

Anger has evolved from displeasure. Or so Asher thinks. Acting is a lawyer's second profession. No sense in telling anyone beyond his office about the taped statement, or the promise to Pena.

The arrests go off like the workings of an expensive chronometer, and the arraignment goes smoothly. The Gutierez boys are represented by two white shoe corporate attorneys. Paul Gane is in Antonio's corner and T. Martin MacDonald fronts for Pedro. The attorneys are senior partners in the biggest law firm in the area. This is the same firm that represents Tampa Bank, as well as business holdings of many of those who sit on the board. The fourth side of the puzzle has just been connected to the other three. Now, Flaherty's job is to fill in the space between the edges. But, not all the pieces have been turned over. And he doesn't have the box in which the puzzle came. He can't see the entire picture he will have upon completion of his task. His heart rate quickens with excitement.

Based on the litany of grievous charges and the real risk of flight, the brothers are remanded without bail. They are placed in isolation at the Orange County Jail. Orlando loves to help solve Tampa's problems. A state official helped the transition. Flaherty will owe the Orlando DA a huge favor. Twenty-four hour protection under bogus names. In a stage whisper, Flaherty cynically muses that they probably won't hire someone to kill each other. They will be safe. Both attorneys approach Pennington and Flaherty on the courthouse steps about a conference tomorrow at 9. They want to discuss the case in detail.

Six-thirty PM and Gene is not home from school. Mrs. Torres was not scheduled to pick him up. He was getting a ride with Ben, a senior who has a car. This occasional transportation process has been functional for weeks. Ben is reliable and prompt. He is a great wrestler. Something Gene is thinking about after this season. Mrs. Torres has prepared Grouper, brown rice and beets. No fat, decent carbs, and good sugars. The fish is about two inches thick. Most people buy by the pound, she buys by the inch. And, it's Gutierez fresh. I feel tired and dirty. A shower and hot tea. Seven fifteen and no Gene. I'm beginning to feel like the sea captain's wife, pacing in front of the window trying to will her love home. But, I can't bring him home any sooner than Ben can. Fire up the laptop and check for messages. Nothing special. Turn on the TV for the news. Prattling about the arrest and arraignment of the Gutierez brothers. An interview with the attorneys and a vigil at Mr. G's house. Eight o'clock and still no son. Nor any call. To relieve my anxiety, I call Ben.

"No sir, Mr. Baker, practice was over at about a quarter 'til seven. I saw Gene outside the locker room and then in the parking lot. He was talking to some guy in a Jeep Wrangler. Gene seemed to know the guy. And he got into the Jeep. They drove away."

"And that's it?"

"I did notice that as they drove off, a third shape appeared in the back seat. And something else. The license plate started HDZ, but the rest of it was unreadable."

"Thanks, Ben. I'm sure Gene is all right and I'll hear from him soon. See you at Districts."

"Yeah, thanks Mr. Baker."

The rock in my stomach is expanding to fill my entire being. My actions are short, choppy and repetitive. I start to really pace. Walk. Sit. Walk. Call Tory at home.

"TC, I won't say I'm sorry to bother you, because I'm too damned frightened to be polite. I'm afraid someone has taken Gene."

"Jacob, slow down and tell me what you know from the beginning."

"I expected Gene home by seven or so. He was waiting for his ride after Ben's wrestling practice. When he didn't come home, I called Ben. He told me Gene got into a Jeep with a guy or maybe two and they drove off. Gene has not called. I'm more than just worried. I'm beginning to panic. I think someone has taken him."

"First, I'll bet he'll be home soon with a story that he went to dinner with some pals. He'll apologize that he didn't let you know. You will forgive him and all will be forgotten."

"I don't mean to be rude, but bullshit. He is gone. Taken."

"Can you think of anyone who would want to take him?"

"No."

"You say he got in the car of his own volition. He must have known the driver. Do you know any of his buddies who drive a Jeep Wrangler?"

"Yeah, two or three. But, he would have called."

"Jacob, listen to yourself. As a teen, did you always call your parents when you went out with your buddies? I'll bet not. So, Gene decides to grab a burger or wings with guys he knows. No big deal."

"I'm real upset by this. I have a bad feeling, something is terribly wrong."

"What can you do about the situation as it now stands?'

"Not a damned thing."

"Exactly. You did the right thing to call me. You vented your concerns. Now do another right thing and relax. He'll be home soon. Then all of this will just be a disturbing memory."

I can't eat and will not drink booze. I can fret. Right now, I'm very good at that. I vacillate between anger and self-pity. I'm angry he is not here. And I feel sorry for myself for what is happening to me. I don't dare think what might have happened to Gene. To go there would be catastrophic.

Eleven-ten and no son. I'm in a full-scale panic attack. Heart palpitations. Lots of nervous motion. Back to the phone.

"TC, what should we do? Gene's missing. I just know he's been taken by someone."

"You could call the police, but what would you tell them? So far, you've not heard from your son. Nor have you heard from anyone who claims to be holding Gene or know where he is."

"We have the first three digits of the license plate. TC, you could trace that. I don't want to wait until I hear from some bastard who took my child. I want you and me to start looking for the kidnapper now."

"If someone took Gene, they probably stole the car or the license plate or both. So tracing the car would be time consuming and probably fruitless. Once again, give me all the details of your conversation with this boy, Ben."

I replay the terrifying telephone call and remember the shape in the back seat and the three letters on the license plate. Soon, he may want to involve the police. This action will not be acceptable. Now I drink. Perchance not to dream.

XX

"As we go move up the crime syndicate food chain, I want to be damned sure the legs supporting our ascent are solid. God, I do love to speechify."

"Jack, often that which drips from your lips has the aroma of bovine waste."

The boys are giddy with the anticipation of victory.

"Paco and Sweat will finger Pena. That's a no brainer. When Pena rolls, we have his testimony against the Gutierez operation. If Pena doesn't roll on the operation, he takes the fall for the Silvera murders, as well as the bribery and witness tampering that followed. We have Jimenez's taped statement about the Silveras' activities, who gave the orders to murder the poor bastards, and the link to the Tampa Bank. Not sure what, if anything, we can get from the Gutierez brothers. I think the old man will do anything to protect them. They know this and will not roll on him. I might be comfortable with nailing them for giving the orders to murder the Silveras, fronting the money for bribery, and their involvement in the coke business."

"That's your problem, Stuart. You think small. You'd climb a tall tree to get to a platform half way to the top. Once there, you'd rest. Ever so proud of your accomplishment. You'd be happy you had arrived at a destination. But, you really hadn't arrived at the true destination, had you? You won't get to a true level of power by thinking small. And, I won't take you to that level if you continue to think that way. I want it all. I want to close down the narcotics business from the top down. I want to crush the enterprise that enriches a few and debilitates thousands. I want to shake the very foundation of the unholy alliance that has permitted this evil to exist for so long. Those are my objectives, and they should be yours. Now let's get digging deeper into the bank and the drug delivery procedure. I firmly believe when we know all there is to know about these two subjects, we will have enough evidence to accomplish my overriding goal of national power and prestige."

✱ ✱ ✱ ✱ ✱ ✱

Somehow I passed through the night. I didn't sleep. No call from Gene. No call from his abductors. Time to call Tory.

"He had on a white golf shirt and knee-length khaki cargo shorts. His shoes are white. They're new. Underneath his shirt he wore a white T-shirt, with his name and his favorite line; *It's not over 'til I win.* His backpack is forest green. On the outside of the bag is stenciled, *Get tough. Be tough. Stay tough.* He's five-foot nine inches tall and weighs 165 pounds. His hair is brown, cut very close. His complexion is fair. No glasses. He sometimes wears a necklace made of small white shells."

As my friend and counselor he listens well, but says nothing. The morning has 24 hours in it. I spend a little time at the office then I go for a swim and work out to divert my anxiety. The message light is on.

> *Well, well, well. How does it feel to be fucked over? We have a lot to discuss. But, not now. Stay tuned for more bulletins.*

I call TC again, and he demands we compare this to the original threatening call. Ross Studio to the rescue. The electronic signatures show Reggie that the first and most recent calls came from the same voice, but that they were made from different locations. Tory stresses we should turn the matter of threats and the two tapes over to the police.

"No! No! TC, I think we can catch this bastard without getting the police involved. Maybe just like we caught English. We can do it ourselves without putting Gene in jeopardy. If we tell the police, it could very likely become news with publicity. Then Gene will be in jeopardy. We don't have to play exactly by their rules. We can catch this bastard just like we caught the other scum."

"Slow down. This voice has made no mention of Gene. We don't even know he has Gene. Maybe he doesn't have your son, but he is just playing an ugly mind game with you. He appears to be vindictive. Can you identify the voice enough to tie it to someone, who you have wronged or who could feel that you wronged him?"

"I have no idea who the caller is? In my business, I have pissed-off a lot of guys. I have always hoped that their anger was insufficient to produce this kind of reaction."

"How about your personal life? Any peccadilloes?"

"None."

"I still think we should turn all the details and the two phone calls over to the police. They can set traps on your phones, trace the next call, and catch the caller."

"No! No! Please listen to me. I'm convinced the caller has Gene or knows where he is. He hasn't said so directly. There is a vast difference between phony blackmail and kidnapping for ransom. In the mean time, we'll just have to sit on this information."

★ ★ ★ ★ ★ ★

"Mr. MacDonald and Mr. Garne, thank you for coming to my office. My hope is that today we can lay out some guidelines for agreement. Our multi-faceted case against the brothers Gutierez is very strong and getting stronger each day. I am confident they will spend the rest of their lives in jail. They would have to be 125 to 150 years of age to live long enough to be released. They may even get a chance to try out the state's new method of execution, lethal injection or Ol' Sparky, the good old fashion fryer. So, what do you have to offer me?"

"Let me speak for both of the wrongfully accused. First, I am appalled at your histrionics. Second, we are not in a position to offer anything, Mr. Flaherty, for two reasons. One, our clients have nothing you would want. Two, they don't know what you are offering."

"Mr. Garne, let me clarify our position. We have statements from two different sources directly linking Antonio and Pedro Gutierez to the murder of Hector and Osvaldo Silvera. They ordered the killing that was performed by others. Then they provided the money to create false witnesses. That's murder, conspiracy to commit murder, obstruction and tampering for both of them. The statements confirming the active involvement by your clients is the criminal conspiracy of interstate drug distribution are independent and therefore are corroborative. That falls under the RICO statute. We have statements detailing the brothers' involvement in the purchase and distribution of cocaine. We have legally obtained wiretaps confirming the distribution. We have tapes from surveillance cameras. These tapes show the brothers and other individuals inspecting crates and baskets of fish. Inspecting the baskets and retrieving packages from beneath the fish. These packages were taken separate from the fish, into the Gutierez market. We have audio evidence that confirms the packages contained cocaine. We have evidence that the brothers ordered these drugs distributed throughout a very broad network. In Florida and throughout the Southeast. Interstate commerce of drugs is not a good idea. Let me reiterate . . . RICO. It involves the feds, who are not inclined to be a generous as I am. So, we got them, until death do we part. Their death."

"All of your allegations are interesting Mr. Flaherty. They make for good tabloid fodder. Not very viable in a court of law."

"Not viable? We'll have to see, then, won't we?"

"Well not exactly. Before you go running before a jury, you should read these motions. Have a nice day."

Paul Garne handed Flaherty a stack of motions. With that, the two very expensive smoothies left. The gist was the same in all eight multi folded blue jacket documents. Suppress the evidence and statements. Obtained in an unlawful manner. Obtained via coercion. Obtained without the advice of counsel. The exercise bore the mark of James Tidmore. And, maybe Solomon Tuggs. Who is the acting puppeteer?

"So much wasted paper. So much wasted time."

"Stu, that's exactly what Tidmore wants to do. He will waste his way into reduced charges. If he can bedazzle a soft-headed judge, he may even get a few of his motions approved. If he can get some of our evidence and statements tossed out, he might push the "fruit from the poisonous tree" precedent. And, who knows how he can confuse a jury. Create doubt in their collective mind. Knowing this, he is at work profiling the most favorable jury. One that is easily confused. We can't let it get to that. Do you see anything strange about these motions?"

"No."

"He has missed Jimenez's statement, because Tidmore thought there was no statement. He thought that, because I wanted him to think that. We will spring this piece of evidence when it will do the most good. I told you Tidmore would not deal. I just wasn't sure why. The why is because he is heading up the defense team for the entire family. Now, Stu, review all the tapes and transcripts from Paco Winny and Ralph Sweat. Make absolutely sure that even the dimmest judge can follow the path of truth from point A to point B. I'm going to work on Roberto Pena."

Before driving out to see Mr. Pena, Flaherty calls the Atlanta office of the FBI.

"May I speak to Field Director Dana Davidson, please? This is Tampa, Florida District Attorney Jack Flaherty."

"Field Director Davidson, how may I help you, Jack?"

"Dana, it always nice to hear your voice. Have you had a chance to review the material I forwarded the other day?"

"Yes, I've gone over it and reviewed it with my supervisors."

"What do you think?"

"We think there might be ample evidence to initiate a federal investigation."

"I know what that means. It means that you will approach the issue with due deliberation. The decision to proceed to investigation could take months. I don't have months. If my estimated time line is accurate, you will be ready to investigate while I am concluding the convictions. Then you'll want to assume jurisdiction because of the interstate distribution. Then my efforts and I will be after thoughts . . . footnotes."

"Our plates are very full, Jack. We want to help you, but we can't move your case ahead of those on which we have already a significant investment of time and money. Move your case simply because of your schedule."

"This is big. Reread the transcripts and follow the path from drug importing to distribution. From checking accounts which fund bribery and witness tampering to expansion of a drug cartel. From financial services to money laundering. From local fortunes to illegal interstate commerce. I was told that your team would be cooperative at the time I needed the big guns. If you can't handle a case of this size, justice might be better served by getting some other department of the federal government involved. Then they can show you and the public how good they are. But, if you and your other task force members want to grab immediate headlines and advance your careers, you'll jump on this. I need to know your answer today. If it's yes, when can you start? If the answer is no, I'll contact a friend in the DEA."

"I'll have to talk to my supervisors. That may take some time."

"No time. Patch me through to your supervisors. Let's discuss this huge window of opportunity that is now open before you. The one that may be rapidly closing."

The silent pause lasts twenty seconds.

"That won't be necessary. I can expedite clearance to proceed. I have been given the authority to make the call on this case. I will move this case to the top of the list, and go out on a limb for you this time. I'm risking this for two reasons. First, what you say has a strong ring of validity for the department and me. And, second, when we succeed, you will owe me big time."

"Speaking of time. What about some time for us when you are in Tampa? For old time's sake? After you just played with my mind, you owe me a dinner. Your treat."

"Don't even think about it. What is past is past. I was young, naive, divorced, and lonely. You took advantage of the situation."

"Yes, I took advantage of the situation for about eighteen months. Not very convincing protestations. But, enough of our history. Let's focus on our future victories and the accolades they bring. I need you to start your on-site audits and file requisitions tomorrow. The timing is important, because I am about to spring a big trap on the lower echelon."

"Not tomorrow. But, we will be in Tampa on Friday, I promise. We need time to assemble. Also, Friday gives us the weekend to be inside the bank and not disturb the regular business transactions. The little people won't get wind of what we're doing. They won't panic. It's good PR for us to keep the little people at ease, while we clean up a mess."

"Concomitant with your invasion of the ivory tower, we will wrap up our attack from the ground level. We can close in on everybody with a pincer movement. Are we Zulu or what? I assume you'll be heading up the weekend's work."

"It's my ass, so I want to see everything first hand. But, I have to let Special Agent Bobbi Pulik be the team leader. She has a history at this type of weekend invasion. She has been successful before. I have to succeed through her work. She gets the ink. I get the promotion."

"This is my second and final offer for a working dinner on Monday."

"I'll see. Can I reach you on your cell phone?"

"Sure. And thanks a lot."

✷ ✷ ✷ ✷ ✷ ✷

I can't sit. I can't stand. I can't go to work. I can't stay home. I can't talk on the phone. I can't be quiet. I have to give Beatrice the details of current events. I call. She responds. Her response is comforting.

"I'm coming home tonight. Be there by eight. Bee-bee will be strong for you. Hugs and kisses."

A virtual tonic. The ring of the telephone slaps me back to reality. Five agonizing rings and the machine picks up.

XXI

*By now some people know. But, they don't really know
do they. They don't know the truth. And, for sure the police
don't know. We think it's time they hear the truth. We think
it's time you tell everybody the truth. The truth will set Gene
free. Stay tuned for explicit instructions.*

No need to contact Reggie, this is the same guy. I know
it. I call TC and play the tape for him.

"Good gawd, Jacob, can we turn this over to the police
now? The man has Gene and he is attempting extortion.
My question is what is he trying to extort from you? What
information does he think you have that would be important
for the public to hear?"

"Tory, we need a face-to-face. Can I come to your office
now?"

"I'll see you as soon as you can get here."

The brightness of the day is seeping into my being.
The drive downtown takes twenty minutes. Now, I'm in an
emotional hurry. My pace from parking garage to Tory's office
confirms my mood. The ceiling in his office seems higher
than before and the furniture seems larger. Have I shrunk?
Or, have I become less significant in light of the growing pain
in my soul.

"Tory, what I'm about to tell you, I do so as your client
and hopefully as your friend. I killed the Silveras. When I was
called to the apartment that Heather and Gene shared, I saw
what her lifestyle had done. I became enraged at what had
happened. I wanted to punish those who were responsible.

I couldn't punish Heather. She had already paid the ultimate price. So, I wanted to kill the guys who killed her. I guess I could never stop trying to protect her. I also wanted to punish the persons who, through Heather, had hurt Gene. I knew she had bought drugs from the Silveras in the past and I bet she bought the killer shit from them. So, I went to see them to let them know that I knew they were guilty of her murder. The arrogant pricks tried to talk their way out of the sale and the deaths of all those people. We argued. Got into a fight. Hector scrambled toward the bed and pulled the mattress and box spring away from the wall. He ripped open a panel and reached inside. I was convinced he was reaching for a gun, so I shot him. I used one of the twenty-five-caliber semi-automatics my dad had left me in his will. Hit the bastard in his left ear. He began to twitch. Blood was spurting everywhere as he started to roll over. Then I shot Osvaldo as he cowered in the corner. I stood real close and shot him in the face. My first shot entered his right eye. He thrashed for a moment. I wanted to really mess up them as payment for the damage they had done to Gene. I was livid with rage. The best way to do that was to create the impression that this was a street crime. So I popped each of them in the eyes. The volume from the CD was high. Something heavy metal. That crap had covered our argument. The apartment was in the back of the building and they had blankets over the windows and door to make sure their business was unknown. So, I knew no gunshot noise would be heard by neighbors. Besides, in that neighborhood gunfire is not uncommon."

"I reached inside the wall panel and found a knife. The knife had a blade about a foot long and two-to-three inches wide. It was serrated on the topside. I also found lots of street grams. Each had a colored seal across the opening. Exactly like the one on Heather's kitchen table. I was on an evil crusade. I took the knife and completed the butchery of Hector and Osvaldo. The really crazy gang hit would communicate loud and clear what would happen if a dealer crossed the line and sold that killer shit. Before I began cutting the ears, noses, tongues and fingers I slipped the gun in my hip pocket. After my handy work, I put the knife inside my shirt at my waist. I walked rapidly from the apartment. I didn't have to run. No one would see me. And if they saw me, I was just another junkie, who came to the 'hood. No one would care. As I was going down a flight of stairs at one end of the hall, I noticed Peter Johnson coming up the stairs at the other end of the hall. I exited the back door, found my car and drove back toward the motel where Gene and I were temporarily staying. On my way to the motel, I stopped at my office, and took off my blood stained clothes, put them into a bag, and changed into my swim trunks. I hid the gun in my desk; I threw the bag of soiled clothes and the knife into the Hillsborough River. When I got to motel, I went from my car to the pool for a swim. It washed the blood from my hands and body, and wiped down the car. The next day we went on our cruise. After the cruise, I returned the murder weapon to the lock box at home. Later, I took the second pistol, drove to Johnson's house during the day and hid the gun under the tarp in the shed. I knew that the police would eventually find the gun and assume it was the murder weapon, but ballistics could not confirm their suspicion. So Johnson would take a ton of shit, but would be released. A small price to pay for helping to ruin my wife's life."

"So you think Peter Johnson is coming after you now because he knew you had been to the Silveras' apartment immediately before he got there. He knows that you are the murderer. He wants money and a confession?"

"Mostly he wants me to confess. The money, I believe, is just icing on the cake. In his own warped way, he loved Heather. And, he wanted to kill the Silveras, her murderers. This would have been the final testament of his love. I would not be surprised if he thought Heather and I might get back together. That would make him doubly angry. She may have even told him so, just to mind fuck him. She was real good at that. His mind must have been a playground for her manipulations. So, if he killed her killers, he could assume the mantle of Heather's true love. Her avenging angel. Very operatic. He went there that night to kill. I beat him to it. I robbed of him of his righteous indignation. Over that past two years, his emotional energy has given way to some form of warped rationality. Now, he may be having second thoughts about being involved in the whole sordid mess. What was once a great emotion is now a bad idea. So, he wants me to 'fess up. He wants the world to know that I am the one who murdered the Silveras. And he wants me to pay for doing what he wanted to do; the crime he wanted to commit, but could not. I stole his glory and now I must pay. I think there is some type of gnarled justification and purification going on inside him. I am convinced he took Gene. Gene would not be afraid to go with him. The guy is so fucked up he may even hurt Gene, because he wants me to pay and pay dearly."

Tory is spellbound, but ever the thinker.

"I think it's time for a big plan. Call the school and tell them that Gene is very ill and he has to stay home. Doctor's orders. You will pick up his homework assignments. Doctor has him on a delicate diet, heavy medication, and full time bed rest."

"Consider it done."

"While you're here now, I'll need you to record the events of that evening. Just like you told me. Leave out nothing. I'll have it transcribed for your signature later."

✴ ✴ ✴ ✴ ✴ ✴

Flaherty visits the lead perp to shore-up his case. The trip the Orient Road is short and sweet. He pats his jacket pocket to confirm a document's presence.

"Mr. Pena. Good day to you, sir. I came all the way out here to try to understand why you won't be a cooperative participant in my investigation."

"I need Mr. Tidmore here, if we're going to talk."

"Let me tell you about your attorney, Mr. Tidmore. Mr. Tidmore now represents Antonio and Pedro Gutierez. Well, to be truthful, and we want to be truthful don't we Mr. Pena, Mr. Tidmore is not listed as the attorney for the brothers. But, he is giving counsel and guidance to the two listed counselors. You see Mr. Tidmore works for the elder Mr. Gutierez. But, you know that. The elder Mr. Gutierez wants only the best attorney for his sons. He thought he could stop the investigation with you and Mr. Jimenez. But, he was mistaken. He underestimated my skill and the power of this office. So, after you promised to be a good boy to Mr. Tidmore, Mr. G. pulls this big and very expensive hired gun off your case and assigns him to the cases against his sons. Blood is thicker than water. And you're water."

"What the hell does all that mean to me?"

"It means that Mr. Tidmore will work very hard to convince anyone who will listen that you and Mr. Jimenez acted on your own for your own benefit. Sort of like independent contractors, who were not employed by Mr. G. or his sons at the time of the murders. The two independent contractors killed the Silveras and bribed witnesses and cops. So the weight of the case falls on you because the case ends with you. You will do time until your appeals have been exhausted and the state fries you. Or, the Gutierez brothers will seek you out in prison and order your throat slit. Maybe they will hang you like they did Jimenez, before Jimmy could protect himself. You can protect yourself by helping me. No matter how you look at it, it's your life. You can help yourself by cooperating. Help me shift the blame onto the brothers and Mr. G. Tell me about the business and the bank. Help me help you save your life."

"What can you do for me?"

"I can do one of two things. I can let certain people know that you have been cooperative, even though you have not. Then I can release you to go home. You will be like a rabbit before wolves. I let them get you. You die. Or, you can cooperate and I tell no one. Then you get to live in Montana free from the worry of revenge. New face, name, papers, job, home, and family. Does that sound interesting? You will get out from under this mess with a little confession and a lot of testimony. Then you simply disappear. The choice is yours, because it's your life."

"My choice is no choice at all. I'll cooperate, but I want the witness protection thing in writing from you."

"In the belief that you are a reasonable man, I took the liberty of drawing up the agreement before I came to see you. Please read it and then we'll both sign it."

The paragraphs of a powerless life insurance policy are on one page.

"Before you start your statement, let me tell you what I want. Please state your name and that you have dismissed Mr. James Tidmore as your attorney. Also I want admission that you killed the Silveras on orders from the Gutierez brothers. The more you tell me, the faster I can put our agreement into place. The faster you'll get your get-out-of-jail-free card."

"I am Roberto Pena and I give this statement of my own free will. As of today, Mr. James Tidmore is no longer my lawyer. I fired him. I have worked for Mr. Romero Gutierez and his sons, Antonio and Pedro for seven years. I did what I was told, when they told me. I made deliveries of drugs. I made pick-ups of drugs. I dealt drugs to the people in the distribution system. Kept these people in line. Antonio and Pedro Gutierez wanted Jimmy Jimenez and me to teach Hector and Osvaldo Silver and all the other street dealers a lesson about selling somebody else's bad merchandise. That kind of shit was not good for the reputation of Gutierez quality. We went to the Silveras' apartment to find out who was trying to move into our territory. Who was selling the boys the bad shit? Yeah, we roughed them up, but they fought us and we had to kill him. The butchery was Jimmy's idea. He liked leaving a message. When we left we saw some guys on the street corner. They were so drunk, they weren't sure of it was day or night. We convinced them to say it was the tall blonde guy we had seen leaving the building. He had run down the walk and got into his car. One of the street drunks said he saw a short guy with dark hair. We told them what to remember. A tall blonde guy. That was easy, because Tampa is filled with tall white blonde hair guys. Antonio and Pedro told us to make sure nothing bad got back to them. The investigation had to end with the Silveras' murder. It took a lot of cash to buy off the drunks and some cops. But, it wasn't our money, so we didn't care."

Roberto Pena's statement went on for two hours. It was clearer and more linear than the ramblings of Jimmy Jimenez. Flaherty called Asher from the jail and requested that Pena be taken from the jail and hidden in the state mental hospital near Lakeland. Flaherty knew other inmates and some cops would become suspicious that Pena was spending so much time alone with the DA. Hiding was the only choice. On the call Asher told him that Officer Melton's body had been found in his car. The car was submerged in the canal east of 56th Street. Two bullet holes in his head. Not a suicide. He had five thousand dollars in his possession when he was murdered. Obviously the crime was not robbery.

XXII

The liveried ex-cop at the Condo's Concierge Desk announces Beatrice's arrival. She is at my door in less than three minutes. Her hug is a powerful tonic. Her kisses are antidotes to the poison of sorrow.

"Tell me everything."

"I will. A lot of what I tell you is black, so listen carefully. As my relationship with Heather was going down the drain . . ."

Over the course of the next hour, I tell Beatrice nearly everything leading up to Gene's abduction. Everything; my failures, recriminations, humiliations, rage, protection of my son, misguided love of something lost, revenge, plan, inhuman brutality, the gun, the knife, the other man, running and hoping no one would know, fear that someone would find out, lies, the taped messages, and most importantly my responsibility. I bounce from subject to subject. From date to date. Sometimes out of sequence. From person to person. As I ricochet deeper and deeper into the pit of soul regurgitation, Beatrice sits before me spellbound. She doesn't speak or nod recognition of what she is hearing. She slowly turns ashen. She is mesmerized.

". . . Tory has advised me that I should do nothing until I hear from Peter Johnson with specific instructions. Tory is convinced Johnson wants me to confess my sin to the world and he is holding Gene for leverage. I am relatively sure Peter will not harm Gene. But he is crazy enough that he just might because he wants me to really suffer as he feels he has suffered from Heather's death. He could go that far to hurt me. Once Peter has contacted me again, Tory and I will enact a plan that saves Gene and keeps the entire mess out of the public eye. There will be no police involvement."

"Excuse me, but holyfuckingchrist! You kept this dark side very well hidden from me. And I thought I was beginning to know you."

"Now you know everything about me."

"There is a part of me that feels sorry for you. You've had to carry the burden of this crime with you for two years. To look Gene in the eyes and pretend to be an upstanding father and not a criminal must have been horrendous. You had to pretend to be an honest, hard working business owner raising his son alone. You had to hide all of the evil that you did, behind the mask of moral superiority. But you knew all along that the understanding and sympathy from others was grossly misplaced. I want to hold you up from the crushing weight of the terrible burden. There's another part of me that wants to get out of this chair and flee. Wash my body and soul thoroughly. Leave you and your mess behind. There is a third part that wants to give you whatever strength I have to help you get through all of this. I fully understand that it's your problem and I am not responsible for your actions. Then or now. But, I want to be your lover nonetheless."

"Thank you. And I understand if you change your mind and flee. If you did, I'd follow you begging you to stay. Right now, I'm no longer lost. But, I need you and your strength. Any more words would be maudlin. Let's go to Bellissimo for dinner. Sort of like going back to the beginning and starting over."

Dinner was akin to a first date. Nervous talking and giggling. Looking at the right-hand side of the menu before ordering. Sharing a dessert. We held hands as we walked to my car. She loves me. At home, once again the message light was blinking

We've decided you should pay. And talk. You should pay first and talk later. We think you should pay $50,000. And no crap about not having that kind of money. We know you hide cash you get from clients. You can get the cash in a day. In a day from now we will call you with instructions about delivery. Now listen very carefully. Do not, I repeat, do not call the police and tell them about our arrangement. If you do, something bad will happen to your son. That would be a shame. First you let your wife die then your arrogance kills your boy. When the money is delivered, we will give you instructions where to find your son. Got the sequence: money, no cops, son, and cops. If you go out of sequence, his blood will be on your hands. Now, here's your son: "Dad, I'm OK. Scared, but unharmed. I miss you. I don't understand what is happening. Come and get me soon." That's enough. Mr. Baker, we'll talk.

Beatrice got a first-hand exposure to my situation. She feels my panic. I call Tory at home and play the tape. We will meet tomorrow morning at his office.

✱ ✱ ✱ ✱ ✱

T. Martin MacDonald arrives at 8 AM. Flaherty is waiting.

"Mr. Flaherty, we'd like to know what arrangements could be made for our clients in the event they were to cooperate with your investigation."

"Any arrangements would depend on the extent of the cooperation. But, before we discuss any cooperation, I am obliged to tell you that I know Mr. James Tidmore is guiding your actions. No personal offense, but Mr. Tidmore is the only one skilled enough to run this complex criminal defense. So many defendants. So many charges. So many connections. So little time. And Mr. Tidmore is in the employ of Mr.

Romero Gutierez, as are you sir. Mr. Gutierez hired Mr. Tidmore to run the defense of his employees, his sons, and his business operations. But, most of all his immediate family. You and Mr. Garne are local faces for the defense of his sons. Window dressing, as it were. Hell, you're not even tested criminal attorneys. You're corporate pin-stripers. I am obliged to tell you that all of your many motions will be dismissed. They comprise a smoke screen to buy time. Time for Mr. Tidmore to work on the complexities of the case. He needs to buy time, because we have such a short court date. I see the stalling, and the court will also. Third, because Mr. Tidmore is now the de facto representative of the brothers, he can no longer be the representative of Mr. Pena. Conflict of interest. Mr. Pena knows this, and he has officially dismissed Mr. Tidmore. I have a tape recording of the dismissal and many critical admissions. And I have a signed transcript of the tape that you may see at trial. Mr. Pena seeks no further assistance from Mr. Gutierez, because he fears Mr. Gutierez. Mr. Pena has decided to assist this office with the investigation. In consideration for the assistance, this office has made a special arrangement with Mr. Pena. Consequently, we have enough firepower to sink Antonio and Pedro Gutierez. And, with a little help from my friends, we won't need statements from the boys to sink the drug enterprise of their father and his associates. The net of all this is that your clients are up the creek and I own all the paddles. But, because I'm a decent man, I'll be happy to put them in cells next to their dad."

"Mr. Flaherty, I am aware you are working on a personal success timetable. You wish to have the entire case wrapped up in a two months. At worst four months. I am also aware that the because of the complexities of the case, a very strong defense attorney could drag out the case well beyond your timetable. Drag out the case so long that you will miss your deadline. Your efforts will be viewed in a less than favorable light. Slow and sloppy. You let the defense control the prosecution. Then will come the appeals in all the proper venues. The recent filing of the motions will help in the appeals. Little by little your case will be eroded. Some charges will be dismissed. Some sentences reduced to ludicrous levels such as time served. All the while those who you really want to be behind bars will be free. Finally, you'll see that all the king's money and all the king's men did put Humpty Dumpty back together again. All of this will happen because you foolishly refused our help. Let us help you make your case against the real villains. Don't waste your time with the soldiers, when you have the chance to conquer the castle. Look, I want you to think about my offer. We're scheduled to see Judge Witmer tomorrow to discuss our motions. Let's talk after the hearing. Now, I know you're a busy man. So I'll leave. Thanks for your time."

Pennington comes bursting in from the adjoining office.

"He's stalling. Putting the promise on the table with nothing to back up his word. Hell, the old man might give up his sons to save his ass. But, the sons would never give up their father. That would set a very bad precedent, particularly in jail. I know he came here with specific instructions from Tidmore. You're right. Tidmore is trying to buy time. And he's also trying to probe our resolve and the strength of our case. The brothers have more years to live. More jail time to give. We're supposed to think they will deal. But, they won't deal."

"Stu, the key is to understand who the final puppeteer is. At the bottom of the marionette family are Sweat and Winny. They are energized by a one-time cash payment. Then come Pena and Jimenez. They are driven by employment and a nice life style. Then Antonio and Pedro. They dream of their empire to be. Then Romero. He lives for control of his world. Each pulls the strings of the ones below. But, who pulls Romero's strings. It would have to be someone or some group, which is very powerful. The only local group like this is the board of directors of the Tampa Bank. Maybe a ruling segment of the board. That board would throw Romero's kids and the old man into the legal gristmill in a heartbeat to protect their fortunes and keep their white shirts clean. If the bank's board rids itself of a cancer like Romero and his boys, they may even hope to be considered good guys, who righted a wrong. They might even hope that investigation would stop with the Gutierez's. Maybe Tidmore was hired by the board and not by the Gutierez family. Can you dig into Tidmore's activity? Find out where he is staying, his contacts, and hell, tap his phone and read his mail. I don't care. We must get a better handle on this Paladin. Also, make damned sure we have considered every contingency for the hearing tomorrow. I can't afford to slip now.

"Your honor, as you can see by our motions, the District Attorney's office has built the case against our clients on a foundation of sand. Their case starts with the murder of Hector and Osvaldo Silvera. No one really knows who murdered these men. First the District Attorney ordered a Mr. Peter Johnson apprehended then released due to the lack of concrete evidence, like the murder weapon. Plus, Mr. Johnson has an alibi. Then, they arrest a Mr. Ahl, who resembles Mr. Johnson. Maybe they were profiling. Who knows? But, Mr. Ahl is released, because he, too, has a solid alibi. There still no murder weapon. Now they accuse our clients of ordering a murder for which there is no murderer and no murder weapon. They don't know who killed the Silveras. Without the murderer or murderers, the entire chain of allegations against our clients disintegrates. We are simply asking your honor to dismiss the elements of the case that depend on the murder, because the District Attorney has no case."

"Judge, despite what Mr. Garne and Mr. MacDonald may posit, the District Attorney has testimony that Antonio and Pedro Gutierez ordered Mr. Jimenez and Mr. Pena to murder Hector and Osvaldo Silvera. Mr. Jimenez and Mr. Pena went to the Silveras' apartment for the purpose of murdering the brothers. A butchering of the Silveras would show other dealers what happens to those who stray. And they did the job. They admit it. Our arrest and subsequent release of both Mr. Johnson and Mr. Ahl were unfortunate. Each was based on erroneous information and zeal of my office to bring the murder case to a quick conclusion. These murders have been unsolved for two years. My predecessor was unable to solve it or didn't want to. Each of the unfortunate arrests and subsequent releases was made prior to the aforementioned corroborating testimony from Messrs Jimenez and Pena. Therefore, we have the murderers and we wish to prosecute those who ordered the murder. Any and all indictments that emanate from the prosecution of the murderers are natural events as to motive. All evidence, physical and otherwise, supporting the charge of conspiracy to commit murder, bribery of an official . . . the police . . . and witness tampering also lead to and support the charges of drug trafficking and money laundering. When take separately, these last two charges fall under the RICO statute, and could be the support of a federal case. The testimonies of Mr. Pena and Mr. Jimenez are complete and they go well beyond the murders. These, in turn, are the basis of a far-reaching case springing from the initial investigation. So, the District Attorney's office knows there is a long chain of illegal and nefarious deeds. The murders are simply the first visible link in the very long and ugly chain. The people of Tampa and the state of Florida deserve to be protected from the murderers of Hector and Osvaldo Silvera, and those that benefitted from the murders, as well as to have the entire drug syndicate up rooted and destroyed. We implore you let stand the indictments, and to dismiss the motions as without merit and frivolous."

"Your Honor, you must uphold our motions pertaining to the testimony of Mr. Jimenez and Mr. Pena. Unfortunately,

Mr. Jimenez suffered and untimely death. He died before his counsel could discuss the case with the District Attorney. Subsequent to that, his counsel, Mr. Bailey Biche, suffered a life-threatening stroke. He has lost some of his mental acuity and much of his physical capacity. He should not be called to testify as to what was discussed with Mr. Flaherty's office. Mr. Pena has not had the benefit of counsel in any discussions with the District Attorney. His counsel has been called out of town for a brief time. However, we have been informed that Mr. Tidmore will be returning in a few days to take up Mr. Pena's cause. Therefore, we urge you to view any and all statements by Mr. Pena and Mr. Jimenez made to this date as inadmissible and to strike them as evidence in the allegations."

"Judge, I have two tapes. Each contains testimony. Tape 'J' is the sworn testimony given to my office the evening by Mr. Jimenez the night before he was murdered. Tape 'P' is the sworn testimony of Mr. Pena given of his own free will after Mr. Jimenez's statement and without knowledge of Mr. Jimenez's testimony. I request that your Honor listen to these tapes and determine if they meet the standards of evidence. If they do, they must be included as such in the murder case and any subsequent indictments brought by my office against members of the Gutierez family. If they fail to meet the standards, they should be given back to my office."

"Your Honor. These alleged tapes come as a surprise to the defense. We request copies of these tapes."

"Not before I listen to them to determine their admissibility. If I find the tapes to be admissible, I'm sure Mr. Flaherty will provide true copies of them as part of the exculpatory evidence. If they are found not to be admissible, they will find their way into a court-approved shredder. As to your motions, Mr. MacDonald and Mr. Garne, I must listen to the tapes to determine their merit. And thus the merits of your motions. All parties will hear from me by tomorrow at five. As of now trial is in four weeks. Gentlemen, have a nice day."

"Jack, testimony coerced from two frightened low-life types then reinvented by your office via the miracle of electronics. God, boy, you're making our appeal before we go to trial."

"Well, ol' timer, we'll just have to see, won't we. Will you be stopping by for coffee at three tomorrow?"

"See you then."

XXIII

I can find the necessary funds from a stash in my office. I hid money from Heather, the IRS, and my employees. Sometimes clients like to pay in cash. I give them a discount off one invoice, and enter revised amount paid . . . less than they actually paid . . . as the final invoice. This is my company and these are my books. I have saved the cash for a personal rainy day. It is pouring outside today.

"Tory, I have the money. What should I do?"

"Mr. Johnson will call with instructions sometime today. When he does, let me know immediately. Bring the money to my office, and I'll spell out how my plan of defensive aggression will work. How's Beatrice?"

"She is my rock. Non-judgmental, non-participatory support. I couldn't ask for more."

"After this phone call, keep her out of all our actions."

Inaction is life threatening. I convince Beatrice to go for a brief run. Then the weight room and the condo's sauna. Keep physically busy. There is something very religious about excessive physical activity followed by excessive heat. Mindless purging of bodily urges and thereby replenishing the soul. Wrapped in towels, we sit on wooden-slat benches, while the electric coil heats the rocks to a Hades-like level. Missing are sulfur smoke and flames from the bowels of eternal damnation. Beads of sweat form on my arms. I look at Beatrice and notice the moisture glow of her shoulders and face. Her legs are smooth save for the baby down above her knees.

"It's too hot for what you're thinking. Besides, one of the maintenance people or another daytime stay-at-home could find us amidst ecstasy."

"Beatrice, the only way you could know what I was thinking is to be thinking the same thing. Shame on you. That's naughty."

"It's not naughty. It's inappropriate. Not the right place."

"Well, let me see what would the right place be? Beside your parents' pool? In their Jacuzzi? At the museum? Tell me where it would be appropriate for us to make love."

"Not here. Not now."

"Is it the time or the place? Is it the time and the place?"

"Place."

"Would the right place be in the double tub of my bathroom?"

"That could be considered an appropriate place, yes."

"What about the time? Would fifteen minutes from now be appropriate?"

"Yes."

"Then let us tarry no longer."

Verbal foreplay. Hastily gathering up our workout clothes and stuffing our damp feet into our sneakers, we head for my condo unit. Inside the condo I cannot wait for the tub. I unwrap Beatrice's large towel, sort of twirling her onto the bed. Our sauna-heated and sweating bodies merge. Love is lost in lust's rush. My thrusting moves her up the bedcover. It's as if I am pushing a sled. Aggression. The urgency to complete the activity is great. The exertion produces more sweat. Seated on me, she continues her rite of joy. Her knees are at my sides and she is bouncing to bliss. She grabs my shoulders and squeezes brutally. Digs her nails. Her head falls to my chest. Panting aloud. Slowly she comes down from the heights. Rolls off me and is still.

"I needed you. And, you are here for me. I love you."

"Jacob, I love you, too. We will survive. First we have to get Gene home safe and sound. Then we have to unstick you from the bad situation. Then we have to begin our lives. I call the tub. No men allowed."

"Already you're taking over my house. While you are luxuriating in gallons of hot bubble bath, I'll prepare some food for us both. This is a good division of effort, since I've seen the damage you can do in a kitchen."

Before she escapes the bed, I kiss her. Passing through the living room, I notice the message light is blinking. My heart rate jumps back up to 90 in the six feet I walk to the machine.

By now you have dug into the numerous cash stashes that you have hidden from everyone. Here is your own special twelve-step program for redemption.

Number 1: No police. No police. No police.

Number 2: Put the bills in a paper shopping bag inside a lawn and leaf bag.

Number 3: By six PM tonight, drive the money in the bags to Pier 60 at Clearwater Beach.

Number 4: Go to the eighth large wire basket to the left of the Pier.

Number 5: Remove the manila envelope which we placed inside the basket.

Number 6: Deposit the lawn and leaf bag with the money in the basket.

Number 7: Take the contents of the manila envelope to the police and stay with them while they review the contents.

Number 8: Confess your sins to the authorities.

Number 9: Request that they announce your arrest.

Number 10: When you are out on bail, await our instructions about retrieving your son.

Number 11: Obey those instructions and your son will be returned unharmed.

*Number 12: Violate the steps and you and your son will
    suffer the consequences.*
See you at six. But you won't see us.

It's 3:30. Two and a half hours to get to Tory's office,
make final arrangements, and head to the beach at height of
the commuter rush. Twenty minutes to get dressed and to
Tory's office. Am I late? I begin to panic.

"Bee-bee it's time for me to leave. The important task is
at hand."

No shower. No tub. I am throwing on khakis and a
bright yellow golf shirt with a client logo over the heart when
Beatrice exits the bathroom dripping water and soap.

"I can't go with you. I know that. My heart can. I'll be
here when you return."

"Thank you for your love."

One last item is in a wooden lock box beneath an old
beach blanket in the laundry room. I retrieve the second
25-caliber pistol, the murder weapon, and stuff it into my
belt at the small of my back. Grab the message machine tape
and head downtown.

Tory is very calm. He knows a way to get to the beach
super fast during rush hour. He spells out his plan. Follow
the instructions from Peter Johnson. Except for Tory's
modifications. One of his associates will drive my car and
make the trash drop in my stead, while Tony and I will be
in a van observing the exchange. My body-double is a good
match for height, weight, and color. By six PM this time of
year the sun will be on the horizon. Twilight's long shadows
and a Brown University cap will complete the masquerade.

After the exchange, a drunk from the beach will follow
Peter Johnson toward his lair. Mayan once said that being
black is sometimes a good disguise in a white man's world.
The trap is set in motion. I give my keys to Tory. He turns

them over to his associate. He leaves. TC and I head for the van.

We arrive at the spot twenty minutes before six. Through tinted windows we can see the beach and the Pier. The rapidly setting sun diminishes our ability to see details. We can see large objects. Trees. Trash baskets. The drunk sitting on the bench. Small paper bag at his feet ostensibly holding a pint of booze. My car arrives and my stand-in exits at the appointed time. He casually strolls on the Pier toward the water. As he comes to each basket he pauses and looks insides as if this were the one into which he would drop the lawn and leaf bag. Four. Five. Six. Seven. Eight. The target has been reached. It is surreal watching someone imitate me. Trying to be me in the eyes of others. An actor on a real-life stage.

He reaches in the correct basket, extracts the envelope, and dumps his very expensive trash. He continues his trip to the water's edge. He will be the second vehicle in the caravan. In less than three minutes a girl comes by our basket and tosses the contents of her cooler. I can't make out the details. About five minutes later, I recognize the tall form of Peter Johnson casually strolling along the Pier. He heads for our drop zone. In one fluid motion, he swoops his hand into the basket and removes the bag. He peeks inside the bag and inserts his left hand to confirm the size of the bounty. He walks on at a quick pace. The drunk stirs and slowly follows Pete. TC's ear piece crackles.

"Mayan is on the trail. Gentleman, start your engines."

We follow Mayan by about a block. My double is right behind Mayan in front of us. They are a block behind the quarry.

"The quarry is getting into a gray Plymouth Horizon, license number HDZ-54J. The car is heading south on Gulf Boulevard. I will continue to follow on foot until you catch up."

With a posted speed of 25, the quarry and Tory must drive like tourists . . . slowly as to check out all the shops and sights. In a few minutes Mayan is beside the van. I slide open the door and he leaps in. The ten-year old van smells of bodies and my anxiety. Nothing fancy. Just good old fashion transportation. Blend in with the many out-of-state vans in the area. As a sprinkle of rain covers the front window and the wipers muddy the vision, the vehicular cat and mouse game continues in earnest. I am handed the envelope that Peter Johnson left in the trash basket.

The envelope contains a single sheet of paper.

After we hear your public confession, we will call with the last instructions.

* * * * * *

The twin-engine jet lands on schedule. The flight from the private airport to Tampa International took less than six hours. The pilot glides the sleek, very expensive transportation into the hanger devoted to the rich and powerful. Engines off. The door opens and three men step gingerly on to the Tarmac. Each is wearing a very expensive Italian suit and carrying an ostrich hide attaché case. The countenance on each man is somber and there is no conversation. They are singular in their appearance . . . short, thin, and dark . . . and purposeful . . . all business. The stretch limo engine is running and the doors are open to receive its cargo. The transfer of human cargo from plane to auto is smooth. The limo screeches into the misty night. Taillights disappear with an exit toward the residential part of down town. The men are silent in the limo.

* * * * * *

Delta Flight #3126 from Atlanta lands on time. From the mid-body of the 737 come four women and five men. Each with a specific aptitude or talent: accounting, computer sciences, securities and banking laws, international finance, corporate regulations. They are dressed in business casual and look optimistically toward their work. They know their jobs and how their jobs mesh to create something greater than the sum of its parts. The team leader has been doing his job for years. She has seen every possible wrinkle and wiggle. She knows the team is going to have fun digging for truth over the next two days.

XXIV

"To follow close enough to see, yet not so close that you are seen is the key to successful tailing. This guy is doesn't have clue he has a tail.

"Where the hell is he?"

"Tory, I see the car. He's three blocks ahead of us and eight blocks north of the drop zone."

My double, in my car takes over lead stalker. He turns left onto Coquina Way, two blocks south of 28th Street. We follow. He is now turning onto Coquina Court. We stop the van two car-lengths from my car. There is a row of non-descript bungalows on the right side of the street. The seawall is on the left. The bungalows appear to back up to some offshoot of the Inland Waterway. We are all there for the party.

The three of us exit the van and enter my BMW.

"Our quarry entered number 12. No one has exited, at least from the front. I don't have a clear view of the rear. So, I can't be sure."

"Mayan, go around to the back to ensure no unfortunate escape. Check every widow. Look for the boy. When you hear us enter the front door, you enter through the rear. If you have seen the boy, go to him directly. We will be with Mr. Johnson. I really don't care about broken doors, locks or glass. If we do this as well, as I know we can, minor property damage is collateral. But there must be no bodily damage. Remember our objective is to secure Mr. Baker's son. His safety is paramount. Go now."

"Jacob, you and I will approach the front of the house. We'll look for Gene through the front windows. If we see him, you must rush to him upon our entry. I will deal with Mr. Johnson. If we don't see him, the chances are he is in the back and will be protected by Mayan when he enters. Remember, be calm and let me do the talking."

The distance from the car to the bungalow is about two hundred yards. Walking as slowly as Tory demands makes the trip seem like two miles. I can hear my heart. Once off the street, a bed of coquina shells forms the front yard. Steps crunch loudly. I check the window on the right. The light from the main room through the door's window reveals a very messy, small room. I look to Tory. He shakes his head. Gene must be in the back. Tory approaches the door and knocks.

"Mr. Johnson. Mr. Peter Johnson. This is Tory Covington. Would you please come to the door? I would like to talk to you."

Silence. Now I hear whispers. Two male voices. I hear shuffling, sliding of some kind as if a large package or piece of furniture being moved.

"Mr. Johnson. Please come to the door. I would like to talk to you. I know you have Gene Baker with you. I would like to return Gene to his father. Come to the door. Let's talk."

"We have nothing to talk about. My dealings are with Jacob Baker. He is a murderer and he must confess. When he confesses, he will be given instructions to find his son."

"Mr. Johnson, I really don't want to stand out here and yell at you through the door. You don't want that either. Soon one of your neighbors will hear us and call the police to complain. The police will arrive and you will be arrested. I don't want that. Mr. Baker doesn't want that. And I assume you don't want that. If the police arrive, Mr. Baker's son and his money will be returned him and all your work will be for naught. Let me come in and discuss this with you. You seem to be a reasonable man. I'm a reasonable man. We can reach a reasonable solution to this awkward situation."

"How did you find me?"

"I followed you after you picked up the money."

"Are you alone?"

"Yes, Mr. Johnson."

"How can I be sure?"

"One, I give you my word. Two, open the door and see."

Tory motions me to stand flush against the building to the right of the door, which opens inward. We wait. The dead bolt is turned. The doorknob is turned. The door is open about two inches. Suddenly, I hear screaming and banging at the back of the house. I see Tory throw his weight against the door. Peter's attention has been diverted by the commotion behind him, so he falls backward as Tory bulls into the main room of the bungalow. I follow by two seconds. Peter Johnson is on the floor with Tory standing over him, feet on either side of the kidnapper. I scan for Gene. See him standing behind Mayan, who has Sammy on the floor. Sammy is struggling to free himself, but Mayan has Sammy in a vise-like grip.

"You fucking lied to me. You said you were alone. You brought this band of thugs to invade my home. I'll sue your wretched ass."

"Yes I lied. I'm a lawyer. I get paid to protect my client. And I do that to my utmost ability. Sometimes I lie. Two of this band of thugs, as you call them, are the boy's father and my employee. As to suing my wretched ass, I doubt you'll want to go to court with the kidnapping and extortion charges hanging over your head."

"My dispute is with Jacob Baker. He is evil. He had me arrested for the murder. He had my friend Sammy arrested for the murder. I just want justice. For Heather, I want justice. Is that too much to want?"

"We all want the same thing, justice. That's good. Here is what we're going to do. We are going to let you and your friend, Sammy, get off the floor. You can sit or stand. I don't care. Then we're going to reunite Mr. Baker and his son. Then we're going to take back the bag of money. The one you've hidden somewhere in this house. Then we will leave. On Monday, Mr. Baker and I will visit the District Attorney's office and Mr. Baker will confess to his crime. Your kidnapping and extortion will be ancient and silent history."

"How do I know you will go to the DA?"

"On this, you will have to trust me. I'll make sure your Public Defender, Sarah Stewart, receives a copy of the meeting notes and any agreement that emanates from the meeting. You will have a signed record. Is that fair enough?"

"Yeah. But, how can I be sure that I won't be prosecuted."

"You have my word, the word of the DA, and the word of Ms. Stewart. Do we have a deal?"

"Yes."

Tory steps away from Peter as the crest-fallen, erstwhile criminal rises to sit at the bar counter. Mayan unlocks his control of Sammy, who walks toward Peter. Suddenly he turns, lunges at Tory, and smashes him in the face. Sammy pulls a fish-gutting knife from his waistband and raises his hand. At Sammy's lunge, I had withdrawn the 25-caliber pistol from the back of my belt and without hesitation I fire two shots. One hits Sammy in the chest and one hits thin air. Sammy's attempted knifing is frozen in time. Then he recoils. The knife falls to the floor. He crumbles to the floor. There are great screams.

"You killed him, you fuck. Is there nothing you won't do to destroy my life?"

Peter stands at the counter and wails like a baby.

Mayan rushes to Tory.

"Are you OK?"

"I'll lib. It's just by nose. Check out Sabby."

Mayan leans over the fallen attacker. Sammy is twitching and bitching.

"He'll live, too. Shot entered top of right shoulder. Small caliber gun and a mass of flesh equal no exit wound. Some Doctor is going to have to extract the bullet and stitch up the wound. Better get him to a friendly Doctor ASAP."

"Here take my card, and call the Doctor whose nabe and number are on the reverse. He will treat you, send be the bill, and not file a gunshot report. Now we have to get out of here. Thank you. Mr. Johnson, get me a small and a large towel. NOW!"

Peter snaps out of his hysteria and fetches the towels.

Mayan helps Sammy to his feet. Folds the smaller towel over the wound and wraps the larger towel around the shoulder.

"Mr. Johnson, take your friend to my Doctor. Not a hospital or clinic. Do you understand? An incident report would require too much explanation."

"I will. Now all of you leave. You've done enough damage for one night."

In all the commotion I hadn't noticed that Gene was standing beside me. Touching me.

"Hey kiddo, are you OK?"

"Sure, dad, I'm fine."

"I have a lot of explaining to do. We'll talk on the way back to Tampa."

"One question. Where did you learn to draw and shoot?"

"My dad taught me."

"Will you teach me?"

"Sure."

Tory and Mayan walk to the van.

"TC, how's the nose?"

"Berry sore. But, I'll lib."

"Thanks for the quick reaction. I'll hold your boney until Bonday. Bayan took it from Sabby as he was trying to exit the rear of the house. We need to talk very soon. I want all the loose ends knotted before I see Flaherty on Bonday. Call be in the borning."

I explain it all to Gene. I confess. Perhaps more than he wanted to hear, but all that he had to hear. He has to know the truth that I had been hiding. He's a good listener. His questions evoke greater explanation. This is not an inquisition. He takes my hand. He wants to know our future. Only DA Flaherty knows that. And he's not aware of it yet.

✱ ✱ ✱ ✱ ✱ ✱

The limo is parked at the rear of the mansion. Recent arrivers have blended in with those who had been waiting. The group sits on the heavy overstuffed furniture, which fills the living room. Discussions are muted, but animated. No decisions will be made in the sub-groups. They seem to be awaiting the arrival of the decision-makers. The triumvirate arrives in a bullet proof Land Rover, a battlewagon. Three older and very somber men. The meeting will now come to order. The senior of the three elders speaks.

"Thank you all for coming here on such short notice. We were recently notified that a federal task force is coming to town to examine the bank records and files. They're here to attack the family businesses that have been supporting this area for years. They're here to gather evidence that they will use in an attempt to close us down. We have called this meeting to determine what would be in our own best interests. We have sought the advice of counsel. Someone we can all trust. Before we decide what we should do, let's hear from him."

"Thank you. Gentlemen, make no mistake about the power of this federal task force. They are free to pillage. And they love their work. They are very good at digging up enough dirt to wreak havoc upon your businesses, as well as yourselves. They will extract from the bank all the things, which you have kept hidden from prying eyes. All the things, which have made your work profitable and strong. As I see your options, there are three. All of the three are severe, because you are in a severe situation."

"First, create a delay by creating chaos. The delay will give me time to determine who can be counted on to be our friends and where are the holes in the federal cases. The chaos is created by destruction of business enterprises. The business records that are the corroborating elements of the investigation. If these factors are not available, the federal cases become weaker. The destruction can take any shape. A fire. An explosion. Any shape."

"The second option is to offer the federal task force some type of olive branch. Give them enough that they will cease the investigation. It would have to be something substantial. They won't take money or threats. They will want something on which they can hang their careers. Something, which they can take to the press and public."

"The third option is to run. Take who and what you have as of this date and leave the country to a haven, a country whose government will let you stay. Your new homeland will have to have a non-extradition policy with our federal government. You'll have to be prepared to pay the new government for the protection."

"There they are gentlemen. Fight, sacrifice, or flight."

Murmurs abound. The elder asks for comments.

XXV

"Good afternoon, we'd like to see Mr. Gracia."

"Do you have an appointment?"

"No, we don't. And we really don't need one. You see these papers give us permission to go anywhere in this building. We are a federal task force. Once we board the elevator to Mr. Gracia's floor, stay off the telephone. Call no one. If we find out you called in advance of our arrival, we will arrest you for hindering a federal investigation. Got that? Now on what floor is Mr. Gracia's office?"

"Yes, I understand. Mr. Gracia's office is in the executive suite on the twentieth floor."

With that commanding approach the nine march past the receptionist's desk, board the elevator, exit the top floor, and stride purposefully down the carpeted hall to the executive suite. The takeover has begun. As they near the office of Marshall Gracia, the president of Tampa Bank, he exits his oak-paneled retreat and strolls past his secretary to greet the intruders.

"Good afternoon, Miss . . . ."

"My name is Pulik, Special Agent Pulik and this is Field Director Davidson. Let's step inside your office so we may talk. Here are our cards and the papers that authorize the arrival of my group and the seizure of any and all bank records. Additionally, the papers require your cooperation and silence. Mr. Gracia, we came here at this day and time to review the bank's involvement in the business of interstate drug trafficking, money laundering and corruption of government officials. Please advise your technical people that we will be using their space and systems to access the files and records we need. Please advise your security people that we have taken control of the building and that we will be here for the weekend. They are to keep open access to all floors and rooms. Nothing is to be locked until we lock it. Please do not advise anyone else of our presence and our purpose. If we find out that information relative to our presence has been leaked outside this building, we will hold you personally responsible. We will then have you arrested and held without bail on the charge of obstruction of justice. If you do as you are told, and we can complete our jobs undisturbed without publicity or public knowledge, and we may not come after you. Do you understand?"

"Yes, Special Agent."

The team leaders know that the admonition will be ignored by someone, somehow.

"Good. Now call the bank's Director of IT and the Director of Security to your office. I will explain our needs to them. In the mean time, it must remain business as usual for all your employees. Let them leave when they normally do, but no later than six. We will commence our work promptly at six fifteen, after we have checked the floors."

Arriving at 4:45, Ms. Pisano of IT and Mr. Sullivan of Security listen intently to their responsibilities as detailed by Special Agent Pulik and Field Director Davidson.

The building is vacant of employees by five forty-five. Many leave unaware of what is about to happen. A few leave frightened by some vague notion of the upcoming investigation. Restrooms and broom closets are checked on each floor. No bank employee remains. The elevator doors are locked off. They can only be operated by passengers with keys. And the only passengers with keys will be the nine team members.

They start their process by developing multiple paths to the mainframe. Fifty files are opened immediately. This is just a start. Checking and savings accounts for the past five years are reviewed page-by-page, month-by-month. Business accounts. Personal accounts. Off the microfilm, checks and drafts are viewed and noted.

The team enters the files of the law firm controlled by the bank. The double password to accomplish this is provided by Mr. Gracia. All of the bank clients, whose files have been accessed, are also clients of the law firm. Documents about the client businesses . . . charters, corporate documents, meeting notes, correspondence, billing statements, and financial records . . . are accessed and down loaded for copying. One team member laughs that at 5 cents a sheet, the copying bill would probably run well over $25,000. A small price for the size of the crime.

For the first eight hours the team is focused on gathering information. As stacks of hard copy are accumulated they are carried to the huge board room and allocated to areas on the table and numerous chairs by company or individual. There is a great deal of cross-reference material. Sheets of paper bearing individual's names are designated to several company stacks. And company transactions appear to find their way to numerous businesses. This is the major step in the process, because it establishes the scope of the team's work during the next days. The objective is to connect the dots. Corporation A, run by individuals X and Y and owned by family Z, does business with corporations B and C, which are run by a member of family Z and owned by families X and Y respectively. The procedure requires attention to the smallest details. The maiden names of wives are the most often used screens. The names of grandparents are next. Minor children, first and middle names only, appear as owners. All of their assets are controlled by trusts, which are controlled by other corporations. These corporations are run by the same group of adults, whose names appear on the checking and savings accounts. Layer upon obfuscating layer. The team has done this type of precise artichoke peeling before. It just takes time. But, they don't have forever.

Food consists of health food bars, trail mix, liquid meal replacement and bottled water. Sleeping will be done in four-hour shifts during the sixty-hour lock down. No one can enter the building and no one can leave. No telephone calls in or out. Isolation ensures efficacy and efficiency.

✱ ✱ ✱ ✱ ✱ ✱

Driving to Tory's office to review my options for retaining my life, I realize that I'm not worried about me, but about Gene. Where will he live? Who will take care of him? How will he manage? What will he think? It's all about him. It has always been about him, because he is I. I am he. He is the lineage of my father and his father, etc., etc. What I have done will destroy that line. I must face the consequences of my actions even if those consequences are detrimental to my own flesh. I must do the time, because I did the crime.

"Don't look so damned glum. I think I have a powerful argument, which will appeal to Mr. Flaherty and his sense of public largess. On the night of the murders, you were distraught at the destruction t your ex-wife and young son caused by the drugs sold by the Silveras. What the evil Silveras were peddling to Heather drove her to economic and emotional ruin. This ruin impacted, not only your former wife for whom you still had an emotional attachment, it also damaged your son. It was harmful to an innocent minor. The most recent batch of drugs purchased by Heather from the Silveras killed her. You guessed from whom she had purchased the deadly drug. You went to the Silveras' apartment to let them know you knew who had sold the killer cocaine, and that you would go to the police with this knowledge. You were grieving the loss of your former wife and the damage to your son. You were not acting rationally. When you confronted them, an argument ensued. You fought. Hector tried to get his knife. You two fought some more. He found his big Bowie-like knife. You shot him in self-defense. You had brought the gun to this rough and tumble neighborhood for protection. Then in extreme rage, you shot Osvaldo and mutilated them with your gun and his knife. Your rage blinded you. We know where you tossed the knife and clothes. I'm sure divers can find the knife. The gun is another story, because it remains in your home. We will paint you as a righteous victim pushed to the edge by the evil destruction of drugs."

"OK, let's say Flaherty accepts this story, what will he do?"

"I am confident your case will not go to trial. Flaherty will accept the fact that you actually did a community service by ridding it of a low life that was responsible for the deaths of eight citizens. He'll probably agree to a guilty plea, a suspended sentence, some form of counseling, and community service. Remember Bernard Goetz. Hell, you're a normal father and grieving ex-spouse. Flaherty needs the praise for closing the case and the public homage for being decent. However, if he does decide to put this case before a jury of your peers, you are a lock to be found not guilty by reason of mental defect. The inability to distinguish right from wrong during a period of extreme emotional or physical stress will be easy to prove. And when I introduce Gene to the jury, there won't be a dry eye in the court room. I'll make sure Flaherty knows this alternate scenario. For him it's a win-lose situation. For us, it's win-win."

"Somehow, I feel relieved, but not good."

"You're supposed to have that ambivalence. You're human. Even in the good man there is sin. The good man confesses his sin and expiates it. Jacob, you are such a man. Are we straight with my approach?"

"Yes."

"Now go home to Gene. Rebuild the bridge that has been damaged."

Beatrice is in the kitchen reading the paper and making a shopping list . . . for me. Gene is in his room.

"Hey, how you doin'?"

"I'm doin' OK. Can we talk?"

"Sure."

"I think I understand why you did what you did. There are so many facts and feelings swimming around in my mind, I'll need time to sort them all out. So, let's make a deal. When I'm ready, let me ask and we can talk. For sure this is going to be a primo topic of discussion in my next Doctor's visit. How about you?"

"The only topic."

Gene's love is pure, because pure love is knowing the worst about somebody and not caring. Pure love transcends all sins.

"I'm also confused. What will happen to you? And if something happens to you, what will happen to me?"

"Mr. Covington has made me believe nothing of earth-shattering consequence will happen to me. He outlined my defense. He is convinced I will not be prosecuted. I will have to plead guilty and throw myself on the mercy of the court. Crime of passion. Character of the victim versus character of the perpetrator. I'll most likely receive a suspended sentence, endure heavy counseling, and have to perform some community service. I'll be fine. Therefore, you'll be fine."

"OK. I love you, dad."

The bridge building started.

XXVI

The bits and pieces of information gathered by the team at the bank are beginning to create a picture. A complex picture of interlocking companies and interlocking finances. Layers from beneath and above. Names of the same people populate the numerous companies. These comprise the "A" list. Twelve companies rise to the top of the cesspool are owned by the seventeen families. And, some names on the corporate documents are outside the "A" list. The inclusion of other names and other banks comprise the "B" list, which gives the companies owned by "A" list an air of legitimacy.

A citrus growing and processing concern owns a piece of and is owned by a trucking company. Another partial owner of both companies has vast real estate holdings, which are, in turned, owned, in part, by the family, which is the financial support of *e-bio,* the biggest high tech company in the area. Money flows forth and back, back and forth. Each time it moves the amount of money gets larger. The bank is a conduit for all the financing and all business.

Loans and lines of credit are extended at the discretion of the bank's board of directors. They have the sole authority to move blocks of money. The money is provided at slightly higher-than-normal rates due to justifiable risk. There are times when one company will provide the collateral for another's loan. This is highly risky unless the companies are so close they are just two pockets in the same pair of pants. Then it's illegal. The federal team marks the occasions in which one company has paid off the note of a borrowing company that appears to the public eye to be independent of the payee. There are situations in which the bank has failed to secure collateral or to document the purpose of the loan. Money was loaned on the good name of the borrower, who just happens to be the relative of a board member. Several instances reveal a borrower paying off a note early, yet not receiving a credit for the interest not due. The phantom interest is paid and provides the bank hefty profits.

Vast amounts of money go from the bank to the companies immediately before the companies expand into a market. Companies and drug distribution are the same; corporate expansion is simultaneous with new drug distribution. This money may be used as tribute to the mob already in the market. The new companies are buying distribution. It's like slotting allowances at a grocery chain. The new seller comes to town, wants to get his merchandise on the street, and has to pay for the right to sell. Then the outlet, the dealer, buys from the new distributor. The new distributor promises to pay for protection. Whom does he pay? The former distributor. A turf war resolved with money and not death. A better system and a better quality of merchandise can benefit everyone. The old distributor is happy to be paid for not distributing. Like the farmers who are paid for not growing.

It is obvious the bank is at the heart of the corporate labyrinth. It is apparent that the twelve corporations are funneling huge amounts of cash from and to the bank. This makes the bank highly profitable. The bank's stock pays obscene dividends . . . 20-25%. And, since the same seventeen families own approximately 95% of the bank stock, they are taking profits from the companies they own with any outsiders. The seventeen are defrauding the outsiders. Details of the sales and profits of the corporations will expose the depth of the fraud. Pulik e-mails Atlanta and speaks to an uber-boss at Treasury. Pulik needs all the corporate tax records for the last five years e-mailed immediately. She has dubbed the group, *The Dirty Dozen.*

All of the information, assumptions, and questions are put on to discs. Documents are scanned onto discs. Then the hard copy is shredded. The shreds are placed into bags, and the bags are put in the freight elevator. When a full load is reached . . . roughly every eight hours . . . the elevator is taken to the delivery level and the bags are loaded into a special federal dumpster, which will be picked up every eight hours by a federal cartage company and burned at a landfill. Tidiness prevails.

The guidelines have been established. Details make the rope, which will hang the families who run the companies and the bank. Team members pour over the corporate tax records. If anyone else were running these money-losing propositions, they would have been fired long ago. Operating expenses are high, visible net income is nearly non-existent, and debt service is staggering. This three-headed monster is found in one form or another in every enterprise. Expansion at all costs. Expansion requires capital. Borrowed capital must be paid back. This seems the first order of corporate finance. Pay the loans. Then pay the company's high operating expenses. The companies are expanding into the same markets at roughly the same time. The companies and people with whom the different enterprises do business in these expansion markets are the same. It doesn't matter if one is selling or promoting computer chips, oranges, diesel repair services, residential communities, or fresh seafood, the same people in the market appear as purchasers. Checks and bank drafts from similar banks appear in different ledgers. But, the money is not enough to pay for the expansion. Just enough to create a smoke screen. The assumption of invisible cash payments is a safe one. Cash for drugs. Then cash returned to the former distributors. Very difficult to prove, because cash leaves no trail, and the guys who are the local dealers don't really like to talk to the police or the feds.

Proving interstate drug trafficking is the goal of the team. Money laundering, fraud and corruption are the whipped cream and sprinkles on the dessert. The feds have the skeletal outline of the total operation. The coke comes to Tampa via the boats. Gutierez's people take the "fish" off the boats and distributed the special items to the citrus packers, the ranchers, the diesel guys and all the other businesses that are expanding from Tampa. Experience tells Pulik that where there is coke, heroin is nearby. Two forms of merchandise with universal appeals and high profit margins. It only makes good business sense. For the import of heroin, there must be a company that does substantial business in the Pacific Rim countries or the Middle East. Computer assembly and chip production are the basic avenues. Drug distribution can move into the 21st Century via the computer. Pulik makes a note to scour *e-bio's* files. As the companies expand, the drug trade expands, because it is pushing the legitimate enterprises. The legitimate businesses are barely able to sustain the expansion even with the ever-increasing credit lines. But these credit lines mysteriously get paid down from time to time with money, which never shows up on the books of the companies paying off the notes. The companies then borrow more. The hard working honest corporate fronts seem to be working toward no end. Like hamsters in cages. Running nowhere, but running rapidly nonetheless.

Certain team members are taking sleep breaks, while others explore specific trails. The team convenes in two hours to summarize, discuss, and redeploy resources.

"We need to put a beginning and end to this entire trafficking operation . . . from the boats bringing in the drugs to the dealers in Memphis, Charlotte, Birmingham, and Atlanta . . . places like that."

"Special Agent Pulik, we can access the seafood company's records to determine which fishing line they pay most often. We have a good idea when the company receives the fish. We'll look for checks at that time. The rest has to be in cash. On the other end, we get copies of invoices and contracts with companies that are dealers in the markets of expansion. The companies pay our Dirty Dozen for goods and services. We can match buying patterns with the date and length of time for shipments to reach the markets."

"That's thin. Without irrefutable evidence that the stuff came in on such and such a boat at such and such time, we will be hard pressed to get in the door that way. Also, without proof that the companies paid for goods and services partially with a traceable check and mostly with untraceable cash, we'll never get in that way."

"I've been told by the District Attorney that we have testimony from Mr. Roberto Pena and Mr. Jimmy Jimenez, and some audio and video recordings about shipment dates and weights. If we can squeeze Antonio and Pedro Gutierez with the Pena and Jimenez testimony, we might be able to get deeper into the system. I'll bet they even know how the deals were done with companies in the expansion markets. Leave this part of the exercise up to me." Davidson has her own contribution to make.

Pulik is still in charge of the operation and all the agents.

"I expect everybody's information in four hours. We must continue to dig at the front end and the back. Go over all the checks again. Pour over any business contracts and sales. More tax data is coming in from Atlanta. Divide it up. You know what to look for. We've been through the initial fact gathering stage. We're now in the understanding stage. By early tomorrow we must gain wisdom. I'm going to concentrate on *e-bio*. They have got to be the source for heroin. Back to work. We've got miles to go before we sleep."

Dana Davidson heads for the ladies room and the last stall. With water running in the sinks she calls Jack Flaherty. Violating the code of silence, she reaches out to her local source to get information. Her risk is worth her reward.

"Jack, listen closely. I have to whisper. We can work together on this next phase. We need you to squeeze the Gutierez brothers as well as Pena and Jimenez to get all the facts about the shipping of drugs across state lines. You must get the information and e-mail it to me on my second phone. Here is the number. 800-393-3218. Now the really bad news. There is no way I can break away from this situation to see you. Nor can I stay an extra day. It would look suspicious to the department and to my fiancé. Sorry. I'll let you know our conclusions before we go public. I make sure you get all the credit for the investigation's success. We are simply working in an area that local officials cannot. We are working in concert with the District Attorney's office. Under the direction of the District Attorney. You will get a ton of good ink. OK? Take care of yourself."

✳ ✳ ✳ ✳ ✳ ✳

"Gentlemen, there seems to be some confusion. This is not an-all-or-nothing situation. We can function as separate entities. Our personal relationship begins and ends with business. If some of you want to extricate yourself from this mess, you are free to do so. If some of you want to stay and fight the investigation, that's fine, too. I think it's clear that offering up an olive branch is a viable option. In fact, if some flee and some fight, the case against each one of us could become weaker. Our defense gets stronger if some people can't be found. The investigators will need all the conspirators to create the picture of an overarching conspiracy. Those that stay can always blame those who leave. And if those who leave can't be brought back to stand trial, there can be no case or a very weak one. Indictments we can defeat. So, I think each of us should think long and hard if he wants to stay or leave the country." The breathing becomes easier as this alternative is explained.

"There is one other item. Speed of decision. Whatever you decide must be decided before we leave here tonight. And, those who are going to leave the country must do so before Monday morning. As I understand it, the federal task force has been able to access all our business records, as well as corporate and personal tax returns. Through the bank they, no doubt, got to the law firm's files. And, while this looks like a violation of lawyer-client privilege, Mr. Tidmore advises me that if the lawyer had knowledge of intended criminal acts, this privilege does not hold sway. He further advises me that this will be a point of contention throughout the entire appellate system. In other words, he can create confusion here and seek reduced charges through pleas, if it ever comes to that. But, the basic decision is yours to make. Let us reconvene in two hours."

The senior elder has spoken and calmed the crowd. The elders adjourn to the den, leaving the others to decide on their own fates.

"Connie, watta you gonna do?"

"I'm going to stay and fight this mess. You, Choo-choo?"

"Not sure yet. Leaning toward getting' out. Hell, I have no interest rotting away my life inside. Foxy, what about you?"

"I'm outta here tomorrow evening. No later. Flight to Barbados then a sea plane and boat ride to safety. My house is already stocked. My wife knows the drill. And my kids are grown. They won't understand at first. They'll be pissed. But, in few years the pain will numb and they may even come to visit me."

"What I really want to discuss is the third option. Sacrifice."

The oak paneled inner sanctum was ominously silent. The whispers in the living room sounded as if they were from men sitting beside the elders."

"What?"

"Why?"

"Who?"

"If we offer a sacrifice to the feds and the locals, we may be able to buy a lot of time or, better yet, give them a spotlight villain. Someone they can blame for the evil.

Someone they can show in public. Someone who will put a gold star on each resume`."

They each knew who that must be.

"Think of the power of their case if they arrest and convict the largest drug trafficker in the Southeast. Think of the national headlines they would grab. Think of their egos. Now, think of how quickly and easily the case will be made. With strong legal counsel, we, who stay at home, will probably become footnotes to the indictment. Remember we hired Tidmore. We pay him. We own him. We have money enough to hire ten Tidmores."

"Connie, do we have to give up Romero and his boys."

"So? Foxy, look at like a buy one get two free sale at the seafood store."

"Romero is godfather to my son."

"Your sympathy could keep the feds on your ass for years to come. It could give the bastards a reason to spy on your kids. No sympathy. Hard action. Choo-choo do you agree?"

"Well, it helps me make up my mind. If we give up Romero and his boys, I'm getting out of town. The boys are hot heads. They'll send their thugs after us. Mutilate us like they did the Silvera brothers. They'll go after our wives and families. If they go down, we go down . . . if we stay. So I won't stay."

"I'm not afraid of the street gangs. I'll have police protection. No, better than that, I'll be a witness against the Gutierez family and its drug trafficking. I'll ask the feds to put my wife and me in the witness protection program. We'll simply disappear to New Mexico or Montana."

"Connie, you can run that risk. I'm just gonna run. Choo-choo, care to join me in my island fortress?"

"I've always been partial to the South Pacific. It'll take me about an hour on the Internet to find an island nation that doesn't need our government and would welcome my contributions to their treasury. I'll have a new home, a new bank account, and a ton of cash in less than twelve hours. So, Connie, you'll have to approach the feds on your own."

"That's why we pay Mr. Tidmore."

The two, soon-to-be-departing elders leave the den and are replaced by James Tidmore. The rite of sacrifice is incredibly simple. The lawyer is given two keys. Connie's driver takes Tidmore to the *24-Hour Stor 'n Lok* near the airport on West Doctor Martin Luther King Jr. Boulevard. Bin number C-2W-6 holds rococo artifacts, furniture, and three throw rugs. Rolled in one of the rugs is a small, insulated box. In the box are computer discs. On the discs is enough information to destroy the entire enterprise and everyone connected with it. It would take the investigators thousands of very expensive hours to gather the information on one disc. Now they will get some of it for free. Not all of it, of course. And certainly not all at once. They will be spoon-fed just enough information, facts, names and dates, to slake their initial thirst, but not their deep hunger. Most of the contents of the discs will be held in reserve. Hopefully, never to be exposed to the bright light of truth.

In the den at the mansion with the doors securely bolted, the copying, cutting, and formatting of selected information, and the downloading of it onto a new disc consumes three hours. In the meantime the flighter and fighter camps, having taken shape, are in the process of disbanding so that each member can go about his business. Tidmore must act with great dispatch. He steps outside on to the lawn to make a very important call. For the second time this night, the ringing of his cell phone awakens Jack Flaherty. He had finished with the first caller and was trying to sleep on the office couch. A meeting with Tidmore is set for four hours.

"Thank you for seeing me at this awkward hour, Mr. Flaherty. Permit me to get directly to the sum and substance of my purpose. My client is acutely aware that your office and a federal task force are investigating business and financial operations of great personal concern to him. My client wishes to cooperate with these multi-faceted investigations for the good of the community at large. My client would hope that his cooperation would engender a reciprocal understanding from your office and the federal agents now housed at the Tampa Bank."

"I cannot speak for the federal task force, but if the cooperation of your client were substantial, if it corroborates existing facts and testimony, and if it seals the case against leaders of the vast drug-trafficking and money-laundering enterprises, I would be most cooperative. I would use my vast influence to extract a similar level of cooperation from the federal task force."

"If my client can make your case completely and a case for the federal task force, which might be a little different than the scope of their investigation, how cooperative would you be?"

"Given evidence of that nature, I think witness protection is a reasonable expectation. Get your client out of harm's way as it were. Please, realize that I can't speak for the federal task force. Hell, I can't even speak to them. At least not until Monday. But, if your client's evidence makes a big enough case for them, I am confident they will cooperate."

"There's one other thing, Mr. Flaherty. This all has to be resolved before I leave here, and I plan to leave shortly. If I may presume to ask you, it would be in everyone's best interest if you somehow, someway contacted the federal task force. If you can't talk to them, perhaps e-mail is the proper medium."

"If you'd like some coffee, there is plenty of fresh and all the additives in the break room at the end of the hall. Would you mind bringing me back a cup . . . milk and one sugar? Thank you."

With the closing of the door, Flaherty sends an outline of the proposition to Dana Davidson. Her response is immediate and affirmative. Anything to make a big case conclude with ease. Who will notice if one or two bad guys don't make the headlines? They will disappear. Dana wants to get Pulik in on the deal. She has to be integral to the decision making, because she will be the face of the investigation and case. Tidmore returns.

"Mr. Tidmore, we have federal cooperation. What information does your client have to offer my office, as well as the federal task force?"

The disc is handed to Jack, who down loads the data, then sends it to Field Director Davidson. The names Gutierez, Trane, and Zorro are in each file on the disc. On nearly every page. This triumvirate ran the entire operation. Imported, repackaged, distributed. Drove the expansion of the twelve companies in to markets outside of Tampa. They were the power driving the Tampa Bank's board of directors. They made decisions for others to carry out. The three-headed hydra must be decapitated. The body of the monster will collapse into the valley of death. The e-mail from Davidson:

> *Witness protection is available to whoever provides the viable information and testifies to it in open court . . . yours and ours. Mr. Flaherty, please secure name and vitals so that we may initiate proper procedure. You have our thanks and respect.*

"There it is, Mr. Tidmore. Your client will have to make a formal statement and testify. The feds can hide him away from retribution. Who is the source?"

"Antonio Consolo."

"Holy shit. How did the mayor get this incriminating evidence? Wait, maybe I don't want to know. If the feds want to know, they'll ask."

"One last housekeeping item, Jack. May I suggest you send officers to the homes of the three miscreants and arrest them immediately? My client has advised me that he has reason to believe the three have exhibited a proclivity to flee the country. If you awaken judge Witmer, I'm sure he will sign warrants of arrest. I also suggest that you post officers at the airport to eliminate the possibility of escape. Consider private and public planes."

"Why are you and your client so helpful? What else do you want?"

"My client is a good citizen, who has seen the error of his ways and is acting responsibly. But now that you ask, my client would like police protection instantly. Tonight. He fears for his life. And the life of his wife and daughter. When the arrests and indictments against the criminals are known, my client has reason to believe certain members of the bank's board will attempt to take his life. Retribution for his good citizenship."

"Antonio Consolo will be under police protection as soon as we can get a patrol car to his house."

The printed list contains the names, addresses, and telephone numbers of all varieties of the three board members, who had just been given up to the police and federal agents. Jack calls Commander Asher and sets him in motion. The second call is to a very pissed-off Judge Horace Witmer. The paper work is taken to the judges' house for signature. Grumpily warrants are approved and distributed to Asher's army of trusted cops. The sweep commences.

XXVII

The game went badly with no Gene and no coach. The Jaguars won 28-7. So the Giants finished second and will play the Cardinals for the right to play the winner of the Jaguars-Steelers game. Most likely the Jags.

Tribune Sun, Sunday February 8
DA and Feds Nab Crime Syndicate Bosses

District Attorney, Jack Flaherty, and a Federal Task Force from Atlanta, arrested Romero Gutierez, Steven Trane and Humberto Zorro, leaders of a crime syndicate responsible for the murder of Hector and Osvaldo Silvera, witness tampering, obstruction of justice, interstate drug trafficking and money laundering. Mayor Consolo and his office are assisting with the investigation. Mr. Flaherty said . . .

Federal Agents Raid Tampa Bank

Federal IRS agents from Atlanta raided Tampa Bank and seized the records of numerous accounts dealing with the vast holdings of the companies controlling the Board of Directors. The seizure was done with the cooperation of District Attorney Jack Flaherty and his office and in connection with the charges of interstate drug trafficking and money laundering . . .

Tory calls at 8 am.

"Jacob, did you read Sunday's paper. It appears that the DA's office has taped confessions, as well as signed and notarized transcripts of the audio from both Mr. Roberto Pena and Mr. Jimmy Jimenez. Both of these men confessed to the murder of the Silvera brothers. Unfortunately, Mr. Jimenez was subsequently murdered while in jail the night after his taped confession. Mr. Pena and his confession have become critical to the lengthy investigation by Flaherty's office into the drug distribution and money laundering cases that further were the steps leading to the federal case of interstate drug trafficking. Mr. Pena will testify, then whisked into witness protection. The murders are the predicates for the entire multi-level investigation."

"TC, that's common knowledge."

"Don't you see the impact and the result of all Flaherty's posturing and preening? The murder aspect of the investigation is closed as far as Flaherty's office is concerned. They have moved above and beyond the simple gangster-style execution of a street dealer. They and the federal task force have effectively closed down a huge illegal enterprise."

"Sorry, I don't understand."

"Their case of the Silveras' murder is the tip of the iceberg, and is nothing more than a local headline-grabbing, promotion-propelling case. If we proved to Flaherty that there is another murderer then he would have to admit that the two men, who he can document, confessed to the crime, lied for the benefit of witness protection and a new life. They, in fact, are not guilty of the crime. And, if the two confessed murderers lied on one aspect of their confessions, these confessions would be viewed as tainted evidence in the overall case. At the very least, in the hands of a good defense attorney . . . say Tidmore and Tuggs . . . the confessors would be perceived as paid informers reading a script. This could create enough doubt in the minds of a judge that might consider the entire confessions bogus. Two really good defense attorneys, defending the Gutierez family or any of their cronies, could lead a judge from point A to point B. Every shred of evidence that was contingent upon the confessions would be useless. Flaherty would ultimately have no case as a result of the general ruling dealing with fruit from the poisonous tree. And the feds would have no case, because their case sprang from his poisoned case. But, the District Attorney's office and the Federal Task Force would have egg on their faces and shit on their shoes. Flaherty's career and that of Mr. Pennington would be ruined. The real bad guys would go free. Hell, they'd probably sue the asses off the city and the DA's office."

Tory was making deadly serious sense to Jacob. Jacob's confession and the evidence would upset the bandwagon of success and advancement.

"Why would they confess to a crime they didn't commit?"

"Well they have a "get out of jail free card" forever, they can start their lives anew, and the old cronies here in Tampa know that the two scumbags pulled a fast one on the legal system. Big street cred with the homies. Hell, they are now heroes, because they pulled a big one over on the DA."

"What does this really mean for me?"

"It means that you will not be going to Jack Flaherty's office any time soon to confess to crimes for which he already has confessions. He has his killers. He has his case solved. All is neat and tidy. Flaherty would not want to dirty up the proceedings with the truth. Some people are good and some people are lucky. You are very, very lucky, my friend."

No sooner does one telephone conversation end than another begins.

"Beatrice, what's wrong? You sound agitated."

"Jacob, I'm getting strange vibes from Tampa. I've read the papers and seen the newscasts. I'm perplexed. What do you know?"

"The Tampa Bank has been taken over by federal regulators. Three members of the board . . . Romero Gutierez, Steven Trane, and Humberto Zorro . . . appear to be the leaders of a very big crime ring. They are being indicted on a long list of state and federal counts. Antonio and Pedro Gutierez have been arrested and will be indicted for murder, witness tampering, drug trafficking, and extortion. Several other members of the Tampa Bank Board of Directors are parts of the syndicate. But, much smaller players. Their arrests are on-going as they are found. Your father is cooperating with the investigation and there has been no mention of your brother."

"I know all that. I don't care about the others. What about *papi* and *mami*? I can't reach them. At home or *papi's* office. His administrative assistant says they are on vacation, then hangs up. I don't know where they are. Do you know what they have to do with this circus? *Papi* has not been on the bank's board for years because of his position in the city government. Bay-Bay sat on the board for *papi*. But he lives in Costa Rica. I can't believe my family had anything to do with these crimes."

"I don't have any answers about your parents or your brother, but I'll ask Tory. He has a reliable source of court house information. By the time you get here, I'll know where they are."

"See you in a few hours. Love you."

Paranoia still runs deep in Jacob's soul. Although her inquiries seemed genuine, there was something, which rang untrue. Had she been prepared to expect these types of events? The crimes and the disappearances. Had she known about her father's involvement? Had she known about her brother's involvement? Was she involved? Or was she kept out of the loop because she was a female and the netherworld was a very exclusive fraternity? She did benefit from the wealth. But, did she know about the source of the wealth, and keep her mind shut? If she turned a blind eye to the crime, is she guilty? Jacob is guilty of a crime of passion. Is Beatrice guilty of a crime of dispassion? Which is worse?

"Tory, I just got a call from Beatrice. She's can't seem to locate her father or her mother. She's aware of the arrests and the multitude of indictments. Her priority is the safety of her family. She is firm about their not being involved in the events that led up to the arrests. My gut says that the authorities are hiding her parents. Could you find out if my assumption is accurate and where the authorities have hidden her folks? Would you tell me so I can tell her they are safe? I guess I really don't need or want to know where they are. Maybe Beatrice will be happy just knowing they're safe?"

"Jacob, I'll ask and get back to you later today. OK?"

Tory questioned himself for the first time since this all began. He has been party to unethical and illegal acts. The kind that could cost him his license and a stay at Club Fed, if the truth were revealed. Or, was he party to nothing more or less heinous than the stupidity and arrogance of the local DA's office? The agreement presently in place will ensure that the big wheels of justice grind the big bad guys into pulp. The high profile evil doers will be punished, because they were in the wrong place at the wrong time this time. They are just paying their dues for former crimes. His client will be free. And the remaining other will be free from worry hiding in plain sight. Jacob will be free to live with the responsibility that he is a murderer. Tory is free to practice law, knowing that he defended his client to the best of his ability. It's just that the confession of the real killer didn't suit the needs of the DA. Prosecutorial expediency. This entire charade is most curious. He calls Jacob.

"What have you learned about the Consolos?"

"The word is that the mayor and his wife are on a well-deserved two-week water skiing and deep sea fishing vacation. According to my source at the courthouse, they are in Costa Rica visiting their son, Alberto. The vacation is part of the plan to keep them out of harm's way until they are needed to testify against Trane, Gutierez and Zorro. Tell Beatrice they are safe and where they are."

"Thanks for all you've done. Giving Gene and me our lives. Call me if you need me to sign any papers. Thanks again."

Beatrice arrives and rests in Jacob's arms. He details what has happened, and what will happen with her parents and brother.

"You have not asked me if I knew of the crimes for which the men have been indicted."

"It is not mine to pry. It is yours to offer."

"I've had a lot of time to think of this whole mess. I accept that *papi* and Bay-Bay are in deep *caca*. They are no doubt as guilty as anyone on the board. I never knew the truth for sure. But, I have been suspicious for a number of years. Suspicious about the amount of money *papi* always had on a mayor's salary, the late night meetings in the den, and the trips to Costa Rica. *Papi* was a very successful and powerful politician. He and his male friends seemed to get richer each year. I figured there was some amount of back scratching. You know, the mayor helps those who help him. It was the details that were left out of the picture. *Mami* never said anything. Maybe she knew. Maybe she didn't. She was a traditional and dutiful wife of a successful Hispanic patriarch with old-fashioned values. The values that he let the public and his daughter see were old-fashioned. God, family, and duty. That's how he kept his political base. His public power. I guess the values his son and his cronies knew were those of a new-age gangster. Greed, power, and money. I'll never know how much of what I had or enjoyed came from *papi's* illegal activities. I was never permitted to know, but I had questions and now I have a guilty conscience. Can you forgive me for doing nothing? For not trying to know the truth?"

"There is nothing for me to forgive. You couldn't do anything, because you knew nothing for sure. Given what I know about your father, I can understand how you knew nothing. He and his buddies kept secrets from everyone. If they were your children, you could be held responsible for their actions. But, there is no way you can be responsible for the actions of other adults. Even if the adults are your family. Sometimes, we don't want to know the truth, because it will shatter our reality. Maybe, you didn't want to know."

"Thank you. I love you. Now tell me what transpired with you and the DA."

"Nothing. He is in a real jam. It seems that too many murderers might spoil his ascent to power. So, Tory never met with him and my part of the case is closed."

"What about Pete Johnson?"

"Tory and I agreed to give him $25,000 and have him sign away his version of the truth. The greedy bastard couldn't wait to count the money and catch a plane to California. Tory has someone who will keep an eye on Johnson for a while. I paid Tory the other $25,000."

Over the next few hours conversation bounces in and out of events and feelings. Beatrice opens her personal history book. Gene will be home shortly. Then he must learn of Tory's strange victory of this morning. It is agreed that Beatrice will tell Gene what she wants when she thinks it's appropriate. The day winds down. Calm prevails. The past is vividly clear, the future is promisingly cloudy

✶ ✶ ✶ ✶ ✶ ✶

These are the playoffs. Gene and I are back ready to win and move on. We will not show the Jaguars what is in store for them when we face the Cardinals. The Defense will be basic and both the first and second teams will play. I want everybody ready for the Jags. Giants 17 Cardinals 0.

XXVIII

This is it. The championship. The title game between #1 and #2. A rematch. A grudge match.

"Listen up ladies. You all know your assignments for Louie, Roger, Stanley, Stanley 2, Loop A, Loop B, Blitz A and Blitz B. These guys like to pass at least once in every other set of downs. This is what I know. If you don't bang the wide receivers and tight ends every play, they will eat your lunch. If you knock the wide receivers on their butts, they will be delayed in going out. Once you bang them, back up five to eight yards. Remember you cannot touch them after they go five yards. Ends push their ends into the tackles. Make them trip over each other. Make the ends' paths to pass patterns very difficult. This gives the D-line the time to get to the QB. When they are in a double flanker set, they will pass. They run two passes off this set. One to the tight end going post, the second look is to the wide out cutting across the middle behind the end. They run this left and they run it right. Never both. So, when they are in a double flanker, we must have both outside line backers drop straight back five yards. This will put you in the path of any pass. You can always close if they decide to run off this set. And they will run off the set, once they learn you are dropping off. Be ready for the ball to come your way. It is a gift. It should not be a surprise. This action could leave us vulnerable to the off tackle trap or sweep. So inside line backers you must be sharp. Gene, the more you live in their back field, the easier we will have it. If you can control two men in the middle, you have done only part of your job. You will be doubled often, so one of the tackles will have an easy task of getting into the back field. All of you listen to the commands I relay through Bobby and Amos. Ready?"

"Ready." In loud unison.

"All the 14 year olds are captains. They have earned the privilege. If we win the toss, we will kick off and receive to start the second half. Now kick some butt."

The stands are filled on this cool fall Saturday. At 5 PM the heat of the sun has dissipated. Beatrice is dressed in team colors. We will kick off and they will receive going into the sun. Easier for the receivers to find the ball in the first quarter. Given this, they will pass often in the opening set of downs. I relay this to Bobby and Amos.

The kick is caught and juggled at the 15. Returned to the 30.

"Amos. Bobby. They will pass on the first play. So run a Stanley with double drop. Gene has to eat the center's lunch and get to the QB. All D-linemen with hands up and screaming like they mean it. We need to create fear and confusion that come from that approach. But do not, I repeat do not, hit the QB in the face or after he has let the ball go. No stupid errors. Make the QB pass up not out. Go."

The Jaguars are in a double flanker as anticipated. At the snap of the ball, all humanity is in chaos. The flankers are hit hard. The right flanker is knocked to the ground. The left flanker just bounces off our wing line backer and continues his delayed route across the middle. The left tight end is caught in the trap of legs and arms that is the defensive line. He takes off on his route too slowly, too little, and too late. Their right end stayed to block. The QB has little time as Gene and the gang are closing in on him their hands are raised. The ball is released above the outstretched hands. Almost a vertical trajectory, the pass is up and down, falling harmlessly at the feet of our outside linebacker. Now the Jags will run for two plays. One sweep. One up the gut.

The sweep will be to the wide side; our left. Two blockers in front. This sets up their reverse that we will see in the second quarter. Amos and Bobby have seen this scenario before. They know to call Louie. The D-end must box to break-up the play and give the blitzing linebacker time to catch the runner from behind. All D-linemen will slant to their left. The Jags have a single flanker to our right. He goes in motion back to the QB. The QB takes the ball from center and drifts straight back as if to pass, but in reality to hand off to the flanker. The new ball carrier. Our D-end is across the line and turned into the backfield as the blockers get to his position. There is a pile up. No place for the runner to go but deeper. He loops out of panic in an effort to reverse his path and is greeted by our blitzing line backer. Eight-yard loss.

The next Jag formation is a power I Right. If history holds, they will run off their left, our right side. Two blockers in the hole followed by the ball carrier. Smash mouth foot ball. Amos and Bobby know to call a Roger. They are like coaches on the field. The Jags use a long count to try and draw us off sides. Our line is like a column of stone pillars. At the count of five the ball is snapped and the O-line tackle and guard on their left cross block to open the hole. But they get only one man, Gene has slipped passed the center and into the backfield. The first blocker takes care of Gene. This is the beginning of the pile-up. Amos steps into the hole and pushes the second blocker to the ground. More pile-up. Bobby is fighting with the O-end in the mouth of the rapidly filling hole. The runner lowers his head and bulls into the blockers and would be tacklers. He stumbles and falls beneath Bobby. Time to punt. Three and out. Now for the offense to score.

We move methodically down field. No passes until they move their corners and safety up. Then a simple screen gains twelve yards. Back to running. Drive stalls on the Jag fifteen yard line. A field goal makes it three to zip. Second quarter.

Jag ball on their twenty-eight. Flanker and split end out on their left. QB takes the snap and drifts back to hand off to the running back who heads left. Flanker runs five yards and cuts inside to seal a running lane. Split end runs eight yards and cuts outside to block our corner. Running back has wide lane, and he is off. We are playing catch-up, which we can't. They score. Extra point is good. Three to seven. Can't let the guys become dejected. Stay with game plan. Make adjustment to that formation. Communication is key. Have inside line backer to the power side drift back and over by three yards to stop the run before it gets too far. The Jags stop our offense. We stop their offense. Half time.

Our ball and not much progress. Just a lot of time off the clock. We punt. Jags move slowly toward our goal line. Three yard chunks. No passes. They know that we know. Run time off the clock. Their drive stalls on the twenty-two. But a lot of time has been chewed up. Their field goal is good. Ten to three Jags. Fourth quarter.

We go nowhere. Three passes. Two short one complete. The third for a first down falls dead. We punt.

We stop them three and out. Their punt falls dead on our thirty-one. Now it is up to the offense. The Jags defense is a gap six to slow up the run and to encourage passing. Our offense obliges. Bubble screen gains six yards. Power sweep nets two. QB sneak garners the first down. After that there is give and take until they give less than we can take. Time is running out for us.

We punt. They do not touch the ball which lies still on their twenty-two yard line.

Jaguar ball with one minute remaining. First and ten. I call the team to me, and make damned sure they do not move until the ball is snapped. The Jaguars will try a long count or some screwy cadence to draw us offside and pick-up an easy five yards.

"Remain stone still and look at the ball. Do not move, cough, spit or fart until the ball is snapped. Do no listen to the QB. Just watch the ball. Got that"

"Yes, coach," in unison.

"Now the defensive set for all the plays will be a Stanley 2X. Hands up and screaming for all we are worth. We will smother them before they can do anything. When we hold them and we have a chance to win. Now go get em."

The Jaguars are true to form. They have the lead and all they need to do is run out the clock. We have two time outs left. As they approach the ball, the Jags are quiet. The QB calls out the set and the phony play at the line of scrimmage. My boys hold. They are stone still. The QB is taking his sweet time. The man in motion is nearly across the field. Still no snap from center. The ref's whistle sounds and his flag flies. Delay of game. That's five yards for us. It is now first and fifteen. Best of all, the clock is stopped until they start the play. No play. No time is run off the clock. We still have a minute.

The D-line is down on their knees awaiting the Jag O-line. There can be no quick count now. Power I Right. The ball is snapped and seven Giants smother the seven Jaguars. Gene has pushed the center back into the QB, who trips as he is handing off to the tailback. The ball is bobbled then controlled. But that confusing split second allows the remaining members of the D to converge on the runner. Loss of three. I call a time out. Now we have 48 seconds. They have second down and eight teen from their four yard line.

Jags line up in a double flanker as if they are going to pass. The ball is snapped and seven screaming Giants with hands held high push into the backfield. We have left the ends alone to get to the QB. The middle line backers have drifted back to cover the crossing wide receiver. Gene and the left tackle are on the QB as he passes. The ball falls harmlessly to the ground, three yards from the intended receiver.

No need for me to call a time out. Third and eighteen. 38 seconds left. I tell Amos and Bobby to not tackle the man in the end zone. Allow any runner to get some minor positive yardage. They look confused. I explain that they may try and take a safety. Give us two points and punt from their twenty. This would kill the clock and any chance we might have of winning. The boys understand.

Jags line up with a flanker and split end on our left plus a flanker on our right. He goes in motion. A sweep will eat up time. They will try that blocking scheme that they used to score. The QB spins and drifts back to hand off to the flanker. At that nanno second, our left end beats his blocker, gets into the backfield on a perfect box, and greets the two Jags. A three-body train wreck ensues. The ball bounces wildly to the ground. There is a pile of flailing arms and legs. All the players are fighting for possession of the ball. Amos raises his hand and pulls himself from the morass. The referee's whistle stops the clock with twenty seconds remaining. Our ball on their four-yard line. Now it is up to the O.

The defense stands around me and we all cheer for the offense to tie the score and get us back into the game. Our O lines up in a tight T. The QB will follow three blockers on a sweep. Very simple, basic play that has been executed by the guys nearly a hundred times in practice and in games. The Jags are prepared for it. They have placed a linebacker and a safety outside their end and middle linebacker has moved over to the D-end so he can come in behind the blockers. This overload will be used to string out the play and use the sideline as a tackler. At the snap of the ball, the backfield swings to their left; the wide side of the field. The line pushes right. The first back curls and cracks into the outside line backer. The second back takes on the safety. All he has to do is delay his approach. But the traffic jam is beginning and the QB is slowing. He must have enough time and space to clear the corner and trot into the end zone. The third running back is slow to get off the mark and the QB is right on his tail. The process has slowed dangerously. The inside linebacker is right there to throw his body into both of them. The QB staggers out of bounds at the two. Eight seconds remain.

Time out. Big huddle. The offense knows their assignments. Back to the field and to line up. Wide side is now to their right. Our flanker is on our left. The Jags have seen this before; it is either a pitch or a QB drift to the right and pass to the tight end coming across the field. They shift their power to our right. Even the deep safety drifts to prevent an end zone catch by our tight end. Flanker starts in motion. The Jags linebackers take a half step to the wide side. They know what is coming. The ball is snapped. The backs start to the right. The QB takes a step back to start the play. Then he lunges forward between the center and left guard. The Jags were caught completely in the dark. The center and guard have created a tight lane for the QB. We score. Jubilation. Chest bumps. High fives and sprinting back to the bench. No time left. Easy extra point for the tie. Then, overtime.

The kicking team lines up. The Jags have overloaded the center and just outside our ends. This is their blocking scheme. The count seems to go on forever. The ball is snapped directly into the holder's hands. But, he does not place it on the kicking tee. Instead, he takes the ball, stays hunched over as if to hide and runs to his left as the kicker goes through the motion of a kick. As the holder runs past the charging Jags, I think he waves. Smart ass. Regardless, he runs into the end zone untouched. The final score is Giants 11 and Jaguars 10.

A great explosion of joy occurs near our bench. Lots of high fives, chest bumps and hugs. I even notice a few tears. The long season and the lessons of team work and brotherhood were worth the effort.

After a shower, pizza for all. I will introduce Beatrice to the other coaches and parents. I am honored to be the boys' coach and proud to be Gene's dad.

XXIX

The dining room table is set for a traditional late dinner celebration. It is now eleven. Two eight-taper candelabras, in the same motif as the silver pattern, create a soft, glamorous glow. Wax has begun to drip onto the table. Jungle flowers in a crystal dish adorn the center of the table. Gold rimmed china in all forms awaits food. Delicate Swedish goblets are partially filled with fine Chilean Merlot. The damask cloth rests between the Irish lace cover and the black oak sixteenth century table. Five high-back chairs are positioned to receive the diners. The diners are late. They're on the patio for pre-dinner cocktails.

The patio overlooks the paddock, stables, and the runway. At night, the high intensity security lights running from the base of the mansion to the end of the runway create a vista of immense perspective. Jungle on two sides. Mountains rising behind the thirty-foot high thicket to the right and left. The wicker chairs and table appear to be mottled by a dark brown stain. Antonio Consolo is slumped forward on the table and blood drips from the three shots in his head. The top of Marguerite's head has been pierced by numerous bullets. Her face is contorted and she is leaning backward on her chair. As he tried to run, Alberto fell to the floor twenty feet from the table. In the back of his head are two holes there are two entry points at his heart. The shards of the glasses he was carrying to make an outline around his bent body. The weapon of choice is a 25-caliber semi-automatic. The slugs enter the head cavity and ricochet around the skull slicing and dicing the brain. The slugs, when their job is done, come to rest and do not exit the body. *Mami and papi and Bay-Bay make three.*

Mari Sanchez, nee Gutierez, Alberto's lover of the past six years, is not among the dead diners. Her throat was slit while she oversaw the kitchen activity. The kitchen help were chased away with the spilling of the first blood. They disappeared into the jungle. They will come back when the new lady of the mansion arrives with her man and child. The tail lights of Bee-Bee's Humvee can be seen heading for the plane on the private runway. The engines begin to rev. When they arrive back in Tampa, the pilot must die. A double tap to the skull. No flight plan. No loose ends. The mayor's former business associates will be blamed for the murders. The automatic pistol will be cleaned and returned to its home . . . a lock box in Tampa. This weapon will have six deaths to its credit.

The queen lives. Long live the queen.